Praise for *Dea*

"Unique, witty, and touching—

—P. C. Cast, *New York Times* bestselling author of the House of Night series

"This book will keep you hungry for more from beginning to finish! You'll know enough to follow the story, but very little is given away throughout the novel, to keep readers constantly guessing. What a tease! If you're a fan of romance and fantasy, you'll definitely enjoy this book!"

—Miss Literati

"Outrageously funny, sinfully sexy, with a cast of characters that steals your heart from the very first page . . . I loved this book!"

—Inara Scott, author of the Delcroix Academy series

"She hits plenty of buttons: impossibly handsome boys, supernatural powers, hot romance, friendship, school rivalries, suspense, and comedy."

—*Kirkus Reviews*

"*Death and the Girl Next Door* is unputdownable. Darynda Jones breathes fresh life into the young adult genre with exciting twists to legends we only think we understand and edgy, compelling characters you can't help but care about."

—Gwen Hayes, author of *Falling Under*

"Only Darynda Jones could make the Angel of Death crush-worthy! Wickedly sharp with brilliant wit, *Death and the Girl Next Door* will leave you craving more!"

—Lara Chapman, author of *Flawless*

"The delightful Jones makes a smooth transition to YA in this really fun read. Her kicky dialogue and great characters are super entertaining, and the story unfolds with some surprising twists. Add in some laugh-out-loud moments, a hot hero, and a satisfying but cliff-hanger-y ending and you've got a hit."

—*RT Book Reviews*

"Snapping with sarcasm and a pitch-perfect voice, Darynda Jones has brought her signature humor and supernatural sass to Riley High. Trust me, there's nothing grim about this reaper!"

—Roxanne St. Claire, *New York Times* bestselling author of *Don't You Wish*

"*Death and the Girl Next Door* delivers a smokin' hot story and a guy to die for. Darynda Jones gives one candy-smacking, awesome read that won't let you go until the end." —Shea Berkley, author of *The Marked Son*

"I loved this book. *Death and the Girl Next Door* is equal parts funny, thrilling, and hot. Teens will fall hard for the hero, an original and exciting take on the Angel of Death."

—Maureen McGowan, author of the Twisted Tales series

ALSO BY DARYNDA JONES

Death and the Girl Next Door
Fourth Grave Beneath My Feet
Third Grave Dead Ahead
Second Grave on the Left
First Grave on the Right

death, doom, and detention

DARYNDA JONES

This is a work of fiction. All of the characters, organizations, and events portrayed in this novel are either products of the author's imagination or are used fictitiously.

 Printed in the United States of America. For information, address St. Martin's Press, 175 Fifth Avenue, New York, N.Y. 10010.

www.stmartins.com

Design by Anna Gorovoy

ISBN 978-0-312-62521-4 (trade paperback)
ISBN 978-1-250-02590-6 (e-book)

First Edition: March 2013

10 9 8 7 6 5 4 3 2 1

For Konner

Red hair, hazel eyes sparkling beneath impossibly long lashes,
a killer smile . . . we are in so much trouble.

ACKNOWLEDGMENTS

If the world were a perfect place, I would remember all the people I need to thank when I write these, but alas . . . Please forgive my absentmindedness.

First and foremost, I have to thank my agent, Alexandra Machinist, and my editor, Jennifer Enderlin. There just aren't enough adjectives to describe the depths of my gratitude to you both. I would end up having to throw in adverbs and we all know where that leads. Thank you, thank you, thank you.

And thanks so much to everyone at St. Martin's Press and

Macmillan Audio. I'm so proud to be a part of this fantastic family.

Thank you *so* much to my beta reader for this project, Hayden Casey. Your enthusiasm for this book sparked a fire inside me. I'm forever grateful.

Thank you to the LERA-lites and my Ruby Slippered Sisters who keep me semi-sane, especially Tammy Baumann, critique goddess extraordinaire. And a special thanks to my assistant, Dana, who keeps me in line and is always ready with a kind word and a virtual cup of coffee. You are the bomb.

And the Grimlets!!! Thank you to the bestest street team ever! Especially you, Mama Grimlet. Just thinking of you makes me smile. You are amazing, one and all.

As always, thank you to my family and friends. You know who you are and you know what you've put up with, and for that you have my eternal gratitude. With that in mind, I have to thank Grandma Pat for reminding me there are no fireflies in the Manzano mountains. (Eek!)

If you are reading this, my last and biggest thanks goes to you, the reader who stays up past her bedtime, the lover of words who spends his or her precious free time devouring books one page at a time. You are the nondairy creamer in my coffee.

death, doom, and detention

PROLOGUE

I was six years old, napping in the backseat of my father's car, when I first saw the end of the world. Granddad had preached that morning about loving thy neighbors, and I fell asleep wondering if he meant all our neighbors or just the ones right next door. Thankfully, Tabitha Sind didn't live right next door. She lived a few houses down from us, so surely I couldn't be held accountable for not loving her. She'd pulled my hair in kindergarten. On purpose!

As my eyes drifted shut on the ride home after Sunday dinner, I figured I'd have to at least try to love her. Granddad said so.

So I pondered how I was going to manage such a miraculous feat as the car swayed and the sun cast shadows that slid across the back glass, coaxing my eyes shut for longer and longer periods of time until I fell into a deep slumber.

Or so I thought. What seemed like seconds later, a vision—so bright, it blinded me; so sharp, it ripped through my skull—flashed hot in my mind. I'd had the vision before, but only in dreams and never with such urgency. Such desperation. This time it had enough weight behind it to seize my lungs.

They were coming.

And they would kill us all where we stood.

I awoke to the sound of my own screams. To Mom draped over her seat, trying to grab me. To Dad swerving off the road, barely missing a semi. He careened onto the shoulder and ground to a stop, the tires kicking up dirt around us until the world outside became a brown haze. Mom unfastened my seat belt and pulled me over the seat, into her lap.

But I couldn't catch my breath. As the dirt settled on the windows around us, I screamed and kept screaming, terrified beyond reason. I didn't understand what was happening. I just knew we were all going to die.

I clutched at my mother's jacket and begged my parents, who were the smartest people alive as far as I was concerned, to stop the darkness from leaking in. They gave each other worried glances before my mother cradled me to her and said to him, "Already? So soon?"

Dad bit down, his bright gray eyes watering as he asked, "Where is it, pix? Where's the gate?"

Trembling uncontrollably and unable to draw in enough air to speak, I pointed a shaky finger. Farther down the canyon. Farther away from our home in Riley's Switch. Around the twists and turns of Abo Pass. Closer and closer to the ancient Pueblo missions. The ruins. The sacred grounds where the beginning of the end was seeping onto Earth.

My father peeled through the dirt and gravel, following my lead, but my mother begged him to stop. To turn around. To go back for help.

"There's no time," he said, his jaw set in determination.

She pulled me closer and I was no longer sure which of us was shaking more.

We rounded a grassy hill, and the gate, as Dad had called it, came into view, but it didn't look like any gate I had seen. It looked like a bolt of lightning that had been split down the center, hovering in the afternoon sky while night seeped out of it. Only it wasn't night. The thick oily blackness that leaked into the bright sky was in fact hundreds of dark spirits escaping onto our plane. I didn't know that at the time. I wouldn't find out for ten years that what I was witnessing was a rip in the fabric of reality. A portal between two worlds that should never have been opened.

The bright edges of the gate sparked and crackled when we skidded to a stop. Wind rocked the car, howling around us like a coyote at night. Dirt and debris hit the glass, making sharp thuds and scratching sounds, but I could not take my eyes off the rip in the sky. I sat paralyzed, utterly confused by what I was seeing, though somewhere deep inside, I knew the darkness brought death.

No, not just death.

Annihilation.

Mom and Dad sat frozen too, looking up in disbelief. Hints of panic flashed in their eyes; then Dad swallowed down his fears and reached into the backseat to grab his journal, the one he carried everywhere, the one with scribbled notes written in cursive, a method I had yet to learn. When he opened his door, Mom lunged for him, clamped on to the pale blue sleeve of his shirt. He stopped and looked at her, and in that moment, I saw the depths of his love. My father, so handsome and strong with his red hair and scraggly stubble. And my mother, so absolutely beautiful, her long cinnamon hair falling over her shoulders and brushing across my wet cheek.

Then he took my face into his huge hands. "I love you more than anything on Earth, pix, do you understand?"

I tried to nod, but fear and dread didn't allow it.

"Forever."

That was our family motto: Forever. It was all we had to say. He leaned over and kissed my forehead before letting go of my face and kissing my mom on the mouth. The kiss was hungrier than I'd expected. More desperate.

When he broke free, he didn't look back again. He tore out of the car with his journal and ran for the rip in the sky. Mom scooped me up and we took off after him, but he was already on a hill just beyond the ruins. She stumbled—the wind was so strong—and we took cover behind a clump of bushes. Dad stood on the hill, reading from his journal as the gale force knocked him to his knees. He recovered and began reading again, shouting over the gusts, his words barely audible and completely foreign to me.

"He'll do it, pix," Mom said into my ear as she held me tight. "He'll close the gate, don't worry."

But I had turned my attention to the dark shadows that darted past us, each one nothing more than a blur before it disappeared over the hills, slithering along the ground like vaporous snakes.

Mom began praying, but again, I didn't understand the words. She closed her eyes, cradling me to her as her hair whipped about and tangled in the bushes. Then everything stopped. The wind.

The noise. Mom lifted her head and looked toward my father. An instant later, she struggled to her feet and we ran.

Her hold was like a vise around my waist as we headed for the car. She told me to close my eyes and spoke words of encouragement, but I knew they were just as much of a lie as the calm was. I'd looked over her shoulder. I'd seen what she saw. The splinter in the sky was now circular, the clouds around it swirling like an angry tornado.

With a loud crack, the wind restarted. It picked us up and threw us to the side. Mom lost her footing and we crashed to the ground. But she didn't give up. Crawling on her knees, she fought the windstorm with all her strength. We were almost to the car, her hand straining for the door handle, when she stopped. I heard soft gasps as she disentangled my limbs and tried to shove me under the car. I focused on the tears staining her cheeks, on her hair falling over her face, on her eyes wide with heart-wrenching fear. The last word she uttered was no more than a whisper.

"Hide," she said, a microsecond before she was ripped away.

I'd been cleaving on to her shirt and was jerked forward with the force. I tripped and fell, the space where she once stood so completely empty. So void of human existence.

The winds screamed around me when I crawled to my knees and looked up to search for her. But a beast stood before me instead. A monster as tall as a tree. He had thick black scales that glistened in the sun. Claws as long as my legs. Teeth as sharp as a snake's fangs. He studied me for a solid minute, and my hands curled into fists. My jaw welded together as I fought the sting of dirt and hair whipping into my eyes.

Then the strangest thing happened. He dematerialized. He became fog, like a dark, glittering mist, and I breathed him in. His essence was hot and acidic. It burned my throat as I swallowed him, scorched my lungs as I inhaled until he was no longer, and we were one.

And then I understood.

"No!"

We turned and saw a man I didn't recognize running toward us. A sight we found most curious.

"No!" he yelled over the wind, skidding to a stop beside us, falling to his knees. He had pale brown hair and pale blue eyes and skin the color of chalk. And he seemed quite unpleasant. "No," he said through clenched teeth, "I summoned you, dammit. Not her."

He was screaming in our face and we didn't like it. We looked over, found a stick, and decided to stab him. With a lightning-quick thrust, we sank the piece of wood into his abdomen. Part of us was surprised at how easily the stick penetrated the material of his shirt, the muscles of his abdominal wall. The other part was pleased.

The dark spirits no longer rushed past us. If they got close, they would turn suddenly and head in a different direction, like fish in an aquarium. We watched as the gate in the sky closed with a wave of our hand. We watched as the wind died down and the countryside settled into complacency. We watched as the man staggered away from us, his eyes wide with fear and disbelief.

Then we lay down and slept. And while we slept, we forgot.

No, I forgot.

For ten years, I buried that memory—the last memory I had of my parents—until a chain of events so unfathomable, so unbelievable, brought it crashing through the surface of my consciousness. And with it, the knowledge of what I'd done.

I'd led my parents to their own deaths. I'd pointed the way. Begged them to go. How would I make amends? How would I ever learn to live with what I'd done?

And how would I ever find my way back to normal?

FUZZY EDGES

"Is this class ever going to end?"

My best friend, Brooklyn, draped her upper body across her desk in a dramatic reenactment of Desdemona's death in *Othello.* She buried her face in a tangle of arms and long black hair for effect. It was quite moving. And while I appreciated her freedom to express her misgivings about the most boring class since multicelled organisms first crawled onto dry land, I wondered about her timing.

"*Miss* Prather," our Government teacher, Mr. Gonzales, said, his voice like a sharp crack in the silence of study time.

Brooklyn jerked upright in surprise. She glanced around as our classmates snickered, either politely into their hands or more rudely outright.

"Is there something you'd like to share with the class?"

She turned toward Mr. Gonzales and asked, "Did I say that out loud?"

The class erupted in laughter as Mr. G's mouth formed a long narrow line across his face. Miraculously, the bell rang and Brooklyn couldn't scramble out of her seat fast enough. She practically sprinted from the room. I followed at a slower pace, smiling meekly as I walked past Mr. G's desk.

Brooklyn stood waiting for me in the hall, her face still frozen in surprise.

"That was funny," I said, tugging her alongside me. She fell in line as we wound through the crush of students, fighting our way to PE. I wasn't sure why. I didn't particularly enjoy having my many faults and numerous shortcomings put on display for all to see, so why I would fight to get there was beyond me.

"No, really." She tucked an arm through mine. "I didn't mean to say that out loud."

I couldn't help but smile despite the weight on my chest, a weight that seemed endless. "Which is why that was funny."

I did that a lot lately. Smiled. It was easier than explaining why I wasn't.

"You don't get it," she said. "This is exactly what I've been talking about. Everything is weird ever since . . . you know."

I did know. Ever since Jared Kovach came to town. Ever since he'd saved my life after a huge green delivery truck slammed into me. Ever since we'd found out he was the Angel of Death and had been sent not to save my life but to take it. To tweak the timing. To take me sooner than nature—or a huge green delivery truck—had intended.

And ever since I found out I'd been possessed by a demon when I was six years old.

Still, that wasn't the worst part of that day all those years ago. The worst part was the fact that my parents were gone. Vanished in a whirlwind when some guy—we still had no idea who—opened the gates of hell. And I'd led them straight to it. The fact that a demon—Malak-Tuke, to be exact, Lucifer's second-in-command—escaped from his fiery pit and decided to crash at my place was just the icing on the cake. But I didn't know any of this until two months ago.

I'd been living with my grandparents since the disappearance, but my semi-normal existence changed forever when I was knocked into the street by a skateboarder and hit by that truck.

That near-death experience taught me a valuable lesson: Never get hit by a huge green delivery truck if I can help it. But if I hadn't, if my life hadn't almost ended that day, then Jared Kovach would not have been sent. And oddly enough, Jared Kovach was definitely worth the risk.

The events that followed were both terrifying and life changing. I learned that there really was a heaven and a hell. That there really were angels and demons. That I was a prophet, the last prophet in a long line of incredible women, descended from a powerful woman named Arabeth. And I'd learned that I had a demon inside me, that I'd had him inside me for years.

Even Jared had never seen anything like it. Most people possessed by evil spirits were lucky to survive. People possessed by demons—a rarity, from what I'd been told—never survived more than a month. Ever. And yet here I stood. As possessed as a girl with a demon inside her could be.

And, yes, things had been weird.

"People are acting strange, and the world has dark, fuzzy edges," Brooklyn continued.

Before I could suggest a visit to the school nurse, an arm snaked around my neck from behind and I felt something poke my temple. A quick sideways glance told me it was a hand shaped to resemble a gun. "Give me all your money," Glitch said through gritted teeth, pulling out his best Clint Eastwood impersonation.

Glitch, a connoisseur of computers, skipping, and coasting through school with less than stellar grades, was our sidekick and partner in crime. We weren't the greatest criminals, so we really didn't partner up for such endeavors often. Glitch and I had grown up together. He was half Native American and half Irish American, and he had the dark skin and hazel green eyes to prove it.

I wasn't sure what I'd done to deserve either of my two best friends. Even when they found out I'd been possessed—was still possessed—they didn't bail on me. That was true friendship. Or insanity. Either way.

I shook off his arm and tossed a grin at him from over my shoulder.

"You cut your hair," I said to him, noticing his blond highlights were missing. The trim left only his jet-black hair, spiked as usual with just enough gel to make him almost cool. He was too much of a geek to be genuinely cool, but he was getting there.

"Yeah." He raked his fingers through it. "So, what's up with you two?"

"Brooke feels fuzzy."

He bounced around until he was facing us, walking backwards with his backpack slung over his shoulder, his brows drawn in concern. "Fuzzy? Really?"

"I didn't say I *felt* fuzzy. I said the world has fuzzy edges."

He looked around to test her theory then back at us. How he managed to walk backwards in this crowd was beyond me.

And rather awe inspiring. If I'd tried that, I would soon resemble a pancake covered with lots of footprints.

He furrowed his brows again in thought. "I don't think it's so much fuzzy as nauseatingly yellow, a color that is supposed to calm us, I'm sure. But did you hear?" he asked, suddenly excited. "Joss Duffy and Cruz de los Santos got in a fight during third."

Brooklyn pulled me to a stop, her expression animated. "What did I tell you? Joss and Cruz are best friends. Everything is turned upside down."

As bad as I hated to admit it, she was right. I'd felt it too: A quake. A disturbance in the atmosphere. Everyone seemed to have short fuses lately. The slightest infraction set people off. We'd been warned about an impending cosmic war. Was this how it would begin?

With a sigh, I started for PE again. Maybe we were reading too much into it. Or maybe the moon was full. People did crazy things when the moon was full. And besides, I didn't want everything to be turned upside down. I'd had enough of upside down when I was hit by that truck. When I was possessed by Satan's second-in-command. When my parents disappeared.

Some days I was almost okay with the fact that a demon had slipped inside my body when I was six, nestled between my ribs, curled around my spine. Other days that fact caused me no small amount of distress. On those days, I walked with head down and eyes hooded as my vertebrae fused in the heat of uncertainty and my bones writhed in sour revulsion.

Today was one of those days.

I'd awoken in a panic to the sensation of being crushed, unable to escape an invisible force, unable to breathe. The remnants of a nightmare still ricocheted against the walls of my lungs, squeezing them until air became a precious but fleeting commodity. At first I thought I was having an asthma attack, then I realized it was only a dream. *The* dream.

And the dream was always the same. In it, I would float back to that day so long ago and inhale the beast all over again, his taste acidic, his flesh choking and abrasive. Since I was just a kid at the time, one would think it was a small demon, possibly a minion or a lower-level employee. Like a janitor. But I'd seen him that day. How his shoulders, as black as a starless sky, spanned the horizon. How his head reached the tops of the trees. "Small" was not an accurate descriptor.

And now, thanks to my pathetic need for sleep, I could relive that memory over and over. Yay, me. On the bright side, I'd ditched that other recurring dream I'd been having since I was five. The one where bugs scurried under my sheets and up my legs. That thing was messed up.

Still, if not for all that, Jared would never have come to Riley's Switch. We may be only a tiny speck on the map of New Mexico, hidden among juniper trees and sage bushes in the middle of no and where, but we were important enough to warrant an extended visit from the Angel of Death. Surely that meant something in the grand scheme of things.

"And Cameron has been acting strange too," Brooke continued, mentioning the fifth member of our posse, if you included Jared. Which I did. But I hadn't seen Cameron in a couple of days, which was odd.

"That's because Cameron has a crush on you," I said without thinking. I cringed when Glitch's eyes widened a fraction of an inch. He caught himself instantly and turned away.

"No, seriously," she said, oblivious. "He keeps asking if I'm okay. If you're okay. If Glitch is okay."

Glitch whirled back around and glared, but Brooke missed it once again.

"We need to practice," she said, pulling a compact mirror out of her backpack. "Try again to get a vision, only try harder this time. Put a little elbow grease into it."

She handed it to me as Glitch glowered at her, his mood taking an acerbic turn. "Really? Here?"

"Yes, really, here. She has to be ready."

Along with all the other magnificent oddities in my life, my shaky status as a prophet meant I had visions. But visions weren't normal, and I was trying desperately to get back to normal. It was my new goal in life, right after grow five inches and get boobies. So as far as everyone on the planet was concerned, the visions had stopped. They hadn't been getting stronger every day, filling my head with images and knowledge I didn't want. Didn't need.

That was my story, and I was sticking to it.

Sadly, my sudden inability to have a vision only made Brooke even more determined. She poked and prodded me into *practicing* nonstop. So I would touch her arm or her hand and pretend to try really, really hard to have a vision, only to be disappointed again.

I had sunk so deep into this lie, I didn't have the heart to tell her that the visions were coming at me left and right—so much so, I had to fight the urge to dodge them. I didn't want to know the future or the past. Normal people had no such luxury, and since normal was my new goal in life since my old one—get Jared Kovach to fall in love with and marry me—had been thwarted by my grandparents. Just one more reason for my smiles to be contrived.

But Brooke, ever the trouper, had done some research. She read that a shiny surface helped psychics and mediums see into the future or the past, hence crystal balls. And according to her research, mirrors worked just as well. Hence her compact.

"I have to get to History," Glitch said, his shoulders tense. "Mr. Burke threatened to skin me alive if I'm tardy again, though I don't think he actually has the authority to do that."

"Later," I said, opening the compact with a sigh. The last

thing I needed was to get a vision every time I looked in a mirror. The experience was bad enough as it was.

As we exited the main building and headed for the gym, I looked down into the shiny surface. Brooke dragged me along so I wouldn't fall on my face. I pretended to concentrate, trying not to focus on the fact that my gray eyes seemed darker than usual and my auburn hair seemed curlier. Curlier? I leaned in for a closer look. Oh, the gods were a cruel and humorless lot. Because that's what I needed. More curls.

"Does my hair seem curlier to you?"

"Curlier than an ironing board, yes. Curlier than a French poodle, no. Now, concentrate." She rubbed her hands together to emphasize her enthusiasm. "It's vision time, baby. We need them now more than ever."

Even at their height, my prophetic visions hadn't been terribly useful. What on earth could I gain from looking into a mirror besides lower self-esteem?

"Are you even concentrating?" Brooke asked as I tripped on a pebble. This took coordination. An attribute I lacked in spades. But she believed with every fiber of her being that my visions were the key to everything. According to prophecy, I was supposed to stop an impending war between humans and demons before it ever started, but how I was supposed to manage that, nobody knew. Least of all me.

And why was I even participating in this ridiculous scheme of hers? She knew better than anyone that I either had to be touching the person I was prophesying about, or have touched him at some point in the recent past.

But she was bound and determined to expand my skills, to widen my periphery so I could have visions on the fly. So far, our attempts with the mirror thing had yielded exactly squat. Unless I was touching said fly, nothing happened.

Kind of like now.

After a solid twelve seconds, I gave up. "You know, it would help if I knew what to concentrate on."

Brooke patted my arm absently, staring into her phone. "Concentrate on concentrating."

For the love of Starbucks, what the heck did that mean?

I lifted the mirror again. Shook it a little to make sure it was working. Held it at arm's length. Squinted. Just as I was about to give up entirely, a vision, dark and alluring, materialized behind me. I sucked in a soft breath at the sight even though, admittedly, there was nothing prophetic about it.

Jared Kovach was standing against the wall of the building we'd just left. Watching me. At least he had been until he saw me notice him in the mirror. He turned away the moment our eyes made contact, and the pain that shot through me was quick and unforgiving.

I snapped the compact closed and handed it back to Brooke. "I think it's broken."

From my periphery, I noticed Jared start our way, and my stomach clenched in agony. I wanted to run. Instead, I stopped and turned to him. Mostly because he could outrun me. He was wearing his requisite jeans that fit low on his hips and a gray T-shirt with a brown bomber jacket thrown over his shoulder. The cloudy day had splashed color across the sky behind him, and hints of oranges, pinks, and purples served as a backdrop to the powerful set of his shoulders, the lean hills and valleys of his arms. Somehow I didn't think that a coincidence. But his exquisite form only drove home the fact that he was so far out of my league, it was unreal.

He'd come to Riley's Switch a couple of months ago to do a job. That job was to pop in, take me a few minutes before I was slated to die anyway, then pop back out again. But he'd disobeyed his orders. He'd saved me instead, thus breaking one of the three rules that celestial beings are bound by. Even the powerful Angel of Death. As a result, he was stuck on Earth. Stuck helping me.

The problem was, I fell in love with him. It was hard not to. And he really liked me, if his mouth pressed against mine every chance it got was any indication. But that made my grandparents nervous. They went behind my back and asked him to keep his distance, so keep his distance he had. Out of respect for their wishes and because he couldn't argue their point, he gave his word that he would act only in the capacity of protector and guardian where I was concerned. Nothing more. Nothing less.

And my heart shattered into a million tiny pieces.

My grandparents and I had been so close. For ten years they, along with Brooke and Glitch, were my world. But now all the communication in our house was strained and full of hurtful innuendo and resentful glances.

"He's the Angel of Death," my grandmother would say. "The most powerful angel in the heavens."

Then my grandfather would join in. "He's not a teenaged boy, despite his appearance, pix. He's dangerous beyond your wildest imagining."

The fact that he'd saved my life—twice!—apparently didn't matter.

As he got closer, I tried to subdue the adrenaline rush I felt every time I looked at him. His dark hair fell over his forehead, emphasizing the sparkling depths of his coffee-colored eyes. The wind molded the T-shirt to the expanse of his chest, revealing the fact that he was cut to simple perfection. And he had this way of moving, this animalistic grace, that mesmerized even the stoutest minds.

"How was your last class?" he asked, stopping in front of me but avoiding my gaze. His voice, deep and smooth like warm caramel, caused a fluttering deep inside me, a flood of heat to my face. How could any being, supernatural or otherwise, be so perfect?

"Pretty boring," I said, pretending to be as uninterested as he. I hoped and prayed he couldn't feel the pain his presence caused. The humiliation would be too much.

He nodded and looked into the forest behind the school. I couldn't help a quick glance at his arms. The bands of symbols that lined his biceps were visible underneath the edges of his sleeves. The designs were ancient and meaningful, symbols that stated his name, rank, and serial number in a celestial language. Or that was my impression. I loved looking at them. Thick dark lines that twisted into curves and angles. A single line of them wrapping around each arm. To me, they looked like a combination of Native American pictography and something alien, something otherworldly.

"Are you okay?" he asked, still looking toward the tree line.

"Me?" I pretended to be surprised. It was his job to check up on me. It didn't mean anything. "I'm great."

"We're both great," Brooklyn said. She put her phone away and draped an arm over my shoulders. "And we have to get to class."

She offered Jared a hard glare, and I felt bad for him. He was only obeying my grandparents' wishes. He watched us leave, his face expressionless, and it was hard to look away from the dark brown depths of his eyes shimmering beneath his thick black lashes, or the full mouth that had been pressed to mine on several of my more memorable occasions.

With a heavy sigh, I turned back toward the gym. Still, a person would have to be blind not to notice all the attention Jared drew every time he made an appearance. And I couldn't help but notice that when he headed back to the main building, more than one girl at Riley High stopped to watch.

Sadly, PE was going to require effort. We were ordered to run the Path, which was a footpath in the forest behind the gym. Fun for some, life threatening for others. I was about as coordinated as overcooked spaghetti. This was not going to end well.

But even the pain and sweat of the Path couldn't take my mind off the enigma that was Jared Kovach. Ever since he arrived in Riley's Switch, he'd been kind of undercover as a student. Partly because we didn't really know what else to do with him without drawing unwanted attention, but mostly because he had to stay close to me, to keep me safe. My status as a supposed war stopper carried enough weight to warrant a guardianship by way of the most powerful angel from heaven.

But my arrival onto this plane also warranted a protector of another kind. The angels had created a nephilim—a part-human, part-angel boy named Cameron—sent to protect me long before Jared arrived. And he was normally right on our heels. Part of that could be explained by his crush on Brooke. But he took his job very seriously and had hardly let me out of his sight. I scanned the area, wondering where he was. I hadn't seen him in days, and after having him as a constant shadow every minute for the last two months, I found his absence a little disconcerting.

I thought about Jared. They hadn't exactly been the best of friends. In fact, they'd torn a goodly portion of downtown Riley's Switch to shreds soon after Jared first arrived. Could he and Cameron have fought again? I should have touched Jared when I had the chance, tried to see what he'd been up to. Not that I could control the visions in any way, shape, or form, but if he'd fought with Cameron, it was emotional enough that it could show up. And I swore to all things holy, if Jared and Cameron were fighting again, there would be heck to pay in the way of very sore shins.

"How are you supposed to practice if we keep having to work in all of our classes?" Brooklyn asked as we jogged along the forest floor, dodging tree branches and navigating the uneven ground. We'd had a dry winter, and leaves crunched under our feet as we did our best to stay vertical. This could not be in compliance with the safety guidelines set forth by the state.

"It's crazy, right?" I asked her, my huffing breaths only slightly wheezy. "To expect such a thing from an establishment of learning." I checked the pocket in my hoodie to make sure I'd remembered my inhaler. Nothing screamed *unattractive* like a face bluing from lack of oxygen.

"Exactly."

I had a feeling Brooklyn reveled in my prophetic status. She talked about it all the time and urged me to practice. To concentrate. To concentrate harder, darn it. Of course, she'd seen almost as much as I had when Jared came to town. She now knew there were things that went bump in the night. They were real and they were scary and they'd almost gotten us killed, so I couldn't really blame her for her obsession. Though I could complain about it every single chance I got.

"He's still crazy about you, you know?"

I was busy concentrating on supplying my red blood cells with oxygen when Brooke spoke again. Depriving my cells, I asked, "What?"

She shrugged, her long dark ponytail flopping over her shoulders. Her dark skin almost shimmered when rays of light would find their way to us. She was stunning. I was white. Chalk had more color than I did. And quite possibly more personality.

"Jared," she continued.

I had to think to put her phrases into one complete thought; then I frowned at her. "If Jared were still crazy about me," I said between huffs of air, "he wouldn't have given in so easily to my grandparents' demands."

"How do you know? Maybe he's just an honorable guy. He's old school in so many ways. Like really, really old school. Like the beginning of time old school." When I didn't respond, she added, "He looks at you every chance he gets."

I skidded to a stop, and a girl behind us slammed into me.

"Watch it, McAlister," she said, pushing past me. I fell forward and caught myself against a tree trunk.

Brooke jumped to my defense, squaring her shoulders and jamming her hands onto her hips. "You watch it, Tabitha."

"Please," she said as three other girls ran past. "Like you could take me on your best day."

Tabitha, also known as my archnemesis, just happened to be about seven feet tall to Brooke's five. She smirked and continued her trek through the forest, her blond head bobbing up and down.

Brooke came to my rescue, offering a hand to steady me as I brushed leaves off my shorts. "How rude."

"When is she not rude?" It was a sad twist of fate that Tabitha had PE with me, the person she most despised and most loved to humiliate. "But I did stop in the middle of the path."

"Why? Did you have a vision?" she asked, her eyes glimmering with optimism.

"No, you've gone mad and I think we should seek help."

She chuckled. "Jared does look at you. Every chance he gets. But not in a stalkery way. More like a pining way, like he misses you."

I clasped my hands behind my head and breathed deep to slow my heart rate. "Brooke, he never looks at me. The minute I look at him, he turns away."

"Exactly, because he was freaking looking at you in the first place. He has no choice but to turn away or get busted like twelve thousand times a day."

Her words, insane as they were, gave me a spark of hope. Then reality sank in. "He's looking at me because that's his job. To protect me, the great prophet Lorelei."

She snorted. "Yeah, keep telling yourself that."

But something in the distance had captured my attention. I squinted past the line of trees. "What is that?"

She scanned the area. "Are you changing the subject on purpose?"

When I pointed deeper into the forest, we both leaned forward and strained for a better look. Two girls walked past, clearly having given up on the whole jogging thing. I was right there with them.

"Well," Brooke said, "I don't see anything, but the way this day has been going, maybe we should get back to the gym, just to be safe."

But I had seen something. An outline. A shape that resembled a head peering from behind a tree about thirty yards away. I stepped closer as a ray of light glinted off a blade. A silver blade.

Before I could comment, something moved inside me. A ripple of displeasure. A quake of something dark and dangerous. Every molecule in my body came alive as I looked at that blade. At the sun glistening off it in the shadowy forest.

"Don't you think?" Brooke asked.

I eased my hand around her arm and stepped back onto the path.

"What?" She looked into the forest again and caught on. In a hushed whisper, she said, "I still don't see anything."

"I do." When the shape emerged from behind the tree, hunched down like a wild animal, I squeezed her arm tighter and whispered, "Run."

RATS AND SINKING SHIPS

Thankfully, Brooke needed no evidence to follow my lead. We took off at the speed of light. Or, well, at about one three-hundred-millionth the speed of light. Give or take. Suddenly traversing the uneven ground and dodging tree branches became the least of our worries. We were running for our lives and we had adrenaline on our side.

But we came to another skidding halt when someone literally jumped across the path in front of us. The movement wrenched screams from our throats and we fell back, clinging to each other like victims in a horror movie.

"It's Cameron!" Brooke said, throwing a hand over her chest to help catch her breath. We scrambled to our feet and watched as he flew through the forest toward the figure. Only then did we realize Jared was on its heels as well. He came from behind us and ran so fast, we could hardly see him. What I could see was a being that moved with the speed and grace of an animal. The fluid motion of a predator.

Jared yelled for Cameron to get us to safety, so he reversed and hurried back, stopping in front of us. And while we panted and coughed and even sputtered a little, he stood there, completely calm, not out of breath in the least. Freaking nephilim.

Cameron Lusk was the other supernatural being at Riley High, only he was born and raised here. I'd known him since kindergarten, since he'd stopped Joss Duffy from pasting my eyelids together, but I only recently got to know the real Cameron. The half-human, half-angel who was created because of me. Apparently, when the heavens realized I was going to be born and the impending war was becoming more and more impending, an archangel by the name of Jophiel had *relations,* as my grandfather called it, with Cameron's mother. And nine months later, out popped a little being who was almost as indestructible as a full-fledged angel and every bit as stubborn.

He divided his time between watching us wheeze and searching the forest, his ice blue eyes sharp, his blond hair brushing his shoulders with the breeze filtering through the leaves. After a minute, he said, "We need to go."

"What's going on?" Brooke asked.

"Later. Let's move." He looked over at me as I took a hit from my inhaler, and asked, "Can you run?"

I put my inhaler back in my pocket and nodded. We took off, following the path back to school. Brooke and I ran so fast, the leaves blurred in our periphery. The ground melted into one solid mass. We were flying.

When I glanced over my shoulder to make sure Cameron was still behind us, I pulled Brooke to a stop and glared at him. "You have got to be kidding me."

He was right on our heels. Walking. With a bored expression on his face.

He examined himself, self-conscious. "What?"

After rolling my eyes, I said between gasps of air, "This is just really disconcerting." We started for the school again, only this time I walked. There was no sense in exerting any more energy than necessary.

Brooke crossed her arms over her chest. "The least you could do is jog a little. Make it look like you're putting some effort into keeping up with us."

He cracked a smile, but his gaze stayed on full alert. "It's not my fault your legs are shorter than my attention span."

Brooke held up a hand, refusing to listen to him, and fell in step beside me. "Boys."

"Right?"

We were almost to the tree line when I heard Jared jog up from behind us. I studied him a moment. Could Brooke have been right? Did he still like me? And if he did, why not just tell me? No. He wasn't exactly the shy type. If he were that into me, I'd be the first to know.

"Well?" I asked.

He shook his head, tossing Cameron a secretive look from underneath his lashes.

"Wait," Brooke said. "Lorelei saw someone."

But that glance he'd offered Cameron spoke volumes.

Cameron nodded at him as though sending a secret message right back. "Let's keep going," he said, and led the way as Jared brought up the rear.

I tugged at Cameron's jacket. "I saw someone with a knife."

"Whoever it was is gone," Jared said from behind me.

"He outran you?" I asked, incredulous. "*You?*"

"There's no way," Brooke said.

Jared didn't respond. Maybe he and Cameron had some secret code, intel they didn't want to share with the rest of the class. They were as bad as my grandparents. I almost argued with them, insisted they spill, but my thoughts had drifted back to two pertinent details: One, Jared was right behind me. So close, I could almost feel the heat of his body, the coolness of his gaze. And two, something had moved inside me. Literally. Like a sleeping dragon had been awakened. I clutched my stomach, worry kneading my brows, and continued onward.

Cameron had parked behind the gym, and he stopped to grab a fresh shirt from the bed of his truck. Not because he got all sweaty or anything. It probably took a lot to make a supreme being sweat. But because, according to him, he hadn't changed from the day before.

"Where have you been?" Brooke asked him as he lifted off his shirt.

She tried so hard. She really did. But her gaze shifted for just a split second when his shirt obscured his vision, and she got an eyeful of muscle and skin.

I forced myself not to grin and focused on a rock at my foot, awkwardly pretending Jared wasn't beside me.

"Are you okay?" he asked.

"Wonderful," I said, offering him my best fake smile.

"I believe you saw someone."

"Great. Thanks."

After a quick glance, he asked, "What's wrong with your stomach?"

I immediately let go of my midsection. "Nothing."

He sighed at my terse responses and turned back to the forest. I realized this was my chance. If the Hardy Boys wouldn't let me in on their secret, I'd try to glean it from Jared for myself.

"I'm sorry," I said. I stepped over to him and put my hand on his arm. The touch was electric, but not because of anything extrasensory. I was touching him again for the first time in weeks. And I'd surprised him. He looked down at my hand; then his shimmering eyes locked with mine. He stepped closer, and I sucked in a soft breath.

His head descended until his mouth, full and sensual, was almost on mine, and he said, "Are you getting anything?"

I sobered instantly and jerked my hand away. "Of course not." I couldn't help the defensive tone in my voice. "I stopped having visions."

He crossed his arms over his chest and pressed his mouth together in doubt. "Really?"

"Yes, really." I tightened my jacket around me and turned my attention to Brooke and Cameron.

"Do you think the world has gotten a bit dark and fuzzy around the edges?" Brooke asked when Cameron closed his tailgate.

"It looks pretty sunny to me."

"No," she said, waving a hand absently, "I mean in general. Like there's something wrong. Something waiting."

Not even I could miss the silent exchange that time. He glanced at Jared and they held gazes for a second too long before he shrugged. "I'm not sure what you mean."

"You know exactly what I mean," she said, her voice accusing.

I had to admit, I was getting exasperated with their furtive behavior myself.

He pulled on his jacket, his brows raised in question.

"Cut it out and just tell us what's going on."

After fidgeting with the zipper, he gave up the charade with a heavy sigh. "They're gone." He scanned the area, deep in thought. "The spiritual elements in this area are gone."

Jared stepped away from me and turned back to the forest, his shoulders straight, his body tense.

"What do you mean?" Brooke asked.

I wrapped my arms around my midsection again. This was bad. I could tell. Though I had no idea what he meant either, I knew it was bad. It had to be if it set the Angel of Death and a bona fide nephilim on edge.

"Like ghosts? Poltergeists?" she asked.

They started walking back to the gym. I followed at a slower pace, wanting to hear but not wanting to know. This was not part of my plan to get back to normal. Anything having to do with spiritual elements was not normal. Normal people talked about homework, the opposite sex, plans for the weekend. They did not talk about the spiritual elements in the area like they were discussing the weather.

Jared brought up the rear.

"Exactly," Cameron said with a nod.

"What do you mean, they're gone? Why are they gone?"

"You know how rats leave a sinking ship? That would be my guess."

She stopped and ogled him. "So, all the ghosts left because this ship is sinking?"

He lifted one shoulder into another halfhearted shrug. "Something like that."

"Riley's Switch," I said, joining the conversation at last. "Riley's Switch is a sinking ship, and they know it."

The moment I said it, the minute the words left my mouth, another ripple of movement shuddered inside me. Every cell from my chin to my knees reverberated like a low chord had been strummed. I tightened my hold, calming the beast within. And wondering, why now? After ten years, why awaken now?

Jared reached for me. He grabbed my arms and looked me up and down, his expression shocked. Did he feel it too? Did he know?

I jerked out of his grasp and said, "Don't look at me like

that." Then, like a silly schoolgirl with hurt feelings—which was true on both counts—I stalked back to the gym without them.

I headed straight for the toilets. Most of the other girls, including Tabitha, were already dressed. The bell would ring in a couple of minutes, and I still had on gym shorts and a hoodie. But being tardy to my next class was the least of my worries. I crashed through a stall door and fell to my knees, heaving into the toilet. But I had yet to eat that day. Partaking in breakfast would have required some alone time with my grandparents, and I avoided that scenario as much as possible lately. So, I heaved several times to no avail. Still, that was better than upchucking actual content.

I stood and weaved toward a sink, my legs weak, my footing unsure, as one girl eyed me like I'd grown another head and a couple of others asked if I was okay. I nodded and proceeded to splash cold water on my face, groaning when the bell rang. No way would I not be late to my next class now.

"Are you okay?" Brooklyn asked, rushing in.

"Yes, but the bell rang. We need to hurry."

"Lor, what's wrong?"

I patted my face dry with a paper towel. "Nothing. We're going to be late is all."

She didn't believe me. I figured that out when she said, "I don't believe you, and we are going to have a very long talk, Lorelei McAlister."

Uh-oh. She'd used both names. I was in trouble.

"Why don't you guys iron out your problems tonight?"

We turned to see my archnemesis walk in. She handed me a pink slip of paper with crude writing and a small map.

"You can come hang and talk all you want."

Brooke ripped the paper out of my hand. "A party? You're inviting us to a party?"

Tabitha checked her long blond hair in the mirror. "Just thought you might like to have some fun. There'll be boys." With a sly grin, she retrieved the paper out of Brooke's grasp and handed it back to me. "And you and I can chat as well. You know, girl to girl." After offering me a playful wink, she turned on her toes and left.

Brooke gaped at me. "What was that all about? And since when do you even talk to the creature whose name shall not be spoken aloud? Especially after she just rammed you into a tree?"

I studied the paper, curious myself, but only a little. "If you noticed," I said, stuffing it into my pocket, "I didn't talk. She did." I left her with that and strolled to my gym locker to get dressed. No need to rush. I was going to be tardy anyway.

My grandparents might have to be called. They might have to give up part of their day to talk to Principal Davis. They might have to worry over what has gotten into me, be bothered by my lack of respect for school rules. What a shame that would be.

As it turned out, I did not have to go to the office for a tardy slip, because the teacher was late as well. She'd had to help break up another fight in the halls, this one between two girls who had the practiced art of hair pulling down to a science. The teacher's absence gave me time to recuperate from my last carpet-bombing of visions. While hurrying to fifth hour, the crush of the crowd trying to see the fight and the emotions running high catapulted vision after vision toward me until I could hardly see where I was going. Most were inconsequential, stuff that had already happened, but one vision—and there was always one—had a Riley High student contemplating suicide. It was a kid I didn't know well, but the rest of my day would be lost inside the hopeless musings of depression like a deep pit I couldn't claw my way out of.

Again.

Brooke and I walked to the Java Loft after school. It was our favorite hangout. Mostly because it served lattes and cappuccinos, but also because it was the only place in our small town that did.

Cameron was right behind us, and when I asked him about Jared, he pointed to the top of an art gallery on Main, where Jared was standing guard.

My life was so weird.

"I think I'll just head home," I said, stuffing my icy hands into my jacket pockets. "I'm kind of tired today."

"On a Friday? Lor, what is going on?" Brooke asked as I watched the silhouette of Jared against the descending sun.

"What do you mean?"

She let a loud sigh slide through her lips. "You've been acting really strange lately. I know it's a lot, everything you've been through with your parents and finding out about what happened to you as a kid, but it just seems like there's more to it than that."

I couldn't suppress a soft laugh, though there was nothing humorous about it. "More than finding out that I led my parents to their deaths?"

She put her hands in her jacket pockets too and lowered her head in silence.

"More than finding out I was possessed by Lucifer's second-in-command and he's still inside me?"

She lifted a shoulder. "It sounds so bad when you put it that way."

"And more than finding out my grandparents sabotaged the only real relationship I've ever had with a guy who could double as a supermodel slash international spy? More than that?"

"Well," she said, looking away, "yeah. More than that."

"You don't think that's enough?"

She stepped closer. "I most definitely think that's enough, but there's still more. I know you. I can gauge what's going on in that head of yours." She tapped my forehead with her index finger. "I just think we should talk is all."

I shook her off. "I can't tonight. My grandparents want to have dinner," I said, lying.

"Oh." She seemed surprised. "Okay, that's good. You guys need to talk. I'll just see you tomorrow, then? It's Saturday. We can watch movies all day and eat popcorn until we're sick."

"Sure."

"Okay," she said with a relieved smile just before she ducked into the Java Loft for a latte.

I started for home, then stopped and looked back at Cameron. "You know, you can stay here with Brooke."

His mouth formed a thin line. "You know I can't."

"Dude, you've been gone for two days. What's another half hour going to matter?"

When all I got in response was a glare, I dropped it and headed home. Cameron followed me as I knew he would. I decided to sneak around back to avoid a confrontation with my grandparents. Our house, or houselike dwelling, was connected to their store, The Wild 'n Wonderful. It was technically a health food store, but we sold a little of everything. All the everyday essentials. Like soap. And Cheetos.

"I'm going back to school for my truck," he said. "Stay inside. I'll be back in five."

"I think I'll be okay in my own house," I said, growing a little annoyed with the constant presence of one of my bodyguards.

He looked over his shoulder. "Whatever helps you sleep at night, shortstop. I'll still be back in five."

I shook my head and opened the screen door as quietly as I could. It was so weird to be at odds with my grandparents. We were always close, almost inseparable. But they had kept so much from me growing up, so much I could have used to understand the visions and other oddities in my life. They'd wanted to wait, to tell me everything when I turned eighteen—the Order, my lineage, the prophecies—but when I was hit by that truck and Jared was sent to take me, everything changed.

Everything.

Only then did I find out that my grandparents were part of the Order of Sanctity, a group of people who believed in the teachings of a powerful prophet named Arabeth, the first prophet in human history to be burned as a witch centuries before it became common practice. Only then did I find out my lineage, that I was apparently descended from her. And only then did I find out about the prophecies surrounding my birth and my destiny. Not to mention the fact that I'd been possessed as a child. That was a kicker.

And now the situation with Jared. Whatever they'd said to him brought a screeching halt to our involvement, and I resented them for it, plain and simple. It all added up to one massive wedge in our relationship. And now I avoided them whenever I could. It was just easier that way.

I crept inside and heard muffled voices coming from the living room off the kitchen. The pocket door was pulled almost completely shut, but I could just make out a heated exchange resonating from within.

"You can't do this, Bill," someone said, his voice angry, desperate. "Not after everything we've been through."

"I can and I will," my grandfather said. "I've already made the plans."

Then a woman spoke, and I recognized the voice as Mrs. Strom, one of the members of the Order of Sanctity. "After all you've taught us, after all you've preached, and now you're going to pull the rug out from under us. You're going to send our only hope away."

"She's my granddaughter, damn it," Granddad said, and a jolt of electricity shot down my spine when I realized they were arguing about me.

"She's also the prophet, Bill," someone else said. Another woman. I didn't know who. "She's the only one who can stop what's to come."

"We'll find another way," my grandmother said, her voice fragile, unsure. It was very unlike her. "We can't risk her. Not like this. Not anymore."

I heard something fall, like a table toppling over, then a low voice so full of anger and resentment, it shocked me to the core. "You're going to send her away when all the signs point to Armageddon? When she's our only hope?"

Send me away? Did I hear that right?

"You need to calm down, Jeff," another male voice said. It was Sheriff Villanueva, one of the many members of the Order. "This isn't our decision. It's Bill and Vera's."

Jeff's voice broke through again. "I hope to God you rethink this, Bill, or we'll all pay for your idiocy. You're gambling with our lives."

The pocket door slid open with a loud crash and Jeff stomped out through the kitchen to the front of the store. The bell chimed when he left. Four others followed him, and I jumped back behind our refrigerator.

"Please rethink this, Vera," Mrs. Strom said. "For all our sakes."

She sniffled into a tissue as my grandmother showed them out. They were scared and angry. Energy sparked and pulsated around them like someone had put it in a blender and set it to puree.

Granddad was still in the living room. I didn't know if he was alone or not. I should have checked. I should have tried to talk to him. Instead, I sneaked around to the stairs and hurried up to my room.

Stunned.

Speechless.

They were sending me away? To where? While I didn't want the visions or the prophecy or, most definitely, the monster inside me, I also didn't want to leave Riley's Switch. And *sending* meant alone. They would not be going with me. No one would be going with me. What would I do without Brooke and Glitch? Without Cameron? Without Jared?

My heart contracted as though I were a cornered animal, wounded and scared.

I pulled out the pink slip of paper from my pocket and studied the map. The party was in the forest about two miles from the store. Maybe a party was just what I needed. I could walk the two miles. I could walk a lot farther if I had to. Running away would be better than being sent away like a criminal, but getting back at someone was not a good reason to run away.

A floorboard creaked on the landing by my door.

"I made dinner, pix," Grandma said.

But she knew the drill. "I'm not hungry," I said, hardening my voice and my heart.

They could have made me go downstairs and eat with them anytime they wanted, and at first I wondered why they didn't. Then I figured it out: guilt. They felt guilty for keeping all that information from me growing up. For my near-death experience. For not telling me about the monster inside. So I was getting away with way more than I normally could have.

"I'll keep a plate for you in the oven," she said. My grandmother was the feistiest, cleverest, most direct person I'd ever known. She never let me get away with even the slightest white lie. The fact that I was getting away with treating them like lepers astonished me. And made me feel almost as guilty as they did. They had given up everything to raise me. When my parents had disappeared, they were nearing retirement. They had plans to travel the world, and then I was dropped into their laps like living anvil—a constant burden, a constant reminder of what they'd lost.

And there I sat, treating them like the enemy. But I was beginning to wonder if they weren't.

THE CLEARING

I waited until after ten. My grandparents had gone to bed an hour earlier, but I had to make sure they were asleep before descending the stairs. I didn't dare take the stairs outside my bedroom window. Since this whole building used to be a store and my grandparents transformed the back part into living quarters for us, there was a fire escape right outside my room. I took those stairs often, but the metal clanged with every step. No way would my grandparents not hear me.

Worse, I had two bodyguards by the names of Jared and Cameron just outside somewhere. Surely they didn't actually stay up all night every night. They had to sleep sometime. But I couldn't risk going out the back door. Jared's house, a small apartment my grandparents had used as storage and remodeled for him to live in, sat right behind the store. If he didn't see me, Cameron—who camped out behind the store in his truck while on sentry duty—surely would. So I decided to sneak out the front door.

I crept down the stairs, through the store, and out the front door. Thankfully, when the lights were turned off, so was the door chime, but I did have to turn off the alarm, which beeped every time I pushed a number. I cringed and waited to make sure no one heard, then headed out into the frigid night toward a waiting car.

"I'm glad you called," Tabitha said when I shut the door to her Honda. Her car was warm and smelled like Tommy Girl.

"Thanks." I strapped on my seat belt and settled in. I felt like I'd wandered into the cave of the enemy, but my curiosity had gotten the better of me. Why would Tabitha Sind invite little ol' me to a party? And where was her entourage? She never went anywhere without Amber, her second-in-command. Maybe it was a trap. Maybe Amber was waiting for us in some remote part of the forest and they were going to beat me to death with rocks and sticks. That would suck.

Tabitha drove down the winding canyon and took the cutoff to the Clearing, which was pretty much party central for high school kids. I'd been there once, but only during the day, never at an actual party. I waited for Tabitha to make a point in her ramblings, hoping she'd fill me in on why she'd invited me, but she went on and on about her hair and her chem test and about who all was going to be at the party. Riley's Switch had taken state this year and we were apparently still celebrating three weeks later, no matter how cold it was.

"Help me with the bags?" she asked.

We got out and she handed me a paper bag with glass bottles in it.

"My dad will kill me if he finds out I raided his liquor cabinet," she said, offering me a conspiratorial wink. But all I could think about was how she was going to navigate the uneven ground in those heels.

The party was everything I'd expected it to be: Couples sitting around a campfire, others standing, chatting and drinking. A few yelling powerful fight metaphors into the night, after which everyone had to raise whatever he or she was drinking into the air. Someone had a car stereo on in the background, the music fairly low. Lots of jocks. Lots of hair-sprayed girls. Lots of popular kids who actually got invited to parties fairly often. I straddled a weird kind of fence at school. I wasn't popular by any stretch of the imagination, but I was friends with most of the kids. And almost everyone I wasn't friends with was at this party. This was going to be loads of fun.

I strolled to a shadowy area and marveled at how it seemed warmer there, though I still shivered underneath my jacket. In what seemed like seconds later, Tabitha found me. She walked up with a cup in each hand and a clear bottle wedged under her arm.

"Here, try this."

She handed me a yellow Solo cup, and I examined the colorless contents inside. "What is it?"

A pleased smirk lifted one corner of her mouth. "Strawberry vodka. You'll love it." She tipped it toward my mouth, and a warning signal went off in my head, much like the blaring alarm preceding an imminent nuclear disaster, but I did what any normal sixteen-year-old would do. I ignored it. And I drank.

The searing liquid trailed like molten lava down my throat. I gasped and struggled for air, and after a small fit of coughs and a sneeze, I said, "Now I know why they call it firewater."

She laughed, pretending to be amused, and I gave her a second to come to her point. We weren't friends. She didn't invite me here to make small talk. And my curiosity was getting the better of me, no matter how hard I pretended otherwise. So I took another searing drink and held my cup out for more.

I could be cool. I could hang with kids who wouldn't give me the time of day. Who quite possibly didn't know my name. I could be normal.

Tabitha refilled my cup, pouring from a tall bottle before Joss Duffy grabbed it from her. She lunged to snatch it back, but he held it at arm's length, just out of her reach.

"Didn't you learn to share?" he asked, clearly having had too much already. He lost his footing, caught himself, then raised the bottle in salute.

"That's from my dad's liquor cabinet," she said. "Don't drink it all. I'll have to dilute it enough as it is."

Joss nodded, then winked at me. "Hey, McAlister. Long time no see." His Riley High letter jacket looked freshly cleaned, the red and black combination striking.

I offered a quick smile. "Actually, we saw each other in sixth today."

"Oh." He snickered. "I don't really pay attention in that class."

He tried to step closer and stumbled into me instead. I braced myself for both a fall and a vision, but nothing happened besides almost getting knocked unconscious. I pushed him off me, spilling half my strawberry vodka in the process.

"My bad," he said, raising his hands in surrender. "You look nice tonight."

"So," Tabitha said, angling her shoulders to block Joss, completely dismissing him. He shrugged and staggered back to the fire, the bottle tipped at his mouth.

"So?" I asked, taking another drink. It seemed the more I drank, the easier it became to swallow the hot liquid.

"You and Jared?" she asked, and I realized she had been biding her time, waiting for the opportunity to ply me with alcohol—a learned behavior—before asking the personal questions. "Are you guys a thing?" she continued. "I mean, it seemed like you might be a thing there for about five minutes, but now you hardly look at each other. And yet he's always near you. So, what gives?" She took a drink from her own cup, eyeing me in question from over the rim.

The world slid to the left a bit as I watched her, the alcohol affecting my equilibrium already. That was really fast. But as much fun as I was having, I just didn't think I could bring myself to have a heart-to-heart with Tabitha Sind.

"We're not a thing," I said, taking another drink so I could hide behind my cup.

She brightened. "Oh, I'm sorry. I mean, I thought maybe—"

"Nope," I said, cutting her off. "We're just friends."

"Jared!" Her tone took on a sharp pitch that cut through the frigid air.

I frowned at her. "Right. Jared. We're not—"

"You came."

She stepped closer, and I realized Jared was behind me. I closed my eyes and let out a long, exaggerated huff of air. How on earth did he find me?

"I didn't think you'd come." She was lying. Was that why she'd invited me? As a way to get Jared to come to her stupid party? I felt so used. And nauseated. Though one had nothing to do with the other.

Before I could even look at him, the world tilted just a little too far to the left. I doubled over and heaved, an act that could not possibly be appealing.

"Uh-oh," Tab said, smiling at Jared, utterly love struck. "Looks like someone isn't feeling well." She reached over and took the sleeve of Jared's jacket. That much I could see through my hair, though the image was upside down. "Why don't we leave her alone for a bit?"

When my gaze finally made its way up strong legs, fit hips, masculine hands, long arms . . . up, up, up to wide shoulders, a beautiful mouth, a perfect nose, and eyes so dark, they glittered—I realized he was looking not at Tabitha but at me. And his expression was not a happy one.

"Who gave her alcohol?" he asked.

"What?" Tabitha asked, placing a hand over her chest. "She's been drinking?"

He shot her a glare so hard, dynamite couldn't have penetrated it. Then he bent down, pulling out of her grip with the movement, and scooped me up. The world spun and my stomach heaved again—thankfully, to no avail—as he carried me a short distance from the fire.

He plopped me onto my feet, then steadied me when I almost crumpled. "What the hell are you doing?"

"What? I got invited to a party."

He grabbed hold of my upper arm. "With everything that's going on, you decide to go to a party?"

With feelings shredded, I jerked out of his grip. "Why are you even here? Why did you come?"

"What do you mean?"

I wondered what I meant as well. Was I talking about the party or just in general? "I can go to a stupid party if I want to, Jared. I can be just as normal as the next girl."

"You're not normal, and you know it."

His words cut for some bizarre reason, no matter how accurate they were. When he tried to take hold of me again, I jerked away again.

His expression hardened. "We need to get you home."

"Why? So I can be a prisoner for the rest of my life? Is this what it's going to be like forever?"

"Until we figure out who wants to harm you, yes. You'll just have to deal with that."

"What are you talking about? You killed that reporter guy who tried to kidnap me."

"And he was sent by someone else. Someone smart enough to make your death look like an accident."

"What do you mean? What accident?"

"Think about it, Lorelei. You're the prophet. The one who's supposed to save the world, literally, yet you're hit by a truck and suddenly slated to die? Does that sound wrong to you?"

I stepped back, growing wary. "What are you saying?"

"I'm saying that your near-death experience was planned. It had to be. Someone wanted to stop the prophecy from coming true. Why else would you have been scheduled to die before you could fulfill it? A centuries-old prophecy?"

I pulled my bottom lip through my teeth. "Someone tried to kill me? On purpose?"

"I believe so. And maybe that's why I couldn't take you when I was supposed to. Maybe I knew. Somewhere deep inside, I knew it was wrong."

"I thought— I thought you couldn't take me, because—" I stopped before I embarrassed myself even further. Admitting that I thought he couldn't take me because he had feelings for me, because he'd fallen madly in love with me. would probably have him in stitches.

I tried to walk past him, but he blocked me and stepped closer. He didn't try to grab me again. With arms at his sides, he watched me through his glittering gaze. His dark irises didn't reflect the light from the campfire so much as absorb it, turn it into something magical, something mesmerizing.

As though fighting with himself, he bit down, locked gazes with mine, then stepped even closer. He lifted a finger and ran it over my mouth, along my jaw. "Your grandparents were right, Lorelei."

The word "grandparents" brought me skyrocketing back to reality. I nodded and swallowed down the bitter taste in my mouth, the same one I got every time he mentioned them. "Right. When they told you to stay away from me."

"They didn't say that. Not really. They just— They reminded me of the truth."

"Of course. And what truth would that be?"

His gaze didn't waver as he said, "That I am not worthy of you."

If the world had fallen out from under me, I would have been less surprised.

"That I have no right to pursue you. I have nothing to offer," he continued. "No future here on Earth."

I was fairly certain my jaw was hanging open at that point.

"That you are destined to do great things. That you were prophesied about over four centuries ago." He closed his eyes. "And I am nothing more than an errand boy."

Maybe it was just the alcohol, but everything faded away except Jared. His startlingly beautiful face. His wide, solid build.

Then his gaze narrowed and darted past me. He scanned the area, suspicion furrowing his brows. "Who invited you to this party?"

I glanced down, embarrassed, and tried not to fall sideways with the movement. "Tabitha."

He wrapped a hand around my upper arm, still examining the black beyond. "And where is Tabitha now?"

"Over there with the in crowd, I suppose." I frowned at him. "Why?"

Jared eased me away from him. "Get her home."

"What?" I asked, but my question was answered when Cameron stepped from the shadows, his footsteps as quiet as Jared's. How was that even possible? I totally wanted that superpower.

"Really?" Cameron asked as he looked me up and down, his

expression full of mirth. "You thought you could sneak away from us by using the front door?"

"Shut up."

"Stealthy. You're like a ninja." He chuckled.

I crossed my arms over my chest, but before I could snip at him again, he stepped in front of me, blocking my view of Jared. When I tried to look around him into the forest, he blocked me again. So I tiptoed, trying to peek over his shoulder. Though I couldn't quite manage it, I did get a good look at his shoulder blade. This was ridiculous.

"What?" I grabbed his arms and finally peered around him. "What are you guys looking at?"

Cameron reached back and took hold of my wrist, then stepped closer to Jared. "This isn't my fight, Reaper. She's my only concern."

He turned back to him. "And why do you think they're here?"

"Who?" I asked, but was ignored again.

They did things like that. Spoke. Argued. Ignored.

And enough was enough. I wrenched my wrist from Cameron's grasp and stepped around him. "No more cryptic crap. I mean it. What is going on? What's out there?"

"A presence," Cameron said, clenching his hands, on full alert.

"I thought you said there wasn't a presence. That the rats left the sinking ship."

Jared spoke then. "The normal spiritual elements are gone. This is something else. Something that shouldn't be here."

Well, that couldn't be good. But if I were as honest with myself as Brooke was, I would admit that I'd felt it too. Something skewed. Something not quite right. Then again, I did just drink strawberry vodka.

"There's a balance," Jared said, turning back to us, "between the physical world and the spiritual one. The light and the darkness. And when that balance is thrown off, when the scales have been tipped to one side or the other, there is chaos. Emotions bubble. Tempers flare. Decades' worth of animosity and resentment surface, and there is a rise in violent crimes. Those who lean toward violence anyway are naturally affected more. And those who don't are seen as weak."

"Humans are swayed by more than just stress and reality TV," Cameron said. "The spiritual world is very much a part of their makeup, whether they acknowledge it or not."

I thought about how my grandparents were suddenly fighting with members of the Order. Were they being affected as well?

"And until we can figure out what is throwing the world off balance," Cameron continued, taking hold of my arm as though afraid I would rabbit, "we need to keep you safe."

"Get her home," Jared said again. "There aren't many entities that can throw the world into turmoil." He turned back to us, his mouth slanting into a menacing grin. "This shouldn't take long."

In an instant, the space he'd occupied was empty. I barely heard him running through the trees as Cameron helped—aka dragged—me back to his truck.

I looked up at him, trying not to trip. "What did you mean, it's not your fight? Why is it Jared's?"

He lifted a shoulder. "Sounded good at the time." He stuffed me into his truck none too gently, then went around to his door.

"How did you guys find me?"

"Your aura isn't exactly subtle," he said as his truck roared to life.

"My aura?"

He cracked a grin. "It's like a freaking bonfire, way brighter than that paltry excuse for a campfire you guys started."

"I had nothing to do with that," I said, defensive, "you know, if the forest burns down because of it."

I so very much wished I could know more. Could see more.

In desperation, I steeled myself for anything, then reached over and grabbed his wrist.

He frowned at me. "I'm nephilim, shortstop. You can't get anything off me unless I want you to. Or I'm so stunned, I can't think straight. Sorry, but you just don't do that to me."

I thought about being offended but couldn't quite manage it.

He pulled around to the back of the house, and I cringed. His truck wasn't exactly quiet. I jumped down after he turned it off and headed inside, only to be brought up short.

"In the bizarre instance that my grandparents didn't hear that beast of yours, we can't go up the fire escape. They'll hear."

"Maybe they should," he said, walking up behind me. He eyed me as though I were a naughty schoolgirl who deserved to be punished.

"Oh, please." I crossed my arms over my chest. "Like you've never drunk a beer."

With a shrug, he hauled me over his shoulder. I squeaked in protest.

"I've had a few beers. They don't do anything for me."

"This is so uncomfortable," I said as he climbed the fire escape as quiet as a church mouse. "I have got to learn how you guys do that."

"Do what?"

"And what do you mean, they don't do anything for you? You don't like the way they make you feel?" I wasn't going to admit it, but I was right there with him. Tipsy, buzzed, drunk—whatever the colloquialism, it sucked. If the world would quit spinning, I would get off and wait for the next one to come by.

He slid open the window and sat me on the sill. "No, I mean they do nothing for me. I don't feel any different. I don't think I can get inebriated like you."

Brooke's voice burst into the quiet like a freight train barreling through town at midnight. "You're inebriated?" she screeched.

I scrambled inside, stumbling over a chair leg, and slammed my hand over her mouth. A single lamp lit the room, casting more shadows than light, but I could see the shock in her huge eyes.

She mumbled through my hand. "You've been drinking?"

"Sh-h-h."

"Alcohol?"

Shushing her with an index finger across my lips, I said, "Only a little."

She broke free of my grip. "Lorelei Elizabeth McAlister."

Great. Time to be judged again. "What are you doing here anyway?" I peeled off my jacket as Cameron climbed in and closed the window against the crisp night air.

"Cameron called me."

I glared at the traitor before sinking onto my bed. Completely unaffected, he turned to stare into the darkness.

Brooke sat beside me. "Why would you go to that party, Lor? What could you possibly have had to gain?"

"I don't know." Leaning against the headboard, I clutched a pillow to my chest. How could I tell her that I just wanted to know what it felt like to be normal? That I just wanted to belong? And that I was super curious why Tabitha had invited me in the first place.

I couldn't miss the hurt that flashed across her face before she reined it in. "Did you think that going to a party without me would earn you brownie points with the cool kids?"

"What? No. Why would you even say that?"

"Why would you even go to that moronic party? Especially with everything that's going on?"

"No," I said, suddenly annoyed. "*In lieu* of everything that's going on. Don't you just want to forget it? To pretend that there's nothing wrong with us?"

She leaned back, clearly offended. "Wrong with us?"

"Oh, my god, Brooke, look at us. The only normal one in our bunch is Glitch, and that's debatable on his best day. We have an angelic being, a nephilim, a girl who was possessed and has a cracked aura to prove it—"

"Don't dis my crack."

"And then there's me. Whoopty-freaking-do. Oh, yes, the world will surely be saved now. And by whom? By us. The misfits of Torrance County. *We* are supposed to stop a war between good and evil? When we can barely make it to school on time, we are destined to safeguard humanity?"

She put a hand on my knee, her face knowing. Sympathetic. "You mean you."

I stilled. Questioned her with my eyes.

"You mean *you* are supposed to stop a war."

I swallowed hard with the reminder. "I just don't want it anymore. I don't want the prophecy, the visions, any of it."

"But why?" She grew animated, her movements exaggerated. "Your visions were so cool. You could've changed people's lives with them, Lor. You could've helped people."

I wanted to scoff at her. To rant and rave about how wrong she was.

She bit her bottom lip in thought, and I could see the wheels spinning. "We just need to practice more. That's it. I'm sure you'll get them back."

My next statement was little more than a whisper, but I couldn't keep going on like this. It wasn't fair to her. To either of us. Gathering my courage, I said, "I never lost them."

"What?" she said, sobering.

I shifted away from her. Plucked at the pillow. "The visions. I never lost them." I looked up to gauge her reaction. "In fact, they're so strong, so fierce, I can't control them. They come at me like missiles. They punch me in the gut. They tear through my heart. They make me sick. Every single one."

She scooted closer. "You're still having them?"

"Yes."

The surprise on her face confirmed she really had no idea. "Lor, why didn't you tell me? Why would you lie about that?"

"Because I don't want them."

"Why? Why would you not want something so miraculous?"

"Miraculous?" That time I did scoff. "You call what happens to me miraculous?" I drew in a ragged breath and readied myself to give her the truth, the whole truth, and nothing but the truth. Curling my fingers into the pillow, I asked, "Did you know there is a student at Riley High who was raped last year?"

Her eyes widened, but I barreled forward, afraid if I stopped, I wouldn't be able to start again.

"She never told anyone, because she thinks it was her fault. She keeps it bottled up inside." I leaned into her. "Do you know what it's like to be raped, Brooke? Because I do. Now I know exactly what it feels like. It is a complete and savage violation of body and soul."

Stammering, Brooke said, "I-I didn't know."

"Then did you know that another student is planning to kill himself?"

Her expression morphed into a mixture of shock and sympathy. "No."

"Not just thinking about it. Planning every moment. He's going to do it with his father's gun. Do you know what it feels like to be that desperate? That lost?" Before she could answer, I asked, "And do you know what it feels like when a bullet enters the roof of your mouth and blows the top of your head off?" I was shaking with the memory of something that had yet to come to pass. My stomach lurched as I heard the gun go off. As I felt, for just a split second, a bullet enter my brain before everything went black.

"Lorelei," she said, her voice faltering, "I'm so sorry."

"And did you know that there is another student who will die in a motorcycle accident this summer? Or another who is almost going to die of exposure and dehydration when he goes rock climbing with a friend in Utah and gets lost in the desert? Do you know what it feels like when your kidneys shut down? When your tongue swells to three times its normal size until you can barely talk? Barely swallow?"

She put a hand on mine. "I'm so sorry, Lor."

"You don't understand. I don't just see what happens to them. I feel it. Every ounce of horror. Every wave of nausea. Every pang of heartache. I'm right there with them. And I get everything—every emotion, every jolt of pain—in a blinding flash that leaves me in a stupor. The aftermath lingers for days on end. I can't eat. I can't concentrate."

Her hand pressed against her mouth as tears spilled over her lashes and onto her cheeks.

I gazed into her huge brown eyes, not wanting to offend her, but hoping—no, praying—that she would understand. I was not prying when I saw what had happened to her. I would never do such a thing. It came to me when I least expected it. When we were working on a science project in lab. It was just there.

"And did you know that another student at Riley High was almost abducted when she was seven? That a man reached out of his car and grabbed her as she was on her way home from the store? That terror filled her so completely, she wet her pants?"

Brooke stilled in disbelief for a second, then she fell into the memory like a skydiver during free fall, her expression blank, void of anything but that moment in time.

"And when she wrenched free of him, ripping her shirt and staining it with the orange Popsicle she dropped, she ran all the way home, too scared to scream, too in shock to cry. But she never told her mother. She wasn't supposed to go to the store by herself. Ever. And she was more worried about getting in trouble for that than turning the man in. So she never told anyone."

After taking a moment to let the memory resurface, Brooke stood and stepped back, struggled to absorb the fact that I knew.

"How would you suggest that I tell her that?" I asked, my voice soft, empathetic. "The student who wet her pants and told her mom she'd fallen in a puddle of water? How should I approach her and tell her that I know one of her most guarded secrets? Do you think she would believe me?"

I hadn't missed the clenching of Cameron's fists when I talked about Brooke's memory. The tensing of his jaw. He cared for her deeply. That much was obvious. And I was glad because of it. To have a nephilim on your side could only be a good thing. He was super strong and super fast and could protect her from so many of life's dangers. Like pedophiles.

"I don't want this anymore, Brooke. Any of it."

She blinked back to me, but before she could respond, Glitch lifted the window. "What'd I miss?" he asked, his gaze bouncing between the two of us. Alarm flitted across his face when he saw Brooke. Then again when he saw me, and I realized I was crying.

I wiped furiously at my wet cheeks and strode to the bathroom. Apparently, Cameron had called the whole gang.

"What happened?" Glitch asked Brooke as I closed the door and swiped at the tears, angry at what I'd seen, angrier that I'd shocked Brooke, that I'd hurt her with a memory she'd tucked into the farthest reaches of her consciousness, trying desperately to forget.

Oh, yeah. These visions were great.

BEEN THERE, DONE THAT

Since I'd been honest with Brooke, I had no choice but to tell Glitch the truth about my visions as well. He was surprised. And then a little hurt. Then a little angry. Then sympathetic. And about twenty seconds after all his emotions boiled and bubbled beneath his coppery surface, he settled on understanding and supportive.

"We're staying over all weekend if we can get away with it," he said. "But seriously, Cameron needs to go for pizza."

Cameron scowled over his shoulder. "Okay, and while I'm

gone, can you protect Lorelei from any supernatural threats that might come her way?"

"I'll go for pizza," he corrected. Thankfully, the Pizza Place stayed open until midnight on Friday and Saturday nights.

An hour later, we were having a slumber party complete with pepperoni pizza, orange soda, and an '80s movie about kids in detention who become unlikely friends.

"Shouldn't Jared be back by now?" I asked Cameron, growing more concerned by the minute.

He took another bite of pizza and shrugged. He was so helpful.

I stood and looked out the window. "My grandparents are sending me away."

Everyone stopped what they were doing and gaped at me.

"They got in a fight with several members of the Order about it, but they're resolute. They think it's become too dangerous, and they're sending me away."

Cameron frowned as though confused, as though the mere thought was unfathomable.

"Did you remind them how insane that is?" Glitch asked.

"I didn't talk to them about it. I overheard."

"Then I'm going with you," Brooke said, indignation raising her chin. "They can't separate us. We're practically twins."

Glitch took the floor. Cameron took Brooke's bed since it was closest to the window seat and he could stare out the window in his broody way and still get some rest. And Brooke had insisted. She slept with me on my bed, and while we were small, we still had to snuggle really close to get comfortable. Twin beds weren't exactly made for two, but it was nice having her so close. About an hour after we all settled in, I still couldn't sleep. I kept thinking about Jared. Was he still out there? Back in his apartment? Was he still on guard duty or sleeping?

Cameron gave it his all, sitting on the bed instead of lying in it, but even he had dozed off. Glitch had joined him, snoring softly into the carpet after stuffing the pillow I gave him between his legs and cradling it. He would have quite the cheek imprint come morning.

Brooke whispered softly into my ear. "What about Glitch and Cameron? Did you see what happened to them on that camping trip that spring break? Have you seen that in your visions?"

I turned to face her, our noses mere inches apart in the dark room. "No," I whispered back, hoping not to wake Cameron, since we were talking about him and all. "I've tried very hard not to, in fact. It's just— It's such a violation."

"But if you're not doing it on purpose, if you're not controlling it—"

"I used to think that too, but it's all I can do to make it through a school day without throwing up or becoming suicidal. I just try my best to avoid visions whenever and wherever possible."

She took my hands into hers and lifted them to her mouth. "I'm so terribly sorry, Lor. All the pushing I've done, all the nagging, and you were just trying to get through the day."

"It's not your fault."

"I just wish I had known. I wish I had picked up on it instead of making your life worse."

I smiled, wondering yet again what I'd done to deserve her. "You couldn't make my life worse if I paid you to."

The smile that widened across her face like the New Mexico sky made me rethink my last statement. She crinkled her nose. "Bet I could."

I laughed softly. "Okay, I bet you could too."

She sobered, bit her lip, looked at me from underneath her ridiculously thick lashes. "Lor, why didn't you tell me?"

My lids closed with regret. "I'd planned to, but when I saw what happened to you, when I saw your past, I just didn't know how. I felt like I was doing something wrong. Something invasive. And I just wanted it to stop."

She nodded. "I understand. I do. But you'll still have to pay. Dearly. You realize that, right?"

I grinned. "I suppose I do."

"And I won't go easy on you just because we're besties."

"I would never expect you to."

"There'll probably be pliers involved. And fire ants."

I shuddered. At least she didn't mention spiders.

"And spiders."

Dang, she was brutal.

By Sunday morning, Brooke was belting out classic tunes to try to cheer me up. It was not working. Jared had never come home, and I had been reduced to a pile of nerves. No, not just a pile of nerves. A *quivering* pile of nerves.

Brooke leaned over to me as we sat in a padded pew, and whispered, "Want me to sing 'Tainted Love' again?"

I frowned. "No."

"'Love Is a Battlefield'?"

"Nope."

"'Love Shack'?"

I couldn't help it. I cracked a smile.

"'Love Shack' it is."

She took a deep breath and I clamped a hand over her mouth in horror, garnering a few admonishing looks from our staunchest members in the process. When Grandma joined in, her expression mortified, we straightened instantly. Brooke pointed to me, rolling her eyes as though I were hopeless. She would pay.

Grandma made eye contact with me. I quickly averted my gaze. I could see the sadness and frustration through my periphery, but I couldn't quite bring myself to pretend everything was okay. They were once again making plans for my life without even consulting me. And just where were they planning on sending me? We had no relatives. We were the last of our clan. I think my grandma had a great aunt who was still living, but that was about it. She lived in Oklahoma. Was that where they would send me? Off to live with an estranged aunt nobody had heard from in decades?

I fought not to focus on that and tried to pay attention to Granddad's sermon. My mind wandered regardless.

Like many churches, this one had an unassuming door behind the pulpit. Ours led to the basement. Or so that's what I'd always believed. My grandparents showed me just how deep the basement went. They gave me the grand tour of the Order of Sanctity headquarters.

Down one level was a shadowy storeroom that looked like any other basement one might find beneath an old church. Dark and dank and a little bit scary. But down another set of stairs was a second basement. Again, it looked normal at first glance. Until Granddad opened the doors to what I could only describe as an underground warehouse.

Room after room flowed through a massive bunkerlike structure. It had tall ceilings with exposed metal framework and rooms divided by half-height partitions. All except one.

One structure was a room unto itself. It had thick walls and a single opening. Inside it, metal drawers and shelves lined the walls. Inside those were the ancient texts and documents of the Order of Sanctity. That was the archive room.

The ancient documents had been passed down from generation to generation. They were very valuable. Some of the texts were prophecies directly from Arabeth or one of her daughters, recorded long ago and translated through the ages by varying scribes. And some talked about the prophets from the other lines. Always female. Always groundbreakers. People like the famous Greek poet Sappho and the awe-inspiring heroine Saint Joan of Arc.

I had to own up to a certain amount of pride, knowing I hailed from such brave and noble beginnings. Though they were both from different branches, we were all related in the end. At least, that's how I saw it.

Unfortunately, I didn't have a lick of bravery or nobility.

With as much stealth as she could muster, Brooke slipped a note to me while keeping her attention focused on Granddad.

I unfolded it and read, *We should come back tonight.*

She wanted to come back to do some research, but I was pretty researched out. And I wanted to know what had happened to Jared.

I wrote, *Been there, done that,* and slid it back.

We'd sneaked into the archive room several times over the past few weeks. It was like some kind of morbid curiosity took hold of me. I didn't want anything to do with this war or the visions, yet I couldn't help but read the prophecies every chance I got. I always hoped they would tell me what to do. How to fight. How to win. But after another fruitless search, I could only close the thick book I'd been trying to decipher with a huff of frustration. Prophecies were weird and boring. The translated texts said things like, "It will take the Last but a moment to undo all that which evil has done." How the heck was that supposed to be helpful? The last what? Prophet? That's what they called me, the last prophet of Arabeth. Which did not bode well for any children I might have. Since the prophets were always female, I supposed if I did survive the war and did happen to have children someday, they would all be boys. So that was one question out of the way.

". . . but a moment to undo all that which evil has done."

If that prophecy was about me, it was nice to know it would

take me only a moment to fix everything. Not. I'd already tried snapping my fingers, to no avail. I'd even tried crossing my arms and blinking. Wiggling my nose didn't help either. Clearly magic was not part of my gift.

I felt the note slide under my fingers again. *We might learn something about your visions. About how to control them.*

At that exact moment, I realized something. None of the translated texts talked about the visions themselves. They recorded only what had been seen, not *how* to see or how *not* to see. Just what had been seen already.

I wrote back. *We couldn't be that lucky.*

After Granddad's sermon, Brooke and I hurried to the back of the church as Grandma and Granddad spoke to a few members of the congregation. They'd called a special meeting of the Order amidst hateful glares and resentful glances. And not just mine. Many in the congregation were angry with them for wanting to send me away. I still hadn't talked to them about the conversation I'd overheard. I was curious how long it would take them to tell me themselves. Or were they just planning to truss me up and ship me off?

Cameron and Glitch were waiting at the back of the church and we rushed out before anyone could stop us. We were going to the forest. We were going to search for Jared.

We wound through the trees and over dips in Cameron's tan pickup. The poor thing looked like it'd been used by war correspondents in the Middle East. It sported a nifty camper shell and several large rust-covered dents. We bounced and lunged until we came to a stop near the clearing. It looked so different in the daytime. I was surprised there wasn't more debris. A few bottles and cans littered the ground, but nothing too significant. And a couple of fallen logs bordered the charred remains of the campfire.

"Okay," Glitch said, zipping up his hoodie. "Where did you last see him?"

I turned full circle, trying to get my bearings.

"Over there," Cameron said, pointing to a patch of trees just past the Clearing.

"That's right," I said. "He went through there."

I was heading that way when Cameron said, "Wait." He stopped and examined the ashes where the campfire had been.

"What?" Brooke asked, following him over.

"Do you smell that?"

Curiosity got the better of me. I went back and sniffed around. An acrid scent, sharp and tangy, assaulted me.

After taking a big whiff herself, Brooke coughed into her jacket sleeve. "What is that?"

"It's like vinegar," I said, crinkling my nose.

Cameron knelt beside the cremated remains for a closer look.

"Well?" Glitch asked, impatient.

Placing his icy gaze on him, Cameron said, "What's wrong with this picture?"

Glitch took offense. "Oh, right, because I'm Native American, I automatically know everything about campfires."

"I was thinking back to Boy Scouts, but that'll work too."

At the mention of Boy Scouts, Glitch hardened. His eyes glittered with anger as Cameron let a malicious grin slide across his face. He'd done it on purpose. Brooke and I glanced at each other, once again wondering what had happened that spring break years ago. Glitch went on a camping trip in the mountains with his Boy Scout troop. Something happened on that trip. Something bad. And I'd known that Cameron was involved, but no one would ever tell me more, including Glitch. It was a constant source of curiosity. What could cause such animosity between them?

Cameron chuckled, giving up the game first, and said, "I just meant, most campfires don't turn the wood blue."

We all stepped forward to look. Sure enough, the charred wood had a blue tint to it, iridescent like a pearl.

"Wow," Brooke said, bending to pick one up.

Cameron grabbed her arm. "I wouldn't," he said, pulling her away from it.

"What is it?"

"No idea. I just wouldn't. And there's blood." He pointed to the side. "A lot of it."

Startled, I rushed forward to examine the area myself. "Do you think it's Jared's?"

"No telling."

"Well, let's look over here," I said, heading to where I'd last seen Jared.

Cameron stood and did a 180. "He's not out here."

I turned to argue, but realized if anyone would know, Cameron would. Disappointment ripped through me. "You're sure?"

He nodded, eyeing the trees like they were about to attack. "I'm sure. And we need to go."

"Why?" Brooke asked.

"You know how you were feeling fuzzy?" he asked her before walking over to me and grabbing on to my jacket.

"Yes." She started to become wary, as did Glitch. They surveyed the surroundings too and started making their way back to the truck.

"Well, it's even fuzzier out here."

Just then, Cameron stopped and put an arm across my torso from behind. He squinted, peering into the forest.

"Is it Jared?" I asked in a hushed whisper.

He shook his head and stepped back, dragging me with him.

We were only a few yards from the truck when I asked, "Cameron, what?"

That's when I saw a kid, a boy around thirteen. Partially obstructed by the trees, he wore a huge green army jacket that was about three sizes too big and a gray hoodie underneath that. It was hard to make out his face. I didn't recognize him from school, but I did recognize his slight shape. And, of course, the blade in his hand.

A razor-sharp tingling raced up my spine. "That's the kid from the other day. The one in the forest behind the school."

"Do you know him?" Cameron asked.

"No, do you?"

"No." He said it purposefully, like he was making a statement.

Before I could question Cameron further, the boy disappeared into the trees. We kept walking backwards past the campfire, the strong scent assaulting us again, before climbing back into the truck.

Brooke clicked her seat belt, then asked, "Okay, what was that about?"

"I'm not sure, but I want a list of everyone who was at that party."

"Um, I'm not sure I can remember everyone."

"Right," Brooke said, " 'cause you were wasted."

I frowned at her. "I wasn't wasted."

"And," Cameron continued, "I want you two to stay inside today." He looked directly at me. "No venturing out for any reason."

"You have to tell me why first."

He put the truck in reverse. "No, I don't, actually."

"Yes, you do," I said, my voice full of false bravado. Army-jacket kid shook me up, and I had no idea why. Probably the fact that he was creepy and carried a knife. But he was young and not particularly big.

Cameron got us headed in the right direction, then floored it as we wound down the mountain. "I want you both to know," he said, sideswiping an overgrown bush, "I have permission to tie you up if you give me any trouble."

Brooke gasped. "You do not."

He grinned. "Call your parents and ask."

She clamped her mouth shut and folded her arms over her chest as Glitch stared out his window. I didn't know if he was still seething over the Boy Scouts comment or the fact that Cameron had permission to tie up Brooke.

"So, what's up with that kid?" I asked Cameron as we pulled behind the store.

He leaned his head to either side, stretching his neck. "It wasn't him I was worried about. How soon can you get me that list?"

"I can work on it now, but I really didn't see everyone and I'm not sure how many I'll remember."

"That's okay. It'll be a start."

"A start for what?" Brooke asked.

"We need to interview them. See if anyone who was there that night has been reported missing or is acting strange."

"Like Lor?" Brooke asked.

I elbowed her.

One corner of his mouth tilted up. "Something like that."

Grandma and Granddad were not happy that we'd left after church without telling them where we'd gone, but I was a little unhappy with them as well, so I figured we were even-steven.

I wondered how the meeting went, if they held their ground about sending me away or if they'd allowed the congregation to sway them to change their minds. After playing twenty questions, we were finally allowed to go upstairs.

And stay there.

Or get tied up.

"You need to rest."

I peered into the darkness toward the window seat where Cameron had set up surveillance, his back against the wall so he could keep watch.

"Cameron, this is ridiculous. You need rest, too. What good are you going to do anyone if you can't stay awake?"

I couldn't see his face clearly in the soft light of the moon, but I was certain he scowled at me. "This is what I do, Lor. I'll be fine. You, on the other hand . . ."

"What is that supposed to mean?"

"Have you seen your hair when you don't get enough sleep?"

He knew my curly red locks were a constant source of concern. I threw a pillow at him. He caught it, then stuffed it behind his head.

"Thanks," he said, the satisfaction in his voice worth the loss of my most cherished possession. Or, well, one of my top twenty most cherished possessions.

"Is he okay?" I asked him, and he didn't have to ask me whom I meant.

"I wish I knew."

I rose onto my elbows. "I thought you guys could, like, sense each other."

"We can. He must be too far away. I haven't sensed him for a while now."

That worried me. "Do you think something's happened?"

His head shake was not a negation, but a confirmation that he had no idea.

"Do you know what's going on?"

"No more than you."

I lay back on my lumpy, less-prized pillow. "Yes, Cameron, if there is one thing I know for certain, it's that you know more about all this stuff than I do."

He settled his gaze on me. I couldn't so much see it as feel it. "What's it like?" he asked, his tone full of genuine curiosity.

"What? Having friends?"

He smiled. "Having a demon inside you."

"Oh." Of course he would want to know about Malak-Tuke. The demon inside. What was it like? That was a good question. "I think at one point I could feel him. I remember knowing he was there. But then I forgot and I honestly don't know that I even feel him anymore. Maybe I'm just used to having him inside me." It was a disturbing thought, but a logical one.

As nephilim, Cameron could see things we couldn't, like poltergeists and auras. It fascinated me. He told me a while back that my aura was different, unusual. He'd never seen anything like it. "Is my aura different because of the demon, do you think?"

"No." He shifted toward me. "Your aura was different even before then."

"You remember that far back?"

"I remember seeing your aura when I was very young. It's one of my first memories." His head tilted to the side. "The girl encased in fire."

Oh, I liked that. Jared had told me that my aura looked like fire. The thought fascinated me. "Did it change after my parents disappeared? After the demon took me?"

He lowered his head as though regretting what he was about to say. "For a while. It got darker. But slowly the fire took over again."

"I wish I could see what you see."

He glanced at Brooke's sleeping form. Her aura was different as well. It was cracked from when she too was possessed. Damaged. Only she was possessed by an evil spirit, not a demon. The way I understood it, if caught in time, a person could survive possession by an evil spirit, but people almost never survived possession by a demon. No idea what happened with me, why I was even still alive with a demon inside. Granddad and the Order exorcised the entity out of Brooke. She almost died as a result. If her family had not brought her to Riley's Switch when she was in the third grade, to the Order, she may not have survived much longer anyway. But apparently, trying to exorcise the demon out of me when I was six would have killed me. Or that was what they feared.

Still, I wished I could see Brooke's unusual aura as Cameron could. "Is she still cracked?" I asked, unable to suppress the smile in my voice.

"I think she'll always be a little cracked."

I chuckled. "I think we should call her that. Crack."

"That's why I call her Moon Pie."

With interest piqued, I asked, "What does a MoonPie have to do with it?"

He stretched and let out a yawn before answering. "When we were in the fifth grade, I saw a MoonPie in a store that was broken. It had a crack down the middle that reminded me of her aura."

I couldn't help it. I burst out laughing. "That's why you call her that?"

He laughed too until Brooke stirred. We quieted instantly, but the image was one I would cherish forever.

I ended up talking to Cameron for much of the night, learning about what it was like growing up with his abilities. Being able to see what he sees. On one hand, the idea of detecting ghosts and auras was fascinating. On the other, the things he saw would have scared my hair straight. I wasn't sure any kid, nephilim or not, should be subject to such knowledge. How did he make sense of it growing up? How did knowing what he knew shape his psyche? His behavior? He'd always been such a loner, never had many friends, and kept to himself pretty much his whole life. Now I understood why.

I looked at the clock as sleep finally settled around me. Two in the morning. I would look horrible for school. Especially since I woke up a little over three hours later to the strangled sounds of my own breathing.

STRAWBERRY SHAMPOO AND CINNAMON ROLLS

A nightmare. I'd had a nightmare, and it was enough to cause an asthma attack. Thankfully, someone thought to put battery acid in an inhaler for just such an occasion.

Standing barefoot in my bathroom, surrounded by a billowing cloud of steam, I wiped condensation off the mirror and leaned forward. Probing. Searching. I studied the pupils of my gray eyes and rapped on the silvery glass. "I know you're in there," I said to the demon lying dormant inside.

Talking to the demon was better than dwelling on the fact that Jared never came home. Even my grandparents started asking questions, to which I just shrugged. If they knew he was missing, they would send me packing for sure. For my own safety, of course.

Then again, maybe Jared wasn't just missing. Maybe he'd been called back. He was the Angel of Death, after all. He had a job to do. Would he leave without saying good-bye?

The thought made my chest ache with sadness.

Since it was Monday and I couldn't sleep anyway, I'd dragged myself out of bed earlier than I thought humanly possible and forced my reluctant body into the shower. The warm water helped, but it didn't dissipate the dream I'd had. The same dream I'd been having for weeks, reliving the possession as though it had happened yesterday. The residue lingered, dark and eerie, like a thick smoke suffocating any thoughts of a normal day.

I narrowed my eyes at my own reflection, hoping the demon inside was looking out, watching me watch him. I didn't want to be rude, but it was my body he was trespassing against.

"If you don't come out of there this instant, I will drag you out by your fingernails and serve you to the buzzards."

"Really?" Brooklyn inched the shower curtain aside and peeked around it, shampoo bubbling down her long black hair. "I got five bucks says you can't take me on your best day."

"I was talking to Mal," I said, staring him down in the mirror.

Mal was our little nickname for the monstrosity within me. Malak-Tuke was just so formal. I often wondered how Satan was getting along without his go-to guy, him setting up shop in my innards and all.

"Is Mal talking back to you?" Brooklyn asked me.

"Not that I know of."

"Well, if he ever does, let me know," she said, seconds before she sucked in a sharp breath, then followed it up with a whole lot of coughing and sputtering. Either she'd accidentally swallowed shampoo or she was coming down with something. Probably something serious like scarlet fever. Or Ebola.

I almost worried when she started making vomit sounds.

"Your shampoo tastes horrible."

"Really?" I asked, feigning surprise. "It smells so fruity."

I turned back to the mirror and saw Cameron standing at my window. He'd gone out early to do reconnaissance. I had no idea what that meant exactly, but it sounded important. I tightened my robe and strode to open the window. A bitingly harsh wind whipped inside as Cameron bent to talk to me through the opening.

"Pervy much?" I asked him before he could say anything.

"Why?" He looked past me into the bathroom. "Is Brooke in there?"

I maneuvered around to try to block his view, but since he was well over a foot taller, I doubted I was doing any good. "Did you find anything?" I asked, referring to our missing team member.

He shook his head. And he seemed worried, which was not like him.

I tried not to let that news push me further into a state of despair. Jared was a big boy. He was a millennia-old big boy. And me worrying about him was like a gnat worrying about the well-being of a guided missile.

"Hey," Brooke yelled to me, "did you take my favorite towel?"

I bit down and tossed Cameron a conspiratorial gaze. "No," I said, slowly pulling the towel off my head and stuffing it behind her bed. "I have no idea where it is."

Cameron grinned. "Maybe I should take her one."

"Maybe you shouldn't." He shrugged, then frowned at me when he realized I was shivering. "I'll meet you downstairs," he said, but I grabbed his jacket sleeve to stop him.

"Cameron, can you feel him? You know, like before? Is he in pain? Is he lost?" Then I voiced the bane of my worries. "Is he gone?"

He shook his head again, sympathy lining his ice blue eyes. "I just don't know."

"That means you can't sense him, right?"

"It doesn't mean anything." He started to close the window, and just before it shut all the way, he said, "Dress warm."

"Are you sure you haven't seen my favorite towel?" Brooke asked, standing in another towel that was not her favorite.

I wrapped my arms around my waist and headed back to the bathroom. "I bet Glitch used it. He's so inconsiderate that way."

"Mmm-hmm." She wasn't buying it.

When we were finally fit to face the world, I braced myself for the confrontation to come. Breakfast with the grandparents. I took a deep breath and headed down.

"Hey," I said to my grandmother as I stepped off the stairs. We always played nice in front of company, and since Brooke was right behind me . . .

Grandma offered a hesitant smile, then looked back at her new phone, a quizzical expression drawing her brows together. "Hey, pix. Did you sleep well?"

"Not really."

"Hey, Grandma," Brooke said, stepping off the stairs with a special kind of bounce.

"Good morning, hon," Grandma said.

Brooke grabbed an apple, bit into it, then continued to talk despite her mouth being completely full. "Neither of us slept well. I doubt we'll make it through the day without lapsing into a coma."

Grandma didn't even spare her a glance that time. "I'm

almost certain you'll make it. If for some reason you lose consciousness, text me. I need the practice."

Brooke giggled as she scooped peanut butter onto an apple slice, then cast me a sympathetic gaze. "How did you ever survive childhood with such neglect? Such indifference?"

She was doing her darnedest to get Grandma and me to converse. It was not going to work.

The back door opened, allowing the crisp breeze to sweep into the room and up the back of my sweater. I shivered in response, offering my grandfather a sideways glance as he peeled off his jacket and hung it up by the door.

"Hey, pixie stick," he said, his voice only slightly strained. "Brooklyn."

"Hey, Pastor Bill," Brooke said. "Do you like your new phone?"

He strolled over and bent to give me a hesitant peck on the cheek. "Not even a little," he said, then offered Brooke a peck too.

"Well, I love mine," Grandma said, her eyes glued to the screen, sparkling with an alarming degree of lust. I never figured Grandma for a techno geek, but she was really getting into that thing.

She pushed a button, and a microsecond later Granddad's phone beeped. With a heavy sigh, he took it out of the case at his belt and worked a few moments to get the message to come up. Then his face morphed into one of his signature glares. The one that reminded me of a guy at a carnival one time when I tried to convince him I was old enough to go on the Terrifying Twister without my parents' consent. I was four.

"You couldn't have just said good morning?" Granddad asked. "I'm standing right here."

"No." She waved an impatient hand at him. "You have to text that to me. Pretend we're on our honeymoon."

Brooklyn choked on her milk and spent the next two minutes coughing. Then she made this gagging sound that was very much like her reaction to my shampoo.

Taking Brooke's sudden fit into consideration, Granddad explained. "We had a huge fight on our honeymoon. We didn't talk for days."

"But if we'd had these phones," Grandma said, shaking it at him for effect, "we wouldn't have needed to talk. These things are great."

His phone beeped again. "Really, Vera? I'm right here."

"What? I can't hear you." Then she giggled like a mental patient, and I almost smiled. Maybe the phones weren't such a good idea after all.

The back door opened again when Cameron strolled in, his blond hair a disheveled mess.

"You look like a tumbleweed," Brooke said, her voice hoarse from her most recent efforts.

Never one to be accused of social graces, he shrugged at her before nodding to my grandparents. "Hey, Pastor, Mrs. James."

"Hi, Cameron," Granddad said, but Grandma was still busy with her phone.

He didn't seem to mind. He stuffed his hands into his pockets and leaned against the wall, waiting for us. But when Brooklyn wasn't looking, his eyes wandered toward her, a glint of interest in them despite the fact that she was in the middle of stuffing the last remnants of apple into her mouth. Then his phone beeped. He fished it out of his front pocket, frowned, then looked up at Grandma, who now wore a satisfied grin on her face. After clearing his throat in obvious discomfort, he mumbled, "It's nice to see you too, Mrs. James."

Grandma nodded. This was getting ridiculous.

"How did you know it was Grandma?" I asked him. "She just got that phone."

He leaned forward to confide in me. "She's been texting me all night."

"Grandma!" I scolded, breaking my vow of silence and giving her my best look of shocked dismay. "You can't go around texting high school kids in the middle of the night. You'll get arrested."

Cameron broke, chuckling before he headed toward the back door. "Are you kidding? I now have your grandma's famous recipe for *chile con queso.*"

"Sweet," Brooke said, scooping up her jacket and backpack and following him out. "You can make some later."

I took an apple to eat on the way to school and grabbed my jacket and backpack as well.

"Can we talk to you, pix?" Granddad asked.

I paused but didn't look back at them. "I'll be late for school."

"We'll talk later, then," Grandma said, her voice soft and sad.

It made my throat constrict. I nodded and headed out of a perfectly warm house into a cold, frigid wind that whipped my hair about and took only seconds to convince me I'd underdressed for the occasion despite Cameron's warning. Bummer that insulated work coveralls and ski masks weren't in fashion.

We hurried into Cameron's beat-up Chevy. He'd kept it running, and it rumbled and shimmied as we climbed in. Despite its haggard appearance on the outside, the inside boasted a toasty warmth that kept the chills at bay. That was all that mattered at the moment.

"I think you should look for Jared today while we're in class," I said to Cameron as we drove to school.

He shook his head, and disappointment rushed over me.

"But why? It's not like you've never skipped."

With a sigh, he leveled a hard stare on me. "He's not my concern, Lorelei. You know that."

Of course he wasn't. I was. And because of that, Jared's best hope was lost.

"But what if he's hurt?"

"Not likely," he said, pulling into the parking lot.

"But what if he is?"

He turned off his truck and said, "Then I'll pay the guy who hurt him fifty bucks to tell me how he did it."

I turned away from him. "That's not nice."

"The truth rarely is."

The icy wind cut through our clothes and had my teeth chattering before we got to the door. Still, I loved the weather. Cold and promising as a thick wetness permeated the air. Maybe it would snow. Few things trumped snow days. Hot chocolate with marshmallows, maybe. And Jared's eyes.

Glitch met us at the side door of the school with a box of his mother's homemade cinnamon rolls, but not even the warm scent of cinnamon and melted butter could bring me out of my misery. Though they did their darnedest.

We dived in, and Brooke moaned when she took a bite. Glitch glared at Cameron when he took two.

"Who's that?" I asked, licking my fingers, then pointing to the side.

"Oh, that must be the new kid," Glitch said. "I heard we were getting someone new."

We stopped to take a look. He dressed in retro attire with thespian undertones. Tweed gray coat, long and loose. Sandy brown hair under a black beret. And he was really, really tall.

At the exact same moment, Brooke and I turned to look at the other really, really tall guy in school. One of them, anyway. There was tall, then there was really, really tall—and the new guy, like Jared and Cameron, was really, really tall.

"Not another one," I said under my breath.

Brooke looked up at him. "Relative of yours?"

But Cameron was also staring at the new guy, his expression guarded. If I didn't know better, I'd say he was taken aback.

The new guy stood talking to Mr. Davis. As the principal pointed down the hall, apparently giving directions, the new guy turned and looked right at us. Right at me.

His face, while handsome, was somehow disproportioned. There was something strange about him. Something out of place. His face was a little too long, perhaps, or the angles a little too sharp, the eyes a little too close set.

The polite thing to do would have been to look away, and yet there we stood. The lot of us. Staring as though we had never seen another human being in our lives. Surely we looked like something from one of those *Twilight Zone* reruns. The guy looked from me to Brooke to Glitch. Then slowly his attention meandered up the length of Cameron, and their gazes locked for a long, tense moment.

Cameron's expression wasn't derisive, exactly. More like wary or just plain surprised.

The kid nodded, an almost imperceptible grin lifting one cheek, then headed out in the direction Mr. Davis had pointed.

Glitch turned toward Cameron. "Do you know him?" he asked.

But Cameron was stunned. I could tell. Brooke raised her hand and waved it in front of his eyes. He blinked back to us.

"Is everything okay, Cameron?" I asked.

"Let's get to class." The brusqueness in his tone should have convinced me to comply without any more questions, but I wasn't feeling particularly compliant.

"Cameron, what is going on?" I asked him when he took off down the hall. It was hard to follow a super tall guy when you had only enough leg to accommodate a five-foot frame. "I get so tired of your cryptic personality."

He regarded me, his expression worried. "There's a disturbance in the air, and that guy is disturbing."

"Really?" Brooke asked. "In what way?"

"In a disturbing way."

She'd had enough as well. She grabbed hold of his jacket sleeve and pulled him to face us. "Who was he?"

Cameron studied her before saying, "I don't know. He was just different." When she scowled at him, he added, "He was fuzzy around the edges."

Of all the teachers in all the schools in all the world, Ms. Mullins was my absolute favorite, and Brooke and I had her first hour. It made my mornings not quite so loathsome, knowing I'd get to see her. I wasn't sure why, what it was about her that set her so far apart. She was a tiny woman with dark hair and sparkling eyes who looked at life like there was more to it than just memorizing the cell structure of an earthworm. We had to know that stuff too, of course, but she also taught us to see science in everyday things. Like survival of the fittest and natural selection. Which, sadly, made any attraction Jared might have for me even more questionable.

"Hey, Ms. Mullins," I said to her when Cameron dropped us off. He'd seemed reluctant to leave us, but what could he do? Hovering in the hall was not an option. He'd simply have to go to class and learn stuff like the rest of us.

Ms. Mullins looked up from her desk and drew her brows together. "You're on time."

I grinned and headed to my seat.

"But it's a Monday."

I tried to feign offense. "I've been on time lots of Mondays." When her mouth thinned in doubt, I added, "Well, I've *thought* about being on time lots of Mondays."

Truth be told, I probably had fewer late passes than any other student in school. I was boring. Predictable. And the new guy had fuzzy edges. What was going on?

The morning progressed with me trying not to touch other students—lest I be bombarded with unwanted visions—and Brooke coming up with a thousand different scenarios as to why the new guy had fuzzy edges. She conjured everything from a rare tropical disease to a zombie attack in the forest the night of the party, thus the horrid smell.

Unfortunately, in the classes we didn't have together, I had to stew in my own musings about what was going on. They were worse than Brooke's. I quickly realized, however, I had nowhere near her creative insight. The only thing I could come up with was that maybe the new kid had bronchitis, because a zombie attack seemed a tad unrealistic. Then again, so did the demon possession of yours truly.

By the time we got to PE, Brooke had decided the new guy was a warlock, a witch turned evil and cast out by his Wiccan clan, thus the fuzzy edges. She'd devised a plan to get him to do a spell on Tabitha. Something bad, like have all her hair fall out or paint her fingernails black so she looked goth. I had managed to avoid Tabitha all morning, and oddly enough, she did the same to me. No prodding. No teasing. The reprieve was rather refreshing.

Brooke was busy detailing her vision while I brushed my teeth in the locker room after class. I'd had an unfortunate incident with black licorice. How could anything taste that bad? Thank goodness I'd stashed a toothbrush in my PE locker. While Brooke explained the ritual where Tab would likely endure any number of painful and degenerative effects, Ashlee and Sydnee Southern walked in.

Ever since we'd broken into their house a few months ago to evict an evil spirit who was haunting them—completely trashing their father's gazillion-dollar mansion and reducing a stunning grand piano to kindling in the process—we tried to steer clear of the Southern Belles. So far, we'd been doing a bang-up job of it. We never really talked to them anyway. Why start now?

But they seemed more than determined to strike up a conversation. I caught on to that fact when they cornered us and said, "We want to talk to you."

"O-okay," I said, needing badly to rinse toothpaste out of my mouth. But I didn't want to be rude. Or give them an excuse to slam my head into the sink like people did in the movies.

Brooklyn stepped beside me—strength in numbers—and crossed her arms over her chest. Sadly, the Southern twins were about a foot taller than us. And they were very flexible. I appreciated Brooke's bravado, but if push came to shove, we would not be the ones doing the shoving. We might get in a gentle nudge here and there.

"You left this at our house." Ashlee, or quite possibly Sydnee, produced a gold pendant of a mother and father with a child in their arms.

I gasped and snatched it out of her hand, eyeing it lovingly. I turned it over and read the word *Forever* on the back. It was the necklace Glitch gave me on the tenth anniversary of my parents' disappearance. The one I hadn't seen since . . . the night we broke into their house. Realization dawned. There was only one place they could have found it. In their own living room.

Playing it cool, I examined it, cleared my throat, then passed it back to them. It was evidence of our wrongdoing. "That's not mine."

Sydnee stepped closer. Or possibly Ashlee. They really needed name tags.

"We know what you did."

I looked at the notebook in her hands, the one with the name Ashlee on it, and took it from there. "I don't know what you're talking about, Ashlee."

"And even if she did," Brooke said, planting her fists on her hips, "which she doesn't, because why would she since there's no way she possibly could, that's no reason to get all up in her face."

Not one of her better comebacks, but it worked. They both relaxed and Sydnee offered me the necklace again.

"We appreciate what you did for us."

I took a mental step back. That wasn't the reaction I was expecting. Taking the necklace warily, I cradled the cool metal in my hand, then glanced back with my brows furrowed in confusion.

"The ghost," Ashlee clarified. "We know what you did for us, and we appreciate it."

Brooke looked over at me. Discomfort prickled along my skin. I shifted, not sure what to say.

"We thought—" Ashlee started to say something, then stopped. She averted her gaze, seeming embarrassed.

"We thought it was our grandmother," Sydnee finished.

"The ghost," Ashlee said, taking her turn to clarify.

But I already knew that. Poltergeists were nasty, manipulative things. It had somehow convinced the girls it was their grandmother, which was disturbing on so many levels.

I decided to fess up. No sense in trying to deny it now. "Sorry about the piano."

Ashlee grinned. "Are you kidding? That got us out of piano lessons for weeks."

"Your house is really nice," Brooklyn said, doing a 180. She dropped her hands to her side. "Most mansions are, I guess."

"Yeah, it's okay, if you like that sort of thing," Sydnee said, lifting one shoulder. She had yet to crack a smile like her sister. "Our dad built it for our mom. Lot of good it did him."

My mouth thinned in empathy. "I'm so sorry about that. It must have been really hard to go through."

Sydnee examined her nails, but Ashlee, the more outgoing of the two, said, "Our mom's crazy for leaving Dad. Seriously, who gives up everything to run off with an investment broker?"

"Dad's not perfect," Sydnee said, "but really? An investment broker? I don't even know what that means."

I never knew the guy, or their mom, frankly, but I had to admit, it surprised me. It shocked the whole town. Quite the scandal. "Well, thank you for this." I clutched the necklace tighter and went back to the sink to spit before I started gagging.

They followed me. And Brooke followed them.

"There's more," Ash said, biting her lip as though uncertain.

Curious now, I rinsed, wiped my mouth, then looked at the clock on my phone. Even if we sprinted, we'd never make fifth hour before the tardy bell. It was too much to hope another fight would detain the teacher long enough for me to sneak in again. I gave the twins my full attention. "What's up?"

"We also know *what* you are."

Brooklyn stilled beside me.

"Really?" I asked, a lighthearted laugh escaping me. "Besides a girl?"

"Yes," Syd said. "And what Ash should have said is, we know what you can do."

"Okay."

Ash stepped closer again. "There's something weird going on."

Syd looked around, then lowered her voice. "Something strange."

I stared cautiously as they closed the distance between us. "I'm getting that."

Inching back to my side, Brooke asked, "What do you mean by strange?"

"A lot of the kids are behaving oddly," Ash said. "Including Syd's boyfriend, Isaac. That's why we're here. We thought you could maybe touch him."

Isaac had been at the party that night. I remembered seeing him with a group of friends along the tree line, barely visible in the low light. One of the few people there I could've called friend, he'd smiled at me and waved.

"You're dating Isaac Johnson?" Brooke asked, beaming with enthusiasm and suddenly tight with the Southern Belles. "That is so sweet. I bet you guys make the cutest cou—"

"Really, Brooke?" I stopped her midstream. She could go on for days.

"I'm just saying." She frowned at me, then did the phone sign to Syd and mouthed the words *call me.*

Syd grinned at last, a shy smile that crept sweetly across her face.

I smiled too, then asked, "How do you know what I can do?"

They exchanged furtive glances; then Ash said, "It told us. The thing in our house. It told us what you are, what Cameron is, and what Jared is." Her eyes rounded a little. "Please don't tell him we know. We won't tell anyone."

"We swear." Syd nodded, her eyes pleading.

"I promise I won't tell him. But he's a good guy. He won't hurt you just for knowing what he is." Their expressions were less than convinced, so I asked, "What is it exactly you're worried about?"

"Isaac is acting strange. He's been acting strange for a couple of days. I think," Syd said, her voice lowering to a whisper, "I think something happened at the Clearing Friday night. I think he's being bullied."

Brooke and I both blinked and waited for the punch line. It never came.

"Wait," Brooke said at last, "you can't be serious."

"Isaac Johnson?" I raised my brows, hoping to give them a clue. "The biggest defensive lineman ever to grace the halls of Riley High? That Isaac Johnson?"

"And he's being bullied?"

They nodded in unison.

"We know how it sounds," Syd said. "But he's not the only one. There are more. Almost every member of the football team in OA is acting strange. Like they're scared of someone."

"Or something," Ash added. "Ever since that night."

To be in OA, or organized athletics, a student had to play at least one sport. Since football was over, the team still got together every day and worked out. And that wasn't all they did. They still partied together. Half the team had to have been at that party. All I remembered was letter jacket after letter jacket.

"Has he said anything? Mentioned any names?" Brooke asked. "Talked about the party?"

"No. That's the other strange part. He just said he doesn't really remember the party. And now he won't talk about it at all."

Brooke and I eyed each other.

Syd wrapped her arms around her waist. "That's why we thought you could touch him. You could do your thing."

"Um, I don't really have a thing."

"That's not what that ghost told us," Ashlee said. "Not in words so much, but in images while we slept."

Sydnee nodded. "It showed us things. About you. About Jared. We never dreamed it was possible until we saw the camera footage."

That brought all thoughts to a screeching halt. "Camera footage?" I asked. As realization dawned on what she had to be referring to, my pulse quickened with a mixture of fear and denial.

"Don't worry," Syd said. "We told Dad the recorder malfunctioned."

"But it didn't." A grin slid across Ashlee's pretty face. "We saw everything. We saw what you did."

"It was amazing."

"Thanks." I glanced at Brooke. She was still at the wide-eyed-denial stage. "Why didn't you tell me sooner? That you knew? That was two months ago."

Ash smirked. "We were waiting for the right moment." She got an evil twinkle in her eyes. "Like now."

My jaw fell open before I caught it. "So, this is blackmail."

"Absolutely," Syd said. "Or, well, technically it's extortion. Same difference."

Ash blinked her long lashes and gazed at me from behind a pout. "You did ruin my very favorite piano."

"You just said . . ." When Ash's face morphed into that same kind of evil, I gave in. "Fine, I'll give it a shot, but my visions aren't really that reliable. I may or may not get something."

"That's okay," Syd said, taking what she could get. "We just want you to try."

I set my jaw. "And I swear, if I come out of this suicidal, I'm coming back to haunt you."

"Deal," Ash said.

THE SOUTHERN BELLE

Brooke piled her plate high with salad for lunch while I went for a more modest version, and Glitch and Cameron went for pizza. Shocker.

"You suck," Cameron said to Glitch as he swiped at his pants. He sat next to Brooke with a scowl lining his face.

"No more than you," Glitch said.

"What did you do?" Brooke let the suspicion in her expression filter into her voice. We knew Glitch too well.

"He spilled his water on me."

Glitch chuckled. "Think you'll survive?"

Clicking her tongue in disappointment, Brooke looked at me. "Boys are impossible." She looked around. "Oh, the school paper's out. I'm going to get us one."

Everyone around us was reading the school newspaper, or at least looking at the pictures. While Brooke went to get us each a copy, I munched on crunchy green stuff with dressing. It was really the dressing I was after. Bacon ranch. Pretty much anything with bacon in it would earn the Lorelei McAlister seal of approval.

"Thanks," I said when Brooke handed me a paper.

She passed one to Glitch, then asked me, "Okay, what do you think?"

"About the newsletter?"

"No. That's just a ploy to make us look normal." She held one up to Cameron, breaking his eye contact with Glitch. Cameron snatched it out of her hands and leaned back to glare at the paper instead of at the crazy boy who thought he could take Cameron on and live to see another day.

"Oh." I nodded. "Good idea."

"The Southerns," she said. "What do you think?"

I picked up my paper as well, going for nonchalance. Like a spy might. "I think we need to check out their story," I said, casting suspicious glances all about me. Like a spy might. "Have you noticed any strange behavior? I mean, stranger than usual?"

Brooke opened her newsletter and spoke from behind it. "Isn't that what we've been talking about?"

"That's true," I said.

"We'll just have to keep a close eye on things. Cameron and Jared said that they'd been sensing something for the last few days. Maybe Isaac saw something at the party."

"Exactly." I spared a glance over the top of my paper. "Something otherworldly. And suddenly that new guy shows up who's *really* tall."

She looked over hers as well. "Do you think they're connected?"

"I wouldn't be surprised. Tall guys and odd things are often connected here."

Glitch finished up his pizza, then picked up his paper as well. Speaking from behind it, he said, "You guys look ridiculous. I was going to speak up sooner, but then what would I have to tell my grandchildren?"

He was right. We put our papers down, but I kept up the suspicious glances. They were fun. And I was hoping beyond hope that Jared would just happen to walk in.

Cameron was busy watching us from over his paper, his brows knitting like he was worried about us.

"Can you even read?" Glitch asked him.

Glitch had apparently become suicidal a while back, taking up the dangerous habit of taunting Cameron. He had to be suicidal to do such a stupid thing. There had been a tension between the boys ever since that Boy Scouts camping trip they went on together in the second grade. We just hadn't known about the tension between them until a few weeks ago.

When Glitch got back from that trip, he was different. I couldn't imagine what had happened on the camping trip that would cause Glitch to become clinically depressed in the second grade, but that was exactly what happened. I'd tried numerous times to find out, to try to get him to open up, but he refused to talk about it.

I'd only recently found out Cameron had anything to do with it, that he was on the camping trip as well. But Glitch knew how strong Cameron was, how indestructible. I could tell he was afraid of Cameron. Who could blame him? But lately he'd taken up the pastime of goading him, egging him on, practically begging him to start a fight. A fight he would be lucky to survive, though he'd probably be in a vegetative state the rest of his life.

And it was all about a girl.

I sighed in wonder. Glitch had feelings for Brooklyn, another fact I'd only recently discovered. I'd had no idea how he felt about her, that he had feelings for her at all other than friendship, until Cameron started paying attention to her. Now, it was all we could do to keep Glitch under control. Cameron could kill him with his pinkie, and he knew that better than anyone.

Brooke kneed me under the table and nodded toward Cameron. He'd stilled. He was looking past me, and when I turned, I realized he was staring at the new guy. He seemed to have made some friends. He was sitting at a table with some of the jocks, but they weren't laughing or joking or even talking. They were just sitting there. All broody like.

Then the new guy's gaze slid over to us and landed right on Cameron. The look on his face was one of glib amusement.

"What is going on with him, Cameron?" I asked.

But he didn't answer. He just stared, his gaze calculating.

"He looks like a Neanderthal," Glitch said. Then he turned back to Cameron. "You guys have to be related."

Before anyone realized what he was going to do, Cameron grabbed Glitch by the front of his jacket and pulled him to his feet with one hand. Or, well, about six inches above his feet.

Glitch tried to fight him, but Cameron was nephilim. Which meant really tall. Really strong. And really fast.

"What do you know about it *Glitch*?" he said, the contempt in his voice evident in every syllable. "Did you learn nothing on that camping trip?"

"Cameron," I said, my voice a harsh whisper, trying not to draw any attention from the teachers on duty. "Put him down this instant."

Brooklyn took a hold of one of Cameron's arms and was trying to pull him off Glitch. She would have had more luck trying to punch a hole in a cinder block wall with her fist.

Unfortunately, the only person in Riley's Switch who stood a chance against Cameron was not there, and Glitch's dark, coppery skin was turning a disturbing shade of red.

"Cameron!" I repeated a little louder.

"Excuse me."

We all turned and saw Ashlee Southern standing there, tray in hand, a shy reverence sparkling in her eyes.

"May I join you?"

Glitch was making these awful choking sounds that didn't so much stop when Cameron dropped him as become more guttural. Cameron didn't give him another thought as he turned to us, his brows raised as though asking us if Ashlee could join us. As though he hadn't been choking one of our best friends nigh to death.

I was the first to gather my wits. "Of course, Ashlee. Sit down."

"I hope I'm not interrupting anything important," she said as she put her tray next to Glitch's.

I couldn't help but notice the sympathetic glances she kept casting his way. Maybe she was worried about him, which was only natural. His wheezing did seem to be growing louder. Brooke placed a hand on his shoulder, but he shoved it away. It was so unlike him.

She gasped, taken aback, but decided to turn her wrath on Cameron. "What the heck was that about?" she asked him.

Cameron continued to direct his scowl at Glitch. "It was about the fact that Blue-Spider doesn't know when to keep his mouth shut."

Cameron remembered Glitch's real name only as a barb.

Glitch scoffed. "Why would anything I have to say bother you?" he asked, his voice hoarse. He looked over at the new guy, who was taking a singular interest in what was going on at our table. "Unless there's something about this guy you aren't telling us."

Cameron seemed to calm then. "Just keep him away from Lor."

"Then there is something you're not telling us," Brooke said, her eyes round with apprehension. "What is it?"

He settled back in his chair and clenched his teeth in frustration. "I told you before. He's fuzzy around the edges." Then he glanced at Ashlee, and I could tell he wasn't sure what he could say in front of her.

"It's okay," Brooke said, "she's trying to help us figure out what's going on."

After a moment, he gave in and said, "I've been sensing all kinds of abnormal activity for days. Stuff I couldn't put my finger on. But the minute Neanderthal gets here, it stops. Everything stops and there's just this low hum of energy, like when you hear the bass of a stereo before you can see the car. Something is coming, and I don't know what."

"So," Brooke said, "he's not a warlock?"

"A what?" When she took another bite of her salad, he asked, "Where did you get that idea?"

"It was just a thought."

Cameron frowned at her. He was worried. He hadn't touched his pizza. Something that never happened.

"Have you sensed Jared yet?" I asked him for the thousandth time.

He pushed his pizza aside and shook his head.

After we sat in silence for a good thirty seconds, Ashlee took an apprehensive bite of her sandwich. "How does it work?" she asked after swallowing. "Your visions. How do you do it?"

Glitch looked at her in surprise. I'd have to fill him in later.

It felt weird talking about it with someone other than my family and friends. I wasn't sure how much to tell her, but she'd kept our secret for weeks. Sure, for nefarious reasons, saving it up for extortion and all, but clearly she could keep a secret.

Once I made sure Glitch was breathing okay, I said, "Sometimes I can touch someone and see something from their past or future, but only if there is something to be seen. It doesn't always work." I stabbed a carrot slice. "And sometimes it works too well."

She frowned. "What do you mean by something to be seen?"

I sat back in my chair. "Well, I don't get a vision every time I touch someone, thank God. If there is something important that needs to be seen, I can see it, but not always. It either happens or it doesn't. I can't really explain it beyond that."

After regarding us with uncertainty she asked, "What about with Isaac? Will you be able to see what's going on?"

"I won't know until I try. I hope so." I really did. If Isaac saw something or had inside info into what was going on in Riley's Switch—or more important, with Jared—I wanted to know.

"I hope so too," she said.

Brooke leaned into me. "Lor, are you sure? From what you told me, this could be dangerous."

"It's worth the risk to my mental well-being. If he knows anything that could help us—"

"I understand. Just make sure I'm around when you try it, okay?"

I'd started to ask her why, when I heard someone off to the side.

"Smile for the camera."

I blinked and looked around, but as my gaze panned to the right, the cafeteria dissolved and in its place, trees formed and playground equipment for small children materialized before my eyes. I was in a vision, but I wasn't touching anyone. And no one I'd touched recently was in it. I looked around and saw a junior—Melanie, I think, was her name—snapping pictures of a group of kids. They were young, probably kindergarteners, with a few high school kids scattered throughout, and they were posing on the playground equipment while holding a banner. It had dozens of tiny handprints with the words THANK YOU written in bright red letters.

The images swam by me, like we were underwater, not crystal clear, but not really blurry either. The sounds were only slightly lower than would be natural. The light only slightly brighter.

"Say yes to literacy!" Melanie said, and all the kids shouted her sentiment as she clicked several pictures in a row. On the last one, just as the banner slipped from one girl's hand, a bright light flashed in my eyes. I blinked again to refocus and saw four people sitting around me, talking. I was back at the lunch table, and Brooklyn was arguing with Cameron about appropriate lunchroom behavior.

Ashlee was staring at me with a curious glint in her eyes. "Are you okay?"

"Did you see that?" I asked her.

Brooklyn stopped talking immediately. "What?" She glanced around, then asked, "Did you have a vision?"

"Yes, kind of. But, it was strange."

She edged closer, as did everyone.

"It was Melanie something-or-other, that junior in Yearbook. She was snapping pictures of little kids on playground equipment."

"Oh, wait a minute," Glitch said, his voice breathy. "I'm getting a vision, too." He held one hand high and pressed the fingertips of the other to his forehead. "Were they holding a banner that said 'thank you'?"

My eyes widened. "Yes, they were."

Brooke crossed her arms and leaned back in disappointment.

"I'm psychic! I knew it!" Glitch said.

Ash smiled dutifully.

"Very funny, Lor," Brooke said, scowling. "I was really worried. If we're going to save the world, you have to take your responsibilities—and your mental state—seriously."

At that point, to say I was confused would have been an understatement. "What are you talking about?"

Cameron tapped on the table, and I realized he wasn't grinning like the rest, but gazing at me with a deep curiosity. I looked down at what he was pointing at. The newsletter Brooke handed me was lying underneath my elbow. The exact picture Melanie shot in my vision, the one snapped just as the banner slipped from that girl's hand, was featured on the front page in an article about literacy. The bundled kindergartners were waving and laughing. The high school students were smiling, each of them holding a different kid. The banner was draped across the front, only the picture was black-and-white, while my vision had been broadcast in glaring Technicolor.

"You're going to save the world?" Ashlee asked.

I clenched my teeth and frowned at Brooke, before saying, "No. Not really. Not the world, so much. More like . . . the . . . coffee shop."

"Yeah," Brooke said, joining in. "The coffee shop. It's in trouble. Financially. With money."

Ashlee laughed softly. "You guys really are the worst liars." She was so lovely, with dark, shoulder-length hair and big brown eyes. I wanted brown eyes. All the cool kids had brown eyes.

Just as I was going to defend my mad skill at lying, the creature whose name shall not be spoken aloud waltzed toward us like she owned the joint. She had blue eyes.

She stopped at our table, unfortunately, and glanced around, probably looking for Jared. When she didn't find him, she turned her attention elsewhere. It would seem our friendship had been fleeting, like two ships passing in the night. Or two planes passing during peak hours, almost colliding in midair, and killing dozens of innocent people.

"Ash," she said, flipping a blond strand over her shoulder, "what are you doing?"

I cringed at the abrasive sound of her voice and tried not to seize. It had some kind of paralyzing superpower.

"What do you mean?" Ash asked her.

Tabitha scoffed. "This is not our table."

"I didn't know we'd bought real estate." Ash indicated the room with a wave. "I just figured I could sit anywhere. Crazy, right?"

"Oh . . . my gawd. Whatever." Then she focused on me, and her expression changed to one of sympathy. "That's so sad about your clothes," she said, her face a picture of faux pity.

Brooke jumped to my defense. "And that's so sad about your face." She was almost getting better with the comebacks.

Tabitha snorted and turned to Amber, her comrade-in-arms. "Wow, I've been put in my place."

"And good," Amber said, agreeing.

Ashlee leaned forward, wearing the same sweet smile she'd offered Glitch. "What's really sad is when girls old enough to know better wear pink and orange together."

Tabitha's breath caught. She looked down at her pink outfit then at her orange bracelet.

"You know," Ashlee continued, "like a third-grader might."

A scarlet tinge infused Tabitha's pale skin, and her mouth thinned as she forced it into the shape of a smile. "I guess it is. I'll see you at practice."

"See you there!" Ash said with a huge grin.

"Wow," Brooke said. "You're my new hero."

Ash smiled again, bashfully. "You just have to know how to handle her. The faster you shut her up, the better it is for everyone involved."

JUICE: ORANGE AND BITTERSWEET

I was a little floored that Ashlee had joined us for lunch, but when her attention kept flitting toward Glitch, I was even more floored. Like carpet on installation day.

Brooke and I had four classes together, and our seventh-hour Foods and Nutrition class was one of them. We walked in about five seconds late, but Ms. Phipps didn't notice. She didn't seem to feel well and decided to show a video on nutrition so she didn't have to teach. Which worked out perfectly, since I didn't want her to teach. My mind was full up for the day.

I poked Brooke in the ribs. We'd scooted our desks closer under the pretense that we couldn't see the video.

"What?" she whispered, eyeing Ms. Phipps, who was sitting at her desk with sunglasses on. If I didn't know any better, I'd say she had a hangover. Then again, I didn't know any better. She could've been a lush, for all I knew. "I'm trying to sleep."

I leaned closer and whispered, "I saw into that picture."

She pointed at the screen and asked through a yawn, "Can food get any more boring? I thought lettuce was supposed to be green. You saw into what picture?"

"That picture from the newsletter. I was touching it with my elbow, and I saw into it. I saw it literally being shot."

She frowned. "I don't understand. What does your elbow have to do with it?"

"No, nothing. Brooke, stay with me. I was there. Melanie what's-her-name was taking pictures. The kids were on the playground equipment. I was there. In the middle of it all."

Brooke's mouth parted as my meaning dawned. "You mean, you had a vision?"

"Yes, only, I don't know. It's like I went into the picture. Like I was just there."

She leaned forward. "Why didn't you tell me?"

"I didn't want to say anything in front of the others. I don't know what this means."

"It means you're the coolest chick I know, that's what it means."

I pursed my lips before saying, "Besides that."

"Oh. Well, I don't know either, but whatever it means, we need to work on it. To hone it." She splayed her fingers in the air. Not sure why. Then she bounced back. "This must be part of your gift."

"I love that you call it a gift," I said.

"I'm sorry. It's just, well, it is a gift. It's just hard for you to see it as such with you becoming suicidal and all every time you get a vision."

"I don't become suicidal every time. And they're counting on me, Brooke. My grandparents are counting on me. Jared is counting on me. Even people who died hundreds of years ago are counting on me, if the ancient texts in the archive room are any indication. It sucks."

"I know. And I'm so sorry, Lor." She gave me a moment, then asked, "But, really, are you finished wallowing in self-pity yet?"

I breathed out a heavy sigh. "Almost. Give me another minute."

"Can't." She did a head dive toward her backpack. "We have to work fast."

"What? I don't want to work fast. Slow and steady wins the race."

Brooklyn reemerged with a grin and a picture. She passed it to me. "Try this. Try to see into it like you did at lunch."

I handed it back. The girl was a menace. "Brooke, it's been a long day. I think I'm visioned out. And I need a break."

"Oh, okay, I can respect that."

She turned back to the program projected on the screen that showed some kind of yellow squishy stuff and swore it was good for building muscle and keeping the body lean, but I could tell from the tone of her voice that this conversation was nowhere near over.

Sure enough, about twelve and a half seconds later, she leaned back to me. "When the apocalypse begins and the world is ending, let me know if your break is over yet, okay? I'd sure hate for you to miss that."

I rolled my eyes until I saw stars, then snatched the picture out of her hand. Without even looking at me, she grinned again. A wickedly conniving thing that would've made Stephen King proud.

"I don't even know what to do." The statement was more of a whine than a . . . well, statement.

"Do what you did before."

"Touch it with my elbow?"

She chuckled, then caught herself and looked over at Ms. Phipps.

"I honestly think she's out," I whispered.

She was sitting up straight, her head unmoving, her body rigid.

"How can she sleep like that?" Brooke asked.

"I don't know, but I want lessons."

We laughed softly together before Brooke grabbed the picture. "Okay, tell me if you get anything," she said. She touched it to my elbow, and we burst out in more hushed laughter that, had Ms. Phipps *not* been taking a siesta, would surely have deserved her attention.

Snatching the picture back before we woke her, I took a deep breath and focused on the image. It was a picture of Brooke at her seventh birthday party, which would have been about a year before I'd met her. A banner hanging in a doorway said HAPPY 7TH BIRTHDAY, BROOKLYN!

She nudged me with her shoulder. "I want you to tell me three things," she whispered. "One, what was in my shoe?"

"Your foot?" I offered.

She grinned some more. "Besides that."

"Okay, sorry. Two?"

"Two, I want you to tell me how it got there."

"You're getting very demanding in your old age."

Then she leaned closer. "Three, I want you to tell me why this picture is so very special to me."

Cool. Intrigue. I looked at it more closely, studied the kids as they ate ice cream and smiled for the camera. It wasn't a posed picture but a candid, random record of the events of that day.

Brooke was running into someone's arms, a tall, African American man's, her mouth open in surprise.

Okay, I could do this.

I concentrated for several minutes, but nothing happened. I held my breath and squinted my eyes. Nothing. I clenched my teeth and ordered myself inside the image. Nothing.

Brooklyn swayed toward me again. "You weren't concentrating today at the lunch table. And you don't concentrate when you get visions throughout the day. Maybe that's what we're doing wrong. Maybe I'm pushing you too hard."

"You think?"

"Smarty pants. Okay, just relax. Think about something else." She paused a moment, then added, "Not Jared, though."

She had a point. I let my fingertips rest on the photo and relaxed with deep and steady breaths, calming my heart and letting the rest of the world fall away. I breathed in through my nose and out through my mouth several times. Then I imagined a sheer curtain over the party. I reached out mentally and pulled it back. It slipped through my fingers a few times like smoke before I got a good grip and swept it aside. I blinked, waited for the image behind the curtain to crystalize, then slid inside.

Everything in my periphery dissolved. The colors melted together, then reshaped themselves, molecules fusing into patterns until they formed the items in the Prathers' living room nine years ago. On the day Brooklyn turned seven.

"Mom!"

I heard a little girl yelling above the roar of grade-schoolers and looked over at Brooklyn, fascinated that I was there, at her seventh birthday party.

"Mitchell poured juice into my shoe again."

Juice, compliments of Mitchell Prather, Brooke's little brother. Two down, one to go.

Brooke's mom, a beautiful African American woman with a

stylishly spiked do, stepped out of the kitchen. Wiping her hands on a towel, she gave Mitchell a withering look. "Mitch, if you can't behave yourself, I'll send you upstairs and you'll miss the party."

"No!" he shouted, his voice edged with the fear of someone facing certain death. His short legs dangled off the chair. He crossed them at the ankles, locking his feet together, and folded his hands in his lap. "I won't do it again. I promise."

Brooklyn's dad chuckled and scooped her little brother into his arms. Mr. Prather was like a sand-colored stick wearing a polo shirt. Tall and slim with pale skin and sandy-colored hair, he was so opposite Brooke's tiny, dark mom that, when I first met Brooke, it had taken some time for me to realize they were married. Then I started noticing little things about them. About their relationship. How her dad doted on her mom. How her mom ordered her dad around. Oh, yeah. They were definitely married.

"There's someone here to see your sister," Mr. Prather said. His eyes sparkled with mischief when he indicated someone behind Brooklyn with a nod.

At her dad's beckoning, Brooklyn glanced over her shoulder and screeched, "Uncle Henry!" She jumped up and ran into a man's arms just as a bright light flashed in my eyes. And just like last time, the image ended when the picture was taken.

I blinked back to the present, my entire body tingling with wonder.

"Maybe you're still concentrating too hard. You need to loosen up." She wiggled her shoulders to demonstrate. "Be a loosey-goosey."

"It was your uncle Henry," I said, astonishment softening my voice. "You were so happy to see him even though your brother had poured juice in your shoe."

With the slow movements of shock, Brooklyn turned and

gaped at me. After a long moment, she asked, "What happened to him? To my uncle?"

The emotion roiling in her eyes wrenched me back to my senses, and I realized who that man was. He was *that* uncle, the black sheep of her mother's family, the one they hadn't seen in years, quite possibly since that very day.

The last time he'd called, he was living in a shelter in South Texas. He'd asked her mom for money and then disappeared. Her mom called the shelter, trying to find him, but they said he'd never gone back. She called the police, but they didn't have anything on him. She called every law enforcement agency in Texas and New Mexico, to no avail.

"You have to go back," she said, her voice rising an octave. She grabbed my arm, her nails digging into my flesh. "You have to touch him and tell me where he is."

"Brooke, I can't touch anyone. I can only see what's going on. It's like I'm not even there, which I'm not."

"But you could try. You didn't try." She jabbed the picture with an index finger. "Just go back through and touch him."

"Okay, I'll try, but I don't think this works like that."

"No, I know. It's okay. Just try."

But by then, I was too flustered. I couldn't get past the curtain again. It was more like a vault door that required a retinal scan and DNA sample. Maybe once I'd entered a picture, I couldn't go into it again.

Despite the failure of every subsequent attempt, I kept trying, over and over, until the bell rang. I shook my head apologetically and handed back the picture. "I'm sorry."

She took it with a disappointed frown.

We stood to gather our stuff and she hesitated, biting her lip in thought. "I'm so sorry, Lor. I didn't mean to freak out on you. This is all just so incredible."

"No apology necessary. I know what your uncle means to

you." We walked past Ms. Phipps, who was still sitting in the exact same position. "Do you think she's dead?" I asked.

"If so, we'll be blamed. We get in enough trouble as it is. Let's get out of here before the homicide detectives come." When we reached the hall, Brooke continued her apology. "I am so sorry again. I kind of lost it."

"Brooke," I said, wrapping an arm in hers, "that's completely understandable. I wish I could tell you where your uncle is."

"This is all just amazing. I mean, I never imagined. We have to tell your grandparents."

"No! I mean, no," I said, a little quieter. "Let's wait awhile, okay?"

The admonishing look she leveled on me could have crumbled a hardened criminal. But I was neither a criminal nor hard. I was kind of squishy, in fact. "Lor, you have to get over what they did sometime. They might be able to explain this."

"It's just, I want to explore it a bit first." I stopped and turned toward her.

"Your grandparents might be able to help."

"It's not just them. Everyone has so much faith in me. There's so much riding on my ability. I don't want to give anyone more hope than they already have. We still have no real idea of what is going on. Of what's going to happen. Why throw this into the mix? Get everyone all excited for no reason?"

She bunched a dimpled cheek. "I guess I can understand that. They do have some pretty high hopes for you, with that whole saving-the-world thing and all. It will suck if you fail. No pressure, or anything."

"Thanks."

"Anytime."

Cameron was waiting for us outside as usual, and we met up with Glitch in the parking lot. He had to go help his dad with some technical thing that I didn't care about, but he promised to be back later. Whatever. I hurried everyone else all along, craving to see if Jared had made it back to his apartment. But after all the pushing and shoving and stuffing bodies into vehicles, I was disappointed yet again.

The skies had turned dark gray, and clouds roiled as I knocked on Jared's wooden front door. Peeked in through his multipaned windows. The small apartment my grandparents had provided him stood empty, just as it had been the last fifty times I checked it. I didn't want to alert my grandparents to his disappearance. They'd ship me off for sure. And the last thing I wanted was to leave Riley's Switch with Jared still missing.

"Can I talk to you, pix?" Grandma called out to me. We'd entered through the back as usual and I was hoping to avoid her. I frowned at Brooke to announce my reluctance, then plopped my backpack on the stairs and walked through the house to the store, bracing myself for whatever may come.

The cash register sang its familiar tune, announcing a sale. "Have a good day," Grandma said. She smiled at Mr. Peña as he left before turning to me. "How are you?"

I grabbed a bar of soap to examine it and lifted a shoulder. "I have homework."

Disappointment lined her face. "Granddad's at the church. He was asking about Azrael."

"It's Jared, Grandma," I said, adding an edge to my voice. "It's just Jared now."

"Pix." Grandma rounded the counter and put a hand on my shoulder.

I stiffened, but didn't step away from her. It was the weirdest feeling, being at odds with my grandparents. It had never happened before. I'd been mad at them before for some perceived infraction, but our relationship never sank to this level of pain and resentment. And it wasn't just about Jared. It was everything. Everything they hadn't told me. Every secret they'd kept and every lie they'd lived. And now they were planning to ship me off without even consulting me? Without asking what I wanted?

"We can't begin to express our gratitude where he is concerned. It's not as though we don't want him here."

For some reason, I asked, "Then what is it?" I didn't want to have this conversation. As infantile as it sounded, I didn't want to forgive them just yet, and having a heart-to-heart would only lead me closer to that end.

"We're just . . . we're worried. That's all. He's so much more dangerous than you can imagine."

"I know." I schooled my expression again. "You've told me. Can I go do my homework now?"

She drew in a deep breath and nodded, and I steeled myself against the hurt in her eyes. "There's fruit in the kitchen."

"Is it in the form of a toaster pastry?" Brooke asked, trying to lighten the mood. She'd walked in after the coast was clear of unwanted sentiment.

"There are those too. Cameron," Grandma said to him, looking past us into the kitchen, "make sure you get a snack. We'll see about dinner in a bit."

He offered a sheepish smile. "Thank you, Mrs. James."

With a sigh, I shuffled off to bake Cameron a toaster pastry. I wasn't hungry in the least. My mood had turned as gray as the skies.

"What are you doing?" Brooke whispered to me.

"Making Cameron a snack."

"At a time like this? We have things to discuss," she said just as I was maneuvering a cherry pastry out of the toaster oven with a fork. Because I could be reckless when I wanted to be. Danger was my middle name.

"And Cameron has to do a perimeter check," Brooke said, pulling at my arm.

"I do?" he asked, taking the pastry from me and blowing on it.

"You most certainly do."

"So, you're kicking me out of the playhouse?" He grinned at us, at her, then took a huge bite, unconcerned.

While Brooke was dragging me up the stairs, she turned back to him and said, "Of course not. We just have girl stuff to discuss."

"I thought you had homework." He said it plenty loud enough for my grandmother to hear. I cringed and glowered at him, but only for a second before I lost sight of him.

"Fingernails," I said as Brooke whisked me into my bedroom.

A storm had moved in. The wind shook the world around us as rain scratched and clawed across my window in massive waves. And again, all I could think about was the fact that Jared was out in it. I could only pray he found shelter.

"Hurry," Brooke said as she rummaged through her backpack. "I know you don't want anyone to know about your new talent, so we have to practice before your bodyguard gets up here."

She was back and in full force. I thought I'd gained a reprieve from her prodding when I told her what I was going through with my visions. Apparently not.

I rubbed the underside of my arms. "I wasn't kidding about the nails. You have a killer grip."

"We need to explore your new talent."

"I didn't really mean that literally."

"You said yourself, you want to understand this a bit more before we tell anyone."

"Brooke, I don't want the visions, remember?"

"But these are safe. You're only seeing into a picture, into what actually happened when it was being taken. No emotion. No scary dreams afterwards or thoughts of suicide. This will be fun. Now sit," she said, completely ignoring my exasperation. She brought out a photo wallet as I sat on the end of my bed. After thumbing through it, she stopped and handed one over. "Okay, see what you can get."

I made sure to exhale really loudly before I scooted until my back was against my headboard. She did the same on her bed, but she leaned against the wall so she could watch me. Which was only a little uncomfortable. I looked at the picture. It was a shot of Cameron at a lake with his dad. He couldn't have been more than twelve, his blond hair shorter and his long frame thinner. He had an almost sad expression in his eyes as he posed for the shot. His dad had an arm around his waist, his teeth flashing white against his dark skin, but Cameron's smile was more reserved, almost cautious.

"Where did you get this?" I asked her.

"Out of Cameron's truck. He wouldn't give me a picture, so I stole one."

"Brooke," I said, my tone admonishing.

"What? He knows I took it. I grabbed it off his visor and stuffed it into my pocket with him watching me." She thought back. "He just gave me this odd expression. Like he couldn't understand why I'd want a picture of him in the first place."

"He isn't the most secure guy."

"True, but the look on his face in that picture has me curious. I just thought you might could see what was going on."

I was curious now too. Darn it. I filled my lungs and concentrated, imagined the sheer veil. My first attempts at pulling it back failed. The veil slipped through my fingers, the only disturbance a puff of smoke where I'd tried. I stopped, shook my head to clear it, then tried again.

Finally, on the fifth try, the veil solidified and gave way to a ridiculously bright day. I blinked and tried to raise a hand to block out the sun. But it seemed I didn't have a hand. I wasn't really there. I had no corporeal manifestation. It was like walking a tightrope a hundred feet off the ground, wanting to grab on to something solid, something stable that wasn't there.

I focused on the surroundings. Cameron stood at the edge of a lake, the water lapping at his feet, his swimming shorts long and bright. He wore no shirt or shoes as he dipped his toes in the water, splashed them around a bit.

"I'm not sure how this thing works," Mr. Lusk said.

I looked over to my left. Mr. Lusk was fumbling with a camera. He was so much shorter than Cameron and had dark skin and hair, very at odds with his son's pale features.

"I think you just push a button."

He glared up at his son teasingly. Cameron laughed softly, then looked out over the mass of blue. When I looked back at Mr. Lusk, he was studying him. His face sad and proud at the same time.

"Got it," he said, balancing the camera on a rock and hurrying to stand beside Cameron. He wrapped an arm around him as Cameron smiled for the shot.

Even as young as he was, he towered over his dad. And they couldn't have looked less alike if someone had paid them to. While Cameron was tall, lean, and very blond, his dad was average height, stocky, and dark, his skin like leather from working out in the elements for all those years. He was handsome like Cameron, just in a very different way.

Of course, he wasn't Cameron's real father. The angel Jophiel was. But he was loyal to his son and supported him in every way.

"I'm so proud of you, son," he said, waiting for the timer. "Of everything that you are."

Cameron shifted in discomfort. "Thanks, Dad."

Just before the timer snapped the shot, Mr. Lusk added, "And so is she."

Cameron's smile faded almost completely as his dad put on his best one. Then a light flashed around me and I was back in my bedroom.

I blinked and sucked in a deep breath like I'd just surfaced from a tank of water. Then I put the picture down, feeling like an intruder.

"What?" Brooke said in alarm. "You have to keep trying. You can't just give up—"

"It worked."

She stopped. "But, you just now shook your head to try again. Like a microsecond before you put it down. And it worked? You went inside?"

"Yeah. I was there for almost a minute, maybe more."

She slumped against the wall in thought. "That is too weird. You weren't—" She glanced up at me, searching for the right words. "—*gone* that long. It's like time is different there. You must be seeing this stuff in one split-second flash, but your mind is interpreting it as longer."

She took out her journal, the one she kept notes in, and jotted down what was happening. I could only pray no one would ever, ever, ever find that journal. Then again, they'd probably think it was fiction.

"Maybe. I don't really know."

"So, what did you see?"

I lowered my head. "Right before the picture was shot, Cameron's dad said he was proud of him."

"Why would that make him sad?" She took the picture back. "He just seems so sad in it."

"Because his dad also said his mom was proud of him too."

"Oh." I'd knocked the wind out of her. "Right."

"Look at the date stamp."

She read the date, then looked back up at me.

"Cameron's mom died nine years before that picture was taken. It was the anniversary of her death."

Brooke let out a ragged breath. "How did I not pick up on that? I'm so stupid."

"No, you're not."

"I'll give this back to him. It's only right."

"I think if he wanted it back, he would've asked for it." I scooted toward her. "I think he likes you having it."

Her mouth formed a hollow smile. "What's it like?" she asked, and I knew she meant the visions, going into the pictures. I thought back and told her about the veil, about pulling it back and sliding inside the image. I told her what it felt like being there, incorporeal, outside my body. It was hard to put into words what I felt, but Brooke was pretty savvy. She imagined it, put herself in my shoes.

"So, every time you come back, there's a flash first? Right when the shot is taken?"

"Yes, but I'm beginning to think the light I'm seeing isn't actually the flash of the camera, but my trip back to the present."

"Lor, I gotta say, this is the coolest thing on earth. Honestly, just when I didn't think you could get any cooler."

I laughed, unconvinced. "I don't know. I mean, what good does it do? It's still not getting us any closer to stopping this stupid war that's supposedly coming. I'm still fairly useless."

"But how do we know that? I think we should tell your grandparents. They'll know what to do. Maybe there's some prophecy that will explain its importance."

"I will." When she cast a doubtful gaze my way, I added, "I promise. I'll tell them."

"When?"

"Soon. Tomorrow maybe."

Her mouth thinned and she crossed her arms over her chest.

"Pinkie swear." Just then my phone beeped. Saved by the bell-like ringtone. It was a text from Grandma. She was ordering pizza. Guilt cut through me. I knew she'd been planning on making enchiladas. She probably thought I wouldn't want any. Which, if it meant eating with them, she'd be right, but it didn't make me feel any less guilty.

Since we were clearly stuck in my bedroom for the rest of the evening, Brooke and I decided to get ready for bed early while waiting for the pizza. May as well be comfy. Cameron came up to check on us twice before heading back outside despite the horrid weather. That guy had chops.

"I wish my parents were here," I said to Brooke. "They would know what to do." I took the picture I had of them off my nightstand. "I have a feeling my dad would have known more about all this than my grandparents do. I mean, he grew up with it. He learned from birth what it meant to be a part of this lineage. A descendant of the prophet Arabeth."

"That's true," Brooke said from the bathroom. "But your grandparents are doing an amazing job, considering they knew nothing about the Order until they met your dad. They've taken a lot upon their shoulders."

She had a point. Maybe I was being too hard on them. "They are pretty great, huh?"

"Yes," she said with a gurgle, clearly brushing her teeth.

"We're about to eat pizza. Why are you brushing your teeth?"

"I don't know. Seemed like the right thing to do." She spit into the sink, then said, "Do you want to try another picture?"

"No. It gives me an awful feeling. Like I'm intruding."

She leaned out the bathroom door. "You're a prophet, Lor. That's what you guys do. Get over it."

She was so brutal when she wanted to be.

Maybe I could try one more picture. I looked at the photo of me and my parents, ran my fingertips along the glass frame. I had just been born. We were still in the hospital, and I looked more like a burrito with a face than like a baby. The nurses had cocooned me in a pink blanket. Mom looked spent but happy, her hair matted and a sleepy smile on her face. And Dad looked so proud as he grinned into the camera, his red hair thick and his eyes captivating.

What if I could relive such moments? What if I could see my parents again as I had Brooke's birthday party? It would be so easy.

With new purpose, I worked the back of the frame off and took the picture into my hands. I was going to lean back against my headboard, take deep breaths, and concentrate. But the moment my fingers touched the picture, I tumbled inside. The sheer curtain drifted apart and I found myself standing in the hospital room while Mom and Dad studied the infant me.

I was sound asleep, probably due to lack of oxygen from being cocooned, as Dad wiggled my chin with a fingertip. "Just like my father's," he said, and I couldn't have explained the pride that welled inside me if I tried a thousand years. My incorporeal chest swelled with emotion.

My parents were right there. Right in front of me. So close, I could almost touch them. I wanted so much to run to them, to thank them for everything. I felt like I couldn't breathe, but could I breathe here at all? In this place of void?

I wanted to stand there forever and bask in their presence. It was like they were back. They were with me. But I had no way to pause the moment, and it slid forward despite my every desire to the contrary.

Mom stopped her cooing and looked over at Dad. "We should tell her when she's older."

I stepped closer. Tell me what?

Dad gave her a sad look. "It's not our secret to tell," he said, shaking his head. "Besides, what good would it do her to know the truth? To know that he's alive?"

What? Who's alive? What truth?

"I think I have this thing figured out," a man said, and just as Mom and Dad looked up, the bright light flashed and I was back on my bed, the picture in my hands, Brooke mumbling something about duty and how spying was a noble tradition. Just look at James Bond.

THE VAGUENESS OF TRUTH

But what were my parents talking about? What truth?

"Mm-hm," I said to Brooke, pretending to listen. I closed my eyes, placed my fingertips on the picture again, and concentrated. But just as before with Brooke's, nothing happened. Maybe one shot was all I got. No replays or do-overs. I tried again and again, but nothing. Then I did as before with Cameron's picture. I took a deep breath and relaxed. A coolness washed over me, starting from my fingertips and fanning out over my entire body. I felt the molecules of my existence fade, become translucent like watercolors. Then fog. Time slipped out from under my feet. The air rippled around me. And the curtain appeared. I reached forward. Pulled. And went through.

Dad sat on the side of the bed and leaned over me to wiggle my chin. My mom cooed and swayed, just barely, back and forth. Beautiful and strangely elegant, like a princess. This time I tried to see more. To extract more from every word, every movement.

"Just like my father's."

The moment Dad said it, a sadness washed over my mom's face. She looked almost pleadingly at Dad. "We should tell her when she's older."

He looked down, shook his head in regret before refocusing on Mom. "It's not our secret to tell. Besides, what good would it do her to know the truth? To know that he's alive?"

Mom bowed her head.

"I think I have this thing figured out." It sounded like Granddad, but I couldn't be certain.

Their dispositions changed as they smiled for the camera. After a quick flash, I was back in my room.

"Are you even listening to me?"

"Of course," I said before diving in again.

I did this over and over, trying to discover something new, a clue, a hint of whom they were talking about. I found that I could manipulate my position. One time I was standing directly in front of them, and the next, I was standing by the window. It took some practice to get there. When I could control my thoughts more, when I could move without being thrown out of the picture, I walked to the window and turned around. Grandma stood pointing at something on the camera as Granddad, younger and leaner, shooed her away.

"We should tell her when she's older," Mom said, and my grandparents exchanged glances—so quickly, I almost missed it.

"It's not our secret to tell. Besides, what good would it do her to know the truth? To know that he's alive?"

Granddad bit down, clearly bothered by something before saying, "I think I have this thing figured out." He raised the camera, and a bright light suffused the area. Then once again, I was back in my room.

They knew. Whatever it was, whatever secret my parents were talking about, my grandparents knew as well. And Mom referred to the secret, something they should tell me, right after Dad had mentioned his father. My dad's parents died before I was born. Is that what they were talking about? Their deaths? Or maybe it was how they'd died. Maybe they didn't want me to know. But they'd said he was alive. I bolted upright.

"Brooke," I whispered, not really sure why.

"Lorelei," she said in the same tone, strolling out of the bathroom in full pajama mode.

I grabbed my pajamas and ducked into the bathroom. "You will not believe what happened."

"Let me guess: You went into a picture of your parents when you were born?"

Peeking around the doorjamb, I said, "How did you know that?"

She held up the picture.

"Oh, right." I went back to changing. "And I can do it over and over."

"The same picture?"

"The same picture."

She hopped up and came into the bathroom to sit on the closed toilet. "Do you know what this means?" she asked, her voice filled with fascination.

"Of course." Then I thought about it. "Well, okay, no. Not really."

After blinking in thought a few times, she said, "Yeah, me neither."

"They had a secret." I pulled my top over my head, then continued. "My parents."

"And you learned this by touching that picture?"

"Yes. They were talking about it. About how someone was alive but they couldn't tell me who." I stopped and gazed at her point-blank. "I think my paternal grandfather is alive."

Brooke's jaw dropped open. "I thought he was dead."

"So did I," I said. "That's what they told me, but they were talking about my chin and how it looked like my dad's father's and then—"

"I love this place." Glitch walked in, his mouth clearly full.

Brooklyn stepped out of the bathroom. "Glitch, you need to knock."

"Hurry, close the door," I said, rushing past him to do that very thing.

He had a slice of pizza in each hand. "Why? What's going on?"

Brooklyn glanced at me, her eyes pleading. "Can I tell him? Please? I'll do your algebra homework."

With a snort, I said, "I would let you kick him in the face for a free homework night. Deal."

"In the face?" he asked, his words muffled.

"Lor has a new talent," Brooke said.

He swallowed hard, then eyed me. "Does it involve pole dancing?"

"No." She rolled her eyes. "Pay attention. Oh, my gosh, that smells so good."

"Fine," I said. "Go get a piece. We'll wait."

"No way." She crossed her arms and refused to budge. "You'll tell him."

"I won't tell him."

"Yes, you will. I'll just take one of his."

"Absolutely not," he said, backing away as though facing a firing squad.

Just then, a knock sounded at the door. Brooke answered it, and Cameron was standing on the other side.

"Hey," Brooklyn said, holding the door close to let him know he was not welcome at that moment in time. "So, are you still checking the perimeter?"

He narrowed his eyes and looked past her. "I guess. Just checking in. Is everything okay?"

"Wonderful."

When she continued to stare at him, smiling for effect, he nodded. "Okay. I'll be outside. Close those blinds."

"You got it." She shut the door, rushed over to close the blinds, then hurried back to the door before turning back to me with an accusing scowl on her face. Like I would risk getting my homework done for free.

"What?" Glitch asked.

"Nothing. Keep her busy until I come back. And don't let her say anything. *Anything!*"

"I cannot believe you don't trust me," I said, but she was gone. So I called out to her. "Bring me a piece!"

Glitch sat at my desk, then yelled, "And bring me an orange soda!"

"Me too!"

I scooted onto the edge of my bed. "It's like having room service."

"So, you gonna tell me or what?"

I looked over at Glitch. He was holding a slice of pizza in one hand and checking his e-mail on my computer with the other.

"Brooke would kill me."

He tossed an evil smirk over his shoulder.

Before I could say anything, Brooklyn burst through the

door, a pile of pizza in one hand and two orange sodas balanced in the other. "Did she say anything?" she asked.

"My god, that was fast."

Glitch's mouth formed a straight line of disappointment. "No, she didn't."

"Perfect." She handed me a slice and sat down to take a bite. After putting her pizza back onto her plate and wiping her hands on her napkin, she focused all her might on Boy Wonder.

"Okay, Glitch, pay attention."

He turned from the computer and took another bite. "'Kay."

Brooke grinned in anticipation and said, "Lor can go into pictures."

He conjured a hesitant smile. "That's great, Lor. I didn't even know you wanted to act."

"What? No, not those kinds of pictures." She waved at him, as though erasing his words. "Like, pictures. You know, photos."

"So you want to be a photographer?" he asked after taking a sip of soda.

With all the flair and drama of a silent screen actress, Brooke plastered her hands over her eyes and threw herself across her bed.

"A model?" he tried. "Aren't you kind of short?"

"For the love of pepperoni, make him shut up."

I laughed at her antics. "Brooke, you have to admit, it sounds a little far-fetched. You're going to have to explain," I said before taking a bite.

"Fine." She sat up and tried again. "Okay, Lor has the ability to touch a picture and go into it. She can see what was happening when that picture was taken. She can enter the scene, look around, hear what people said."

"But once the camera flashes," I added, "I'm thrown out. I can see only the events that led up to that image in the photo."

Glitch sat staring at us. We let him take it all in. Absorb. "That's kind of cool," he said, his voice uncertain.

"Kind of cool?" Brooke asked. "It's the coolest thing ever. Well, okay, besides Jared being the Angel of Death. That was a tad cooler."

I glanced at her and we shrugged in agreement.

"No, it is," he said. "But what does it mean?"

"That's what we'd like to know," Brooke said.

"Have you told your grandparents?"

"No, not yet. It's all still in test phase. As soon as I know more, I'll go to them."

"You said you'd go to them tomorrow," Brooke said, accusing me with her eyes. "You pinkie swore."

"I will."

"Lor—"

"Brooke—"

"Can we get back to the picture thing?" Glitch asked, still absorbing. Wet newspaper was more absorbent.

So we spent the next hour explaining everything and going into a couple of pictures to prove I could do it. Everyone was a skeptic. But Brooke brought out some pictures from our grade school days. I went into a couple and recounted what happened in each. I was getting better. I could manipulate my position, could see the environment outside the frame of the picture.

Glitch didn't know what to think. I wasn't sure why this was any harder to believe than my having visions or Jared being the Angel of Death, but for some reason, he seemed to be having a difficult time with it.

Then he asked, "What about digital images? You know, like a picture on a phone or a computer?"

I hadn't thought of that. "I don't know. Let's try it."

He brought up a picture on his cell phone of him riding his dirt bike in the mountains.

"Who took this?" I asked.

He grinned. "You tell me."

With a grimace of doubt, I touched the screen and concentrated. And just as before, I drifted forward, into the picture, into the scene, a curtain of pixels parting to let me inside. The shrill sound of his motorcycle as he kicked up an unnecessary amount of dirt hit me like a cannon blast. I covered my ears. Or at least, I felt like I covered my ears. No one else was around. Before I got cast out of the photo, I stepped to the side to see who was taking the picture, but his phone sat on a log. He'd propped it up and set the timer.

A split second before the picture snapped, I looked past the camera and saw his dad standing in the distance.

The light flashed bright and I was back. I blinked at him. "You took that picture. And really, must you stir up that much dirt?"

His smile faded.

"Wait, how did he take the—? Oh," Brooke said. "Your phone has a timer?" She took it from me and started punching buttons.

"Yeah, but how did you know?"

"We just told you," she said. Then she gaped at me. "He never listens."

He stared at her. "No, I know what you said, but . . . that's amazing."

"Know what's more amazing?" I asked, offering him a knowing grin. "Your dad was watching you that day."

His mouth fell open even farther. "How did you—?" He caught himself. "You're right. He came out to watch me. I didn't even know it until later." Leaning back in the chair, he furrowed his brows in thought. "But what does this mean?"

I breathed out a heavy sigh. "That's just it. What does any of it mean? I can touch someone and get a vision. I can look at a picture and see what was happening. But honestly, in the grand scheme of things, what good do those things do anyone?"

"Lor, you're selling yourself short." Brooke almost glared at me. "As usual."

"I'm not selling anything. It was sold to me. I had no choice."

After whining a bit longer, I told Glitch about the conversation my parents had when I was born.

"And you think they were referring to your grandfather from your dad's side?" he asked.

"Who else? My dad said, 'She has my father's chin' seconds before my mom said they should tell me when I was older. It has to be him. Which leads me to Plan A."

"Oh, crap," Glitch said. "Whenever you guys start lettering your plans, trouble always follows. And by the time we get to Plan E—because every single plan before that has failed—all hell breaks loose."

"Does that mean you're out?" Brooke asked, a knowing expression on her face.

He snorted. "No way. I'm so in, it's unreal. I just wanted you to know that if we make it to Plan E, I'm running. Far away. And possibly changing my name."

We laughed. "It's not that bad," I said to ease his mind. "I just know where the records are stored. As soon as my grandparents go to bed, I'm going to sneak down to the basement and get all the information I can on him. Surely, they'll have something."

"Then we can do an Internet search," Glitch said. "I can start now, actually. What was his name?"

"I only know his nickname, what they called him."

"Oh." Brooke looked disappointed. "That probably won't help."

"You never know." He turned the chair to face my computer again. "Okay, give it to me."

"Um, they called him Mac."

They both looked at me. "Seriously?" she said. "A guy with the last name of McAlister and they called him Mac? How bizarre."

"Well, I can at least use that to do a search. Do you know anything else? Like where he was from?"

"I just know that he was from the Northeast. Possibly Maine. But they moved to New Mexico long before my dad met my mother."

"Okay, well, keep thinking."

Brooklyn checked the clock. "What time do your grandparents go to bed?"

"Nine or ten, depending. We still have hours." Then I grinned at her. "Plenty of time for you to do my algebra homework."

"I've already done the assignment. Why don't you just copy mine?"

With a gasp I said, "That's cheating. Besides, that would require work on my part." I handed her the homework sheet and a pencil. "Remember, try to write like me."

"Lorelei?"

I turned toward the voice and tried to swim to the surface of sleep.

"Lorelei, wake up."

It was Cameron. I recognized his voice and the not-so-gentle nudging. Was I late for school?

I pried open an eye. It was still dark outside, and the wind and rain had yet to let up. Surely there were special contingencies set aside for such mornings.

Then I bolted upright. "I fell asleep!" I said, my gaze darting about the room. Brooke was asleep too, and Glitch was sprawled on the floor, his hand resting on a pillow where his head should have been. Poor guy. He couldn't possibly be comfortable. "I didn't mean to fall asleep. We had a Plan A."

One corner of Cameron's mouth lifted. "Your plans don't always work out for the best. It's probably good that you fell asleep."

The last thing I remembered was Brooke demonstrating the quadratic formula as she did my homework. Which would explain the sudden onset of narcolepsy.

"Lorelei," he said, his expression grave, "are you coherent?"

After rubbing my eyes, I gave a weak, "Kind of. Are we late?"

"No." He took hold of my chin until I looked at him.

My brows rose in alarm. "What's wrong?"

"He's back."

No further explanation was needed. I scrambled out of bed and hustled into my robe as Cameron went to nudge Brooklyn awake. No time for nudges.

"Brooke!" I yelled, causing Cameron to jump a solid foot. I felt bad about that.

"Do you want to wake up your grandparents?" he asked.

He had a point. Before I could even question where Jared was, I kicked Glitch to wake him and tore out of the room, but Cameron grabbed hold of my arm.

"He's outside."

"He's outside? In this weather?"

He nodded toward my window and I rushed to open it, hurtling Glitch in the process as he stirred to consciousness. Jared lay on the ground at the bottom of the metal fire escape, unconscious.

"Oh, my gosh," I said, climbing out. A bitterly cold rain slashed across my face as I hurried down and knelt beside him, but nothing compared to the alarm I felt at seeing Jared unconscious.

"Lor, what are you doing?" Brooke called to me, but she

quickly shushed and ducked back in for something other than pajamas to wear.

Cameron jumped down and landed beside me as I examined Jared. Blood streaked down one side of his head and from his swollen mouth.

"Hurry up, Blue-Spider," Cameron said, trying to be quiet but shout loud enough to be heard over the pelting rain. I realized Glitch was right behind him, still in his jeans and sweatshirt.

In one smooth movement, Cameron scooped Jared up and draped him over his shoulder. Jared couldn't have been light.

"Get the door," Cameron said, and I realized he was taking Jared to his apartment.

Glitch ran ahead of Cameron and jumped to get the hidden key from over the door. He unlocked it and held it wide enough for Cameron to get through with his charge.

"We need medical supplies," Cameron said, reaching out to turn on a light.

Just then, Jared started to stir. "What are you doing?" he asked, his words slurred and groggy. Then, in a flash of strength that my mind couldn't quite register, he twisted up and off Cameron. One minute Cameron was carrying him to his kitchen; the next Cameron was underneath him in a maneuver that left me breathless.

He lodged a knee under Cameron's chin, his face wary and full of rage.

"Jared!" I rushed forward, and before I had time to blink, a large hand shot out and encircled my throat. I felt the earth move. Saw the room blur. And in the next instant, I was on the floor right next to Cameron. Fighting for air. Fighting to stay conscious.

Cameron wrapped his legs around Jared's chest and threw him off balance long enough to get out from under him. "It's just us," he said, his voice harsh.

I gasped for air as Jared scurried back onto all fours, crouched, and eyed us like we were his next meal.

Cameron dragged me behind him, then held up his free hand in surrender. "It's just us."

Jared fought for balance, then pressed a palm to his head wound. Blood trickled between his fingers as he doubled over and growled in pain.

I wanted to go to him, but Cameron kept his iron grip on my arm.

Brooke crept in behind me and wrapped an arm in mine, keeping a wary eye on our opponent.

After a moment, Jared blinked back to us. He took his time, measuring us with his feral stare. "What happened?" he asked at last just as his gaze landed on me.

"We don't know," I said. "You disappeared. You've been gone for three days."

The barest hint of surprise flashed across his face before he caught himself.

"Are you with us?" Cameron asked, waving a hand in front of his face. When Jared scowled, Cameron flipped him off and asked, "How many fingers am I holding up?"

Half an hour later, Jared sat at what passed for a kitchen table, a blue blanket from our linen closet draped over him as Cameron sewed up a huge gash in his arm. An array of medical supplies sat splayed across his countertop along with bloodied gauze and towels. Towels I would have to wash before Grandma saw them.

Jared's hair, soaking wet, hung in clumps over his bruised brow. The wound on his head that had been bleeding profusely was now stitched and on the mend. It ran along his hairline, and I could hardly see it now.

Brooklyn and Glitch had gone to change out of their soaking-wet clothes, but I couldn't bring myself to leave. What if Jared disappeared again while I was gone? So instead, I stood, assisting Cameron with shivering hands.

Jared raised his lashes and locked his gaze with mine, unblinking even when a drop of rain-soaked blood dripped from the tips onto his cheek. The rich browns of his eyes seemed darker than usual as he stared, more intense.

He reached out and touched my neck, his hands warm and soothing. "Sorry about that," he said.

"I'm okay. I was just worried about you."

Before he could say anything, Brooklyn tapped my shoulder. "I brought you some clothes," she said, wincing as Cameron tugged on a stitch to tighten it.

Jared also had a huge gash on his arm that required sutures. My knees almost gave beneath my weight every time Cameron stabbed. Tugged. Tied. Clearly nursing was not in my future.

"They were waiting for me," he said without releasing my gaze. "A group of them."

"Who?" Cameron asked. At his nod, I took the scissors and cut the suture. "A group of what?"

Brooke took the other seat at the tiny table as Glitch scooted onto the counter.

"Unless it was a group of charging water buffalo, I'm stumped," Glitch said. "Because anyone, even a group, bringing you down is a little hard to believe."

Jared finally looked back at Cameron, his expression grave. "They were descendants."

Cameron stilled. I wondered why. What were descendants? And whom were they descended from?

"I didn't think there were any left," he said, voice thick with apprehension.

"There are quite a few, actually, but the real question is, why would they attack me?"

"Your guess is as good as mine," Cameron said as he plunged the needle again.

The world spun. Brooke took the scissors and sat me in the chair, taking over. I couldn't help but notice Glitch fold his arms at his chest and glare when she started helping Cameron, but when Jared took my hand into his, a movement that both shocked and pleased me, I lost interest in his annoyance. After weeks of avoidance on Jared's part, the warmth was nice.

"I wish I could remember," Jared said. "I can't. Everything after that initial attack is a blank. I was fighting—and winning, I might add—then I was here."

"Glitch-head's right," Cameron said, tying off another stitch. "Even a hundred descendants would have trouble bringing you down. How did they take you?"

Jared turned his attention toward him so slowly, so methodically, I was certain he did it to goad Cameron. "Why?" he asked at last, planting a humorous and, if I didn't know any better, taunting gaze on him. "Looking for pointers?"

"It's just a little hard to believe."

"So is reality TV, but there you have it."

The tension between them simmered, thickened, blanketed the room in silence.

"What are descendants?" I asked, breaking it. They had been getting along famously—or, well, semi-famously. Now was not the time for tempers to flare. When they were at odds, architectural structures paid the price. "And why on earth would they attack you? Surely they don't know what you are."

After a long moment, Jared tore his gaze away from Cameron. "They know exactly what I am. And they are descended from the original nephilim that were created centuries past."

"They're nephilim?" Brooklyn asked, her voice soft with

astonishment. "Like Cameron?" She snipped the last suture and cleaned off Jared's wound with peroxide.

"They're diluted versions of Cameron," Jared explained, "descended from the original nephilim, so there's a lot of pure human mixed in. It's like taking a single drop of food coloring and adding a gallon of milk. The food coloring will alter the color slightly, but for the most part it's still milk. There simply can't be that much seraph DNA left in the breed."

"There's not," Cameron said. "I would be able to tell if there were. I would be able to feel them."

Brooke smoothed antibiotic ointment onto the stitches and covered them with a bandage.

"In an effort to contain the purity of the race," Jared continued, examining her handiwork, "there has been a lot of inbreeding as well. From what I understand, they're not right in the head."

"Then you are related," Glitch said to Cameron.

"Their attacking Jared proves they have a screw loose," Brooke said, ignoring Glitch. "What did they hope to gain?"

"To leave Lorelei vulnerable," Cameron said.

"Me?" I asked, alarmed. "What do I have to do with the descendants?"

"I have no idea what they would want with you, unfortunately," Jared said.

Cameron raked a hard gaze over him. "They tracked you here. When you showed up a few weeks ago, they tracked you."

"Or they were invited." Jared's accusation was as smooth as caramel. He settled a withering stare on him. "You're the hybrid. You're like them."

"I've never even seen one of those things." Cameron bit down in an effort to control his temper. "I didn't even know for sure they existed until you showed up."

"And yet here they are."

"And here you are," Cameron volleyed, baiting the only one in the room who could kill us all with a thought. He was looking at Jared like he'd never seen him before, like he was different somehow.

After a moment, Jared leaned back in his chair and scrubbed his face with his fingertips. "They must have an agenda. They attacked me for a reason." He looked at me, his brows drawn together. "They have to be after you. It's the only explanation."

I really hated to hear that.

"I still think we should get you to the hospital," I said, switching the focus off me. "You could have a concussion."

"Hey," Cameron said, clearly offended. "I got this."

The corner of Jared's mouth lifted into a lazy grin. He let his gaze drop to my robe. I pulled it tighter, smoothed my hair down, and tried not to concentrate too hard on the dark sparkle in Jared's eyes, the powerful set of his shoulders. Even injured, he exuded authority, his supremacy so absolute, so pure. "I know this is going to sound dumb, but are you sure you're okay?" I was still floored with the attention he was giving me. It was like the old Jared was back. Scraped up. Bruised. Covered in wounds. Yep, it was definitely the old Jared.

His grin widened, and I realized his gaze was glassy, as though he had a fever. "I'm fine. I'll be ready for school in a couple of hours."

"School?" I asked, stunned. "I think you can miss a day or two, considering the extent of your injuries."

"She's right. You should stay home today," Cameron said.

I brightened. "See."

"You're no good to us injured," Cameron continued.

"That's not what I meant," I said.

Jared looked at Cameron. "We need to figure out what's going on."

Cameron nodded. "There's a new kid at school you need to meet."

Brooke gasped. "You think he's one of them? A descendant?"

"I wouldn't be surprised," he said, his expression grave.

EXPRESSIONLESS

The next morning, we got ready for school in relative silence. Except for the howling from Glitch when he got the last shower. At least cold water was invigorating.

"Would you kids like some breakfast?" Grandma asked when we made our way downstairs, shuffling off the landing one by one. She sat by Granddad at the table, drinking coffee and reading the sports section. I didn't know why. She never watched sports.

I avoided eye contact. "We'll just have cereal."

"Think healthy," Granddad said, referring to my culinary

choice. I was actually thinking more along the lines of chocolaty, but okay. I took down a box of something with the word "wheat" in it. Brooke crinkled her nose and went for a toaster pastry as Glitch raided the refrigerator.

Since Plan A had gone awry, our sleuthing adventures would have to wait until tonight. At least Jared was back. That single thought occupied 98 percent of my brain function. The other 2 percent was on Plan A. It didn't hurt to do a little investigating. To grill the authority figures for intel. I wondered what Grandma and Granddad knew about my other grandfather, the one on my dad's side. They didn't tell me the truth about my parents' disappearance for ten years, and even then, I had to practically force it out of them. I doubted they would have told me if not for Jared's appearance and everything that happened six months ago.

I cleared my throat. "So, I was looking at some pictures and I realized I don't have a single one of my other set of grandparents."

Grandma choked on her coffee, coughing a full minute before recovering, and I didn't know if her seizure was due to my question or the fact that I was talking to them.

Granddad patted her back, his eyes rounding in surprise, when he said, "I'm not sure we have any. Your dad didn't bring much in the way of personal effects when he and your mom moved back here."

I took a bite of cereal, going for nonchalance, then said, "I wonder if my chin is like his."

And with that, Grandma and Granddad leveled the most shocked expression I'd ever seen on me. So I continued.

"I mean, you know, I don't really have either of your chins, so I thought maybe my chin came from the other side of my family."

Granddad recovered first. "Yes, well, you definitely have the cleft from your dad's chin. That's a signature McAlister trait if I ever saw one. Right, Vera?"

When Grandma didn't answer, he elbowed her. "Right," she said, jumping to attention. "Signature. Spitting image. You know, chin-wise."

"Do you think there are pictures of them somewhere?"

"Well, there are some records stored in the basement," she said. "There might be something in there."

"Cool. I might check it out later. Just out of curiosity." I practically had their permission to snoop now and felt better for it.

Brooke thinned her mouth, admonishing me with her furrowed eyebrows. I stuck out my tongue, then proceeded to ignore her.

At least until Cameron came in. "The truck's warm," he said.

"If you guys don't get cold," Brooke said to him, picking up her backpack, "why do you wear jackets?"

"It's frowned upon in society to walk around without a jacket. I used to catch all kinds of heck in grade school. Now I just get odd looks. It's easier to conform."

"Oh." She strolled out the door with the rest of us behind her.

"Have a good day, pix," Grandma said, her voice full of hope.

"You too," I whispered without looking back.

Jared met us at Cameron's truck, wearing his bomber jacket and jeans. His wide shoulders filled the jacket so nicely, and the brown color went well with his height.

"Hey, you," he said, and I melted a little inside. He was already almost completely healed, at least the parts of him I could see.

"Hey."

He reached out and brushed a thumb over my mouth.

An electrical current shot through me with the contact.

"You look nice."

His hand was warm against the crisp day. "Thank you."

He looked past me. Cameron had stopped and was assessing him with his signature glower.

With a boyish smile, Jared raised his hands in surrender. Then he opened the door for me, but from the corner of my eye, I noticed him look back at the house as though checking to see if my grandparents were watching. Then he turned and spit into the mud. A very guy thing to do, but just odd.

"At least the sun's out," Brooke said when she climbed in through Cameron's side.

Glitch strode to his car without so much as a by your leave. He was getting so moody.

I scooted to the middle to make room for Jared. He slid in and closed the passenger-side door. The warmth of his body seeped into my clothes.

"So, these descendants don't sound very smart," I said, trying not to let my worry filter into the tone of my voice. "I mean, who would be dumb enough to jump you? Besides Cameron, that is."

Cameron tossed me a scowl as he pulled onto Main. He was a master of scowls. Probably invented several of the more defiant scowls so popular with kids today.

In response, Brooklyn flashed her version. "She's just being honest. If you'll remember, you guys made a mess of downtown Riley's Switch a while back. Not just anyone could have done that."

Brooke was right. When Jared showed up a couple of months back to take me when I'd been dying, Cameron knew what he was. And since Cameron had literally been created to protect me, he didn't take kindly to Jared showing up to take my life. Not without an appointment at least. The two of them fought like two gods hell-bent on destroying our small town.

They may have laid aside their differences to figure out this war thing, but the animosity between them hadn't subsided completely.

With a shrug, Cameron conceded to Brooke's logic.

But Jared was still eyeing him, a hint of provocation in his expression. "I guess there were just more of them than I'd expected. I let my guard down."

Cameron spoke then. "What kind of archangel can't handle a few watered-down descendants?"

Jared latched on to that like a bully trying to pick a fight. "The kind that can stop your heart before you have time to blink."

Brooke looked over at Jared as we pulled into the parking lot. School was only three blocks away from the store, but riding in Cameron's warm truck was way better than not riding in Cameron's warm truck.

"Could you guys not start this crap again? It's been weeks. Why the sudden animosity?" When Jared turned to look out the window, she said to me, "See, everybody's acting strange."

And she was right. When we got out, everything got even stranger. Well, not immediately. For the most part, it was a typical Tuesday. Kids standing in their respective groups. Teachers hustling to their classrooms, massive coffee mugs in hand. Principal Davis glaring. Just a regular day at Riley High.

Until we stepped inside. While kids were there as usual—raiding their lockers, walking to class—unlike usual, the halls were deathly quiet. Eyes were cast downward and movements were hurried, wary.

"Dang," I said, suddenly uncomfortable. "Is there a new no-talking rule in the halls?"

"I hope not," Brooklyn said, reading a text on her phone as we wound through the stoic crowd. "Your grandmother says hey."

"She's texting you now too? That woman is a menace."

"She's funny," Cameron said, sticking to us like a Post-it note. He took his job as protector very seriously.

"I'm glad you think so."

Spotting Hector Salazar, a kid I'd known since kindergarten, leaning against his red locker, I waved a quick hello. He was a bona fide nerd and proud of it to the point of arrogance, but I never held it against him. He was smart. He knew it. Who was I to argue? Super smart or not, though, he usually waved back. Instead, he lowered his head and stared at me, his gaze expressionless.

"What the heck did I do to Hector?" I asked no one in particular.

"What?" Brooke barely looked up from her phone, but Cameron took hold of my arm and pulled me to a stop. He was really strong. Like supernaturally strong. So I stopped fairly quickly.

"What did you say?" he asked.

I looked up in surprise as Brooke turned back to us and Jared came closer to hover and stare menacingly at Cameron.

Suddenly self-conscious, I said, "Hector gave me a really odd look."

Cameron straightened and eyed the crowd from his perch atop his shoulders. Man, that guy was tall. "What kind of look?"

Jared did the same before giving me his attention again.

"A look. I don't know. I waved and he just stared." I lifted a shoulder. "I haven't done a thing to him since the first grade. And that was totally his fault. I mean, I'm all for sharing, but there's sharing and then there's robbing your classmates blind."

Brooke laughed. "What did he want from you?"

"My blue construction paper. *All* of it. Honestly. It's not like construction paper grows on trees."

Cameron appraised the crowd before parking his gaze on Jared. Jared returned the sentiment and the glower-fest began anew.

I elbowed Brooke and she glanced up to take in the staredown before questioning me with raised brows.

While Cameron's eyes were filled with uncertainty, Jared's were narrow, challenging. Again, it was so unlike him and, well, more like Cameron. Their roles had been switched. What on former planet Pluto was going on?

"Where's Glitch?" Brooke asked, checking around.

"He had to go straight to class," Cameron said before stalking past us.

We followed. "Really? He didn't say anything."

"I don't see the new kid. Let's just get you to science." Normally, getting to class was not one of Cameron's priorities.

The boys seemed to be lost in thought as they walked us to first hour. We stopped outside the classroom, and I turned to say good-bye to them. Well, mostly to Jared. I wondered if there was a chance I could see what had actually happened to him.

"Are you sure you're okay?" I asked him, inching closer.

His smile faltered and he camouflaged any emotion behind an empty expression. "I'm certain of it."

"Can you tell me what's going on?"

He crossed his arms at his chest. "No."

I leaned forward and put my hand on his. "You know you can tell me anything, right?"

He raked his teeth over his bottom lip and stared intently. It was the sexiest thing I'd ever seen. Then, with his beautiful mouth tilted up at one corner, a playful grin sparkling in his eyes, he asked, "Are you getting anything?"

I dropped my hand and rolled my eyes.

A deep laugh, soft and gorgeous, sounded in his chest.

"How do you always know?" I exhaled loudly and gave up. "Never mind."

He took my jacket and pulled me closer to him. "You're giving up?"

The world tumbled in my periphery, dissolved into nothing. "No." Then when I could catch my breath, I said, "Never."

"We need to get to class," Cameron said, completely breaking the spell I was under.

We turned in unison to look at him. Mostly because he was standing really close.

Brooke stepped closer as well, shouldering between Cameron and Jared. "Are we in a huddle for a reason?" She glanced at each one of us in turn. "I don't want to be left out of the loop."

Jared's mouth softened into a breathtaking grin. He reached over Brooke and shoved Cameron backwards. Not hard, just enough to let Cameron know he was not welcome.

But Cameron came back. He leaned closer and said, "I'm not leaving until you do, reaper."

"I'll see you later," Jared said. "I'd hate for blondie to stroke."

Cameron scoffed and stepped back, waiting for Jared to follow.

"Are you going to tell me what's going on?" I asked.

"Not until I know more."

"Fine." I shooed him away with both hands. "Get to class. History awaits."

He laughed. "I don't think Mr. Burke likes me."

"That might change if you'd stop correcting him."

He raised his hands helplessly. "Your history books are full of errors. I'm just trying to help."

In science, the class was studying the effects of sugar on cellular structure. I was studying the effects of Jared's presence on my nervous system. It was kind of scientific. Jared was the stimulus and I was the test subject. Oddly enough, every time the stimulus was presented, the test subject's cells flooded with adrenaline. Clearly it was a valid test. I should publish.

But I couldn't help but wonder what had happened exactly. It would take something very powerful to bring down Jared. He was almost indestructible. Who could do that? What could do that? And his behavior was different. To deny that would be infantile.

But still. That grin.

I was busy replaying that grin of his in my mind for the seven thousandth time when I felt a sharp jab from behind. I sprang to attention. Ms. Mullins was standing in front of the classroom, her expression questioning, her gaze focused directly on me.

"Um, yes?"

She smiled. "You're right, Lorelei. At least someone studied."

When she turned back to her slide show, I sank back and rolled my eyes in relief.

Brooke leaned forward from the desk behind me. "Nice save."

"I'm going to pass out your papers now," Ms. Mullins continued, "and based on the scores I saw last night, I'm going to present you with a prediction: I predict that at least eighty percent of the class is going to fail the test on Friday if it doesn't study. These scores leave a lot to be desired."

When she got to me, she looked down in disappointment. "You can do better, Ms. McAlister."

I scrunched farther into my seat and took the paper. My grade wasn't horrible. I wouldn't be grounded for a 78. But I would get a good talking-to. Mostly from Grandma. She freaking loved A's. But I'd had a horrid vision that day when I brushed against a senior with bulimia. Surely that counted for something.

"Score!"

Brooke, another A freak, must have aced the assignment. Again. I turned back to her. "I'm totally copying next time."

"I wouldn't suggest it," Ms. Mullins said, coming back through the aisle.

With a startled gasp, I glanced up at her, unable to curb the guilt in my expression fast enough. I laughed breathily instead, trying to recover. "Oh, right. I was just kidding."

Her sparkling eyes crinkled with mischief before turning back to the class. "Okay, we have ten minutes. I suggest you use that time wisely."

She brushed past me as I studiously opened my book, going for another save. Was it too much to hope for two in one day? But the contact as Ms. Mullins walked past shifted gravity. Like a wind that blew one direction one minute, then another the next, the world tilted to the side.

In the next instant, I heard a muffled pop. I grasped for my desk, but my fingers slipped on something warm and sticky. My chair disappeared out from under me and I toppled back, arms searching blindly for something to grab on to. I landed hard. My spine and shoulder blades hit the tile floor with a thud a millisecond before the back of my head cracked against the hard surface. I looked around, wide eyed. The desks vanished. Students ran for cover, screaming and crying, and I found myself lying next to the prone and lifeless form of Ms. Mullins.

THE AVALANCHE

I realized instantly I was having a vision, but it hit like an avalanche, knocked the breath out of me, and stung my eyes like an arctic wind. I'd never had a vision so vivid, so uncontrollably real. I could feel the slickness of blood as I slid in it, struggling to get to Ms. Mullins. I could hear screams and cries of absolute terror as students rushed for cover. I could hear the splintering sound of gunshots, could smell the gunpowder and see the smoke.

Suddenly Mr. Davis came into view. He was trying to get to us, to Ms. Mullins. He glanced around, wild eyed, and came face-to-face with the shooter a split second before the gun went off again, hitting him in the chest. It didn't stop him. He barreled forward, determination locking his jaw. It took five bullets to bring him down. He spun toward me and sank to his knees, his tie, a brilliant red, matching the stains spreading across the front of his shirt, his face frozen in shock. My bloody hands shot to my mouth in horror.

In all the chaos, I never got a clear view of the shooter. I saw a wrist. A hand. A gun. My line of sight stopped there, because the barrel was turning toward me and I couldn't seem to look past it. A boy stepped into view, but he was simply the blurry backdrop for the gun, hazy and out of focus. When he pulled the trigger again, I could almost make out a sneer on his face before the bullet hit its mark right between my eyes. My head jerked back with the force as pain exploded inside me, splintering my skull and my thoughts; then everything went black.

"Lor?"

I heard Brooke's voice—so casual, so unfathomably calm amid such devastation—as I fell back in my chair. My arms reached blindly until my head bounced off the concrete floor.

"Lor! Are you okay?"

Brooke was beside me in an instant. I'd tipped my chair back, and a few kids were laughing as I looked around in shock. I lifted my hands—turned them over, searching for blood—then glanced up at my classmates' faces, suddenly untrusting of them all.

"Lor, what happened?"

Despite the pain in my head, sharp and hot, I scrambled to my feet and turned on the class, searching for the culprit. But I hadn't seen him. Not clearly enough to pick him out.

"Lorelei," Ms. Mullins said. She was sitting behind her desk but rose slowly, watching me with a wary expression. Like she knew I hadn't just randomly fallen. She glanced at the other students as well, and their faces turned from entertained to confused.

Before I could gather myself, a wave of nausea washed over me, the smell of blood and gunpowder so vivid in my mind. I doubled over and emptied the contents of my stomach, the adrenaline rushing through my veins too much for my body to handle. I left my breakfast on Ms. Mullins's floor. It was very unappealing.

"Oh, man," I heard one kid say. Nathan Ritter. He jumped up and put as much distance between himself and the acrid pool as he could, as did everyone else close by. A few students gagged. A few others groaned in disgust.

Ms. Mullins, who wasn't much taller than Brooke and me, took one of my arms and helped me toward the door. "Nathan, go get Mr. Gonzales to watch the class. This is his prep period. And get the custodian."

"Anything to get out of here," Nathan said, jumping to do her bidding.

After threatening the class with dire warnings of quizzes and extra homework should they misbehave, she walked me to the nurse's office. Brooke gathered our stuff and followed. She didn't say anything, clearly understanding what had just happened, but Ms. Mullins kept asking me questions, wanting to know if I'd had a fever that morning or if I felt dizzy.

I stopped and looked at her. At the concern in her eyes. She'd been lying there beside me, her skin ghostly pale, her body drained of blood in seconds. A sob escaped my throat before I could stop it. She glanced around, patted my arm, and urged me forward.

"It doesn't matter, sweetheart."

But it did matter. How could something so heinous happen? Who would do such a thing to Ms. Mullins? To Mr. Davis?

Just before we went inside the nurse's office, she turned to me, her expression grave. "It doesn't matter," she repeated. Then she placed her hands on either side of my face and whispered, "It doesn't matter what you saw. Nothing is inevitable."

Surprise glued me to the spot. I gazed at her questioningly, my lips parting, then closing abruptly, afraid to say anything. But how did she know I'd had a vision? Ms. Mullins wasn't a member of the Order. She didn't even go to our church, not that every churchgoer was a member. Far from it. But how did she know about my visions?

With a smile both grim and knowing, she patted my shoulder again and ushered me inside the nurse's office.

Within seconds of my entering the nurse's office, Jared and Cameron were outside the door, Cameron keeping vigil in that weird, predator-like way of his, and Jared watching me through the doorway. He refused to leave when the nurse told him to get back to class, taking in her every move as she took my vitals, scrutinizing her every decision, all the while keeping tabs on me from underneath his dark lashes. His gaze was so intense, it warmed me to the marrow. I'd been shaking uncontrollably, but with him near, my body seemed to calm. I hadn't realized I was on the verge of hyperventilating until I started breathing normally again, rhythmically.

Nurse Mackey checked me for a concussion. "I'm going to go call your grandparents. Get them over here."

Wonderful. I would be shipped off by nightfall.

She gave Jared and Cameron an admonishing frown. "You kids really need to get back to class," she said before giving us the small room. It had a desk, one cot whose edge I was sitting on, and a couple of chairs.

After she left, Cameron asked, "What happened?"

"I had a vision."

"Did anyone hurt you?"

I blinked up at him in surprise. "In the vision?"

He shook his head. "No, just now."

Confused, I said, "No. I just had a vision. Why?"

Before he could answer, Glitch burst through the door. I jumped a solid foot. "I'm here," he said, panting as though he'd just run with the bulls. He put his hands on his knees and swallowed hard, trying to catch his breath. "I made it," he said between gasps for air. "I'm good. What's going on?"

"Lor had a vision," Brooke said, and every face turned toward him.

He paused. Straightened. Looked at us like we were all crazy. Then said, "A vision? That's it?"

"It was a bad one." Brooke took my hand into hers and squeezed.

"No, really. A vision? Doesn't she have those all the time?"

"Not like this," I said, the memory flooding back in another nauseating wave.

He finally started to get the picture.

Cameron turned to Jared, his expression wary.

Without even looking his way, Jared asked, "What?"

Cameron bounced back and refocused on me. Someday those two would be friends. Until then, we had to put up with their squabbles. They were like first-graders fighting over the only red crayon in the box.

"So, are you guys back to hating each other?" Glitch asked, still out of breath. How far had he run? "'Cause I'm good with that."

"Glitch," Brooklyn said. She pointed a warning finger at him.

"What?" he asked. "It's a legitimate question."

With a sigh of resignation, Cameron stepped back. "I don't know what's caused this imbalance, this turbulence in the air, but it's clearly affecting you, Lorelei."

"What happened in your vision?" Brooke asked.

After a hard swallow, I told them everything. About Ms. Mullins. About Mr. Davis. About the kid and the gun. The only things I left out were the little details like smells and the sounds. I had never had a vision quite that realistic before.

"And Mr. Davis had on his red tie." It was odd that I would remember that, but I did.

"Oh," Brooke said, surprised too. "Well, he always wears that tie on game days, so if this does happen, it won't happen at least until Friday, right? But it could be any Friday. What was Ms. Mullins wearing? We can keep an eye out."

"Blood," I said, sparing her an exasperated look.

She cringed. "Do you remember what color she was wearing? Her shoes?"

"Red and red. Honestly, all I remember seeing was blood. It was hard to get past."

"We have to find that new kid," Cameron said.

"Surely that doesn't have anything to do with him, potential descendant or not," I said. "I mean, this was a high school kid. An angry kid who wanted to take out his frustrations on the world."

"Not the world, Lorelei," Cameron said, stepping closer. "You."

I looked around in alarm. Glitch's head was bowed in thought. Jared's arms were crossed over his chest. Brooke's face was almost pale.

"No," I said, refusing to believe it. "He shot Ms. Mullins and Mr. Davis. He wasn't after me."

"And yet he aimed the gun point-blank at your head," Cameron said. "Shot you with a particular kind of purpose."

Jared fixed a hard gaze on me. "Most likely, he only shot the others because they were in the way."

Cameron took over again. "He was after you, Lor. The

prophet. The only one, according to prophecy, who can stop the coming war before it starts." He kneeled before me. "I promise you he wanted you dead, and I can also promise he was sent by someone else."

"Is it the same guy causing this disturbance you're sensing?"

"Possibly. Or the man who opened the gates of hell in the first place. We still believe he was the one who sent that reporter who tried to kidnap you. We have to figure out who he is."

"And you're the only one who's seen him," Brooke said.

"Right, when I was six." The only plausible solution to stop this war lay in the fact that I had seen the man who opened the gates of hell ten years ago. Maybe it was that simple. Me remembering who he was or recognizing him at some opportune moment. How else would I stop a supernatural war?

Glitch brought me an orange soda, and it helped with the whole nerves and vomiting thing. I convinced them I felt well enough to stay at school.

"She can't be here," Cameron said to Jared. "At school. It's too dangerous."

"Cameron, Ms. Mullins's life is in danger. Mr. Davis's. I can't possibly leave now."

Nurse Mackey came back in just as Grandma and Granddad showed up. She frowned, perplexed, when Grandma called Jared "Your Grace." Grandma insisted on calling him by his celestial title, though Jared swore the angels, arch or otherwise, never really went by such titles. Nurse Mackey shook it off, then explained what had happened, trying to calm my grandparents down before leaving us alone in the room again.

Brooke jumped up and offered her chair to Granddad, but he waved her back into it as Grandma sat beside me on the cot. Jared and Cameron joined us as well, closing the door behind them.

"What happened?" Granddad asked as he sat in the vacant chair before me, his face a picture of concern.

"Nothing. I just got dizzy." The vision flashed in my mind and made me start shaking again. Grandma sat on the bed beside me and wrapped me in her arms. I let her, but only for a minute. Her gaze darted occasionally to Jared, and it angered me, so I leaned out of her grasp. She was so worried about him. What was he going to do? Incinerate me right then and there because he was so dangerous?

Well, okay, he was dangerous, but clearly there was something else out there even more so.

She dropped her arms in disappointment, and guilt crashed into me. I decided to let them in on one secret. One that I was hoping wouldn't get me shipped off. I looked at them all sheepishly, and said, "Ms. Mullins knows what I am." When every set of eyes around me widened in surprise, I continued. "She told me that nothing is inevitable. No matter what I saw, nothing is inevitable. She knows."

"That's impossible," Grandma said, her face a picture of shock.

"No." An astonished smile slid across Granddad's face. "No, it's not. She's the one. Why didn't I see it?"

"See what?" Brooklyn asked.

When he grinned at Grandma, she sputtered in disbelief, thought a moment, then her mouth dropped open in realization. "You're right. Oh, my goodness."

"What?" I asked, fairly bursting to know.

Granddad looked at Jared, who stood with a knowing expression on his face. "You knew, didn't you?"

"Yes, but only recently. She slipped one day. I caught it."

"Granddad, really," I said, growing annoyed.

"She's the observer." He laughed softly. "She's always been the observer."

"I just can't believe it," Grandma said. She looked at me, a loving expression in her eyes. "Your father told us there was always an observer, a person on the outside looking in who makes sure the power of the Order of Sanctity is not being abused or misused. And nine times out of ten, nobody within the Order knows who it is. Once that person is brought to light, another one must be sent, else the position be compromised."

"It has to be her. She moved here right after your parents married. She'd just graduated from college with a teaching degree. But she became friends with your mom," Granddad said to me.

"No," Grandma corrected. "Carolyn became friends with her through that book club. Remember how many times she had to ask Ms. Mullins out for coffee before she accepted?"

Granddad's face brightened in remembrance. "That's right. And that explains why she wouldn't go to coffee with your mom for so long."

Grandma nodded and glanced at me. "She was trying to do her job, and your mother just wouldn't give up."

I couldn't help but let a smile dawn. "What happens now that we know?"

Granddad patted my hand. "She'll be disassociated. She can't be the observer if we know who it is."

"We got her fired?" I asked, suddenly concerned.

"Well, perhaps, but now she can join us. She can be a part of the Order, if she wishes." He cast a hopeful expression on Grandma. "She'll be a great asset."

I hoped they were right. And that Ms. Mullins wouldn't be upset that she'd just lost her job as observer. At least she still had her teaching job. But my question was, to whom did Ms. Mullins report?

Fortunately, our next class was PE, where I had a toothbrush waiting for me. I couldn't wait to wash the taste of vomit out of my mouth. And I had a note from the nurse not to suit up for the rest of the week. Sweet. Thanks to Nurse Mackey, fourth went fairly smoothly, as did fifth. But the day was only a bit more than half over.

"Could this day get any weirder?" Brooke asked as we headed to lunch. Glitch ran up behind us, and Cameron met us on the way.

"What? Did something else happen?" Glitch asked after he tossed a quick glower at Cameron. Just in case Cameron didn't know how he felt about him, because clearly the seventeen thousand other glowers he gave him weren't enough to get his point across.

"No," Brooke said, her voice blasé, "just the usual unexplained events and near-death experiences that seem to be happening a lot here at Riley High. Speaking of which, we've got to practice your new trick more. I've worked up a schedule."

She handed me a schedule with specific times that we would practice. Or, well, I would practice and she would prod me onward. I felt so abused. She was bound and determined to expand my new skill, since it was safer than the visions themselves. I would've bet Glitch's college fund Nostradamus wasn't prodded.

After gracing her with my best grimace, I asked, "Really? Sunday mornings at seven?"

She grinned. "This will give us an excuse to sleep over all weekend."

Wow, she was good. I looked at Cameron. "So, where is Jared now?"

"Why do you always ask me that?"

"I don't know. You guys are like cosmically connected," I said. "You each seem to know where the other one is at any given moment, except when he's been attacked by unscrupulous descendants and is lying somewhere unconscious."

"And you're stealthy," Brooke added.

I nodded in agreement. "That's true. And strong."

"And really tall."

Cameron didn't seem impressed. "So, I'm supposed to keep tabs on the reaper because we're both tall?"

"Something like that," Brooke said.

"Are you going to tell us why the sudden animosity between you two?" I asked him.

"Nope."

It was worth a shot.

"It's not animosity. Or I don't think it is. I'm not sure what that means."

When we left the main building and rounded the corner that led to the cafeteria, Cameron grabbed our arms and pushed us roughly against brick.

"Hey," Brooke said in complaint, but Cameron pressed his back against us as Jared literally fell from the sky in front of us, landing solidly on his feet, the muscles in his legs powerful enough to keep him upright with just enough bend to regain his balance.

He grinned at Cameron, then inclined his head to look at Brooke and me. "I was just going to scare them."

"Were you on the roof?" Brooke asked, astonished.

He had refocused on Cameron and didn't spare her a glance when he replied with a simple, "Yes."

I sidestepped past my barrier. "And you were on the roof because?"

When Jared stepped closer, Cameron ran interference by blocking me again. "Are you good?" he asked Jared, holding me back with an arm made of steel.

"Cameron, what the heck?"

"Why are you asking?" Jared took the challenge in Cameron's expression with a particular kind of glee.

"You don't seem yourself today," he responded, pushing me farther back.

"And you know me so well."

What the heck? I tried to push past Cameron. I failed.

"I want to talk to Lorelei," Jared said. "Alone."

Cameron angled his head. "I don't think so."

"Cameron." I socked him on the arm. "What are you doing?" They hadn't behaved so aggressively toward each other since Jared first showed up in Riley's Switch. They'd almost killed each other that time. And they tore half the town apart in the process.

"Okay, guys," Brooke said, putting on her supervisor's hat. She held up her palms for a cease-fire. "Clearly everyone's blood sugars have dropped to dangerous levels. Let's just go to lunch." She grabbed Cameron's sleeve. Cameron grabbed mine, and I grabbed Glitch's.

Jared stayed back a solid minute, measuring Cameron like he was sizing him up for a coffin.

"Jared, come on," I called out over my shoulder. I didn't know what to think, what to say. Admittedly, Jared was acting different. His movements. His expressions. Even his countenance was full of something strange, something foreign.

He finally followed us, his steps slow and methodical.

We each got our lunch and sat at our table, but the boys hardly touched theirs. Except for Glitch. He inhaled his burger. It was amazing to watch. I didn't bother asking Jared and Cameron what was up between them again. They clearly weren't going to spill. Instead, I brought up another subject that had continued to elude us. The new kid.

I took a drink of my water. "I can't believe we haven't seen him at all today."

"We need to find out his name," Cameron said, "find out where he lives."

"We could break into Davis's office."

"Can I join you?" We looked up at Ashlee. She was becoming a regular.

"Sure," I said.

I moved over so she could pull up a chair.

"Jared, you remember Ashlee."

He nodded. I was grateful for at least that, considering his mood.

She gave a bashful smile, then said, "So, when?"

"When?" Brooke asked.

"When are we breaking into Davis's office?"

Brooke and I chuckled, then Brooke said, "Probably not for a while. But I like your attitude."

After glancing under her lashes several times toward Glitch, who was too consumed with the amount of ketchup he got on each fry to notice, she said, "I didn't mean to interrupt your conversation. It sounded interesting."

"Oh, no big," Glitch said. "Do you know who that new kid is? We need a name and address if possible."

"His name is Vincent," she said with a soft laugh. "But I don't know his address. I can try to get it, though. I'm an office aide last hour."

"Awesome," Brooke said. "That would be great. And it would save us from getting arrested for breaking and entering."

I agreed and took a bite of my turkey sandwich just as the creature whose name shall not be spoken aloud appeared. Out of nowhere. She was just there. And my mouth was full and unattractive.

Shockingly, her eyes alighted on Jared. They always alighted on Jared. Like he was the last source of water in a scorched desert and she was parched. "Hi, Jared."

He watched me chew a few seconds, then smiled up at her. The fact that it was more congenial than genuine wouldn't matter to Tabitha. Either way, a smile would only encourage her. "Have you thought about my proposal?"

Proposal? I swallowed hard and took a drink to wash it down. Holy cow, she irked.

"What proposal is that?" I asked him.

He smiled at me, the same congenial smile he'd just offered Tabitha. I gasped softly, then caught myself. Surely we were beyond congenial, but showing any emotion in front of Tab was dangerous.

"Tabitha asked if I could pose for her drawing class," he said.

Oh, for Pete's sake. "You're taking drawing?" I asked her, trying to unglue my teeth.

"Yes, at the community college. And we need models." Her eyes glittered with the prospect. "I knew Jared could probably use the money, living on his own as he does, so I offered to get him an application."

Despite the fact that Jared had been in pretty much every thought I'd had for the last few weeks, I hadn't taken into account that he might actually need spending money. Everything he needed was supplied to him by the Order. Mostly through our store, of course, and the members of the Order. Honestly, those women baked more than Sara Lee.

But he was a guy. Surely he needed guy things. Like, I didn't know, shoe polish or something. I had never even thought about offering to help him find a job or have him do things around the store to earn some extra cash. He was always busy watching and lurking, his habits frighteningly similar to Cameron's. They took their jobs very seriously.

"Actually, I'm still considering it. Can I get back to you?"

She brightened. "Absolutely." She handed him a card. "Call me when you decide."

She had a card?

Offering the rest of us a smile at last, she said, "Hey, Lor. Hope you're feeling better."

"Thank you. I am."

"See you at practice, Ash."

"Not if I see you first."

Brooke snorted out a laugh, but I was a little too shocked. Ash was now officially my hero.

Tabitha laughed too, then wriggled her fingers at us. "Tootles."

In all the years I'd been on planet Earth, I never actually heard anyone use the word "tootles." The cultural diversity in New Mexico was amazing. We had everything from *Hágoónee'*, which was "good-bye" in Navajo, to tootles.

I looked at Jared from underneath my lashes. He hadn't turned her down. That knowledge stabbed me somewhere deep inside. Probably my pancreas. But who was I kidding? Jared was a supermodel who deserved to be with others of his kind.

The creature whose name shall not be spoken aloud may have won this round, but I would be avenged. Or at least, thought of nicely when I died. How would people think of her? Not nicely, I was positive.

"It's interesting to find you here, Casey." I was so deep in thought, I literally jumped when Mr. Davis walked up.

Glitch wiped his mouth, then gave the principal his full attention. "Why is that, sir?"

He folded his arms over his broad chest. "Because you've been marked absent all day."

"What?" He scoffed. It was a little too fake. Brooke gaped at him, clearly disappointed in his attendance record. "There must be something wrong. A *glitch* in the system." He chuckled at his own joke.

No one else did. Jared was eyeing him suspiciously while Cameron was gazing up at the principal with the same faux innocence.

"I guess I could just talk to your teachers. Get this straightened out."

"Sh-sure," he said, his confidence stumbling.

Mr. Davis nodded. "I'll get back to you." But before he left, his gaze flitted to Jared's arms, lingered there a second, then moved on to me. "Glad you're feeling better," he said. He turned to leave before I could thank him.

Though Jared was wearing the bomber jacket, Mr. Davis knew about the bands of symbols around his arms. He'd seen them when Jared and Cameron got in a fight in the parking lot a few weeks back. And he remembered them even though he'd only been around ten when he saw Jared with his older brother, Elliot, seconds before Elliot dropped dead. Then Jared had disappeared before his eyes.

I wondered what seeing that did to him. How growing up with that unsolved mystery affected him. His brother had died of natural causes. Jared didn't actually kill him; he just tweaked the timing in answer to someone's prayers. Kind of like he was supposed to do with me until he went all rogue and saved me instead of taking me. A fact for which I was grateful.

"All right," Brooke said to Glitch when Mr. Davis left. "Fess up."

"What? It's a mistake. I can't help it if the teachers can't see me. I'm dark. I blend with the wood."

"You're skipping again, aren't you?" she asked.

"Why would I skip? Why would I want to miss all this?" He spread his hands, indicating our surroundings.

While Glitch proceeded to lecture us on the perils of skipping, I couldn't help but notice the lowering of Jared's lashes as he watched him. The sharp slant of his brows when he looked at Cameron. Cameron looked right back in challenge.

I would never figure those two out.

ISAAC'S ARTWORK

As Brooklyn and I entered our sixth-hour History class and took our seats near the front, Brooke riffled through her bag and brought out the photo wallet.

"This is my chance," I whispered to her.

She looked up from what she was doing. "What chance?" I nodded to the back of the room and she glanced over at Isaac Johnson. "Oh," she whispered back, "right." She continued to thumb through her photo book until she came to one that would apparently work for whatever torturous plan she'd schemed up. "So, how are you going to do it?"

I was busy trying to get a good look at the photo, knowing what she was about to ask me. "I'll just touch it like usual."

"No, Isaac." She leaned closer. "How are you going to get close enough to him to try to get a vision?"

He sat in the back of the room, surrounded by friends. Several football players were in History with us. Normally they were horsing around and taunting one another into this or that. But today, utter silence. Joss Duffy sat slumped in his desk, staring at his hands. Cruz de los Santos was playing with a string on his letter jacket. And Isaac Johnson, Sydnee's boyfriend, sat huddled over his desk, shielding his face with his massive arms. He was huge. He'd made the varsity football team his freshman year and was now the star defensive lineman. Talks of scholarships had already made the rounds, but I'd heard he wanted to go into the military like his dad.

He was such a nice guy. Polite. Gracious. So when he lifted his head and locked gazes with mine, a grimace I couldn't quite decipher hardening his features, I had to admit I was taken aback.

"I don't know yet," I answered Brooke. "I'm not sure I want to get close enough to touch him. He seems testy today."

She turned back, but he'd inclined his head again and went back to doing whatever it was he was doing. "Well, try this first. I want you to work on expanding your vision. See if you can go further back in time, see more of the scene before the shot was taken."

Mr. Gonzales walked in, so she quickly handed me the photo, then stuffed her bag under her desk.

I turned to face front and center. For some reason, Mr. Gonzales didn't like it when I sat with my back to him and talked to Brooklyn during class. Weird.

He plopped some freshly printed papers on his desk. "I'll give the first person who guesses correctly what we're doing today ten extra credit points on the *pop quiz*." He winked, letting us in on the clue.

While most of the kids sank in their desks, Brooklyn raised her hand with the enthusiasm of a cheerleader on X. I looked back and grinned. She was such a nerd.

"Are we having a pop quiz?" she asked, a disturbingly happy smile on her face.

He pointed to her like a game show host. "Bingo! Ten points to Miss Prather. Class, take out your pencils and clear your desks."

A hapless moan filled the room as students followed orders. I stuffed my backpack under my desk, remembered I needed a pencil, dragged it back out, and repeated the process. With a quick glance behind me, I realized the football players weren't complying. They were just sitting there. Isaac's head was still down, his shoulders hunched over whatever he was working on. Brian Klein wasn't doing as told either, but he never did.

Seeing my chance to get close to Isaac, I raised my hand. "Would you like me to pass them out, Mr. Gonzales?"

"Sure."

I was careful to start on the other side of the room, and while normally one would simply count out the required amount for that row and have the students pass them out, I went from desk to desk, handing out the quizzes hurriedly so Mr. Gonzales wouldn't feel the need to suggest I do otherwise for time's sake.

Most of the students took them with a grimace, but the football players just sat there, neither accepting nor declining the paper offered, so I laid them on their desks and moved on. Brooklyn cast me a knowing grin when I passed her, and nodded her head in encouragement. I planned it just right, and Isaac was my last stop. I tried to hand him the paper, but he didn't look up from what he was doing. How could I accidently-on-purpose touch his hand if he didn't take the paper?

I decided to tap him on the shoulder, though that wouldn't

help me get a vision. He was wearing his letter jacket, and in order for me to see anything, the contact had to be skin-on-skin. But he still didn't look up. Running out of time, I decided to try to push the paper under the arm he had draped over the desk. The one he was using to shield his activity. I scooted it under his elbow, tapping it further—when he grabbed my hand and pinned me with a hateful stare.

Electricity shot up my spine. I tried to step back, but he had a death grip on my wrist, and while I didn't get a vision, the sight before me was enough to stop me dead in my tracks. He was carving into the desk with a pocketknife, the deep gashes resembling barbed wire. When taken line by line, the vandalism looked like nothing more than sharp angles and thick, angry lines. But when taken as a whole, I had to admit, I was a little surprised.

He'd carved my name, each letter looking more like a first-grader did it than a straight-A high school student. I realized he was still glaring at me, his grip tightening with each passing moment. I tried to pull out of it, but he squeezed his fingers around my wrist so hard, I was certain he would break it.

I gasped and looked back at Mr. Gonzales. He was busy reading a message on his desk and didn't see what was happening.

"Isaac," I whispered. I didn't want to get him in trouble—he was a good friend—but his grip was really strong. "Please let me go."

Instead, he jerked me closer until my nose was almost touching his. I noticed a smudge on his forehead, a dark crimson stain. Then his expression changed, became almost apologetic. He was holding the knife with his other hand, his fingers locked around the blade itself until droplets of blood decorated his artwork.

"Isaac—"

"They want you dead, Lor," he said, a hint of panic in his voice.

I couldn't say anything. Any words that formed in my mind got stuck in my throat, and all I could do was stare into Isaac's frightened face.

"Isaac!" I heard from the front of the room. It was Brooklyn. She must've seen what was happening and came running down the aisle.

That caught Mr. G's attention. He stood and started toward us, but it was Brooklyn's outburst that startled Isaac into letting go. He stumbled to his feet, shock on his face as he looked at the knife in his bloody hand like he'd never seen it before.

"What is going on?" Mr. Gonzales asked. He stopped short and gaped, his gaze traveling back and forth between Isaac's hand and his carving. He had good cause to look shocked. Isaac was one of the nicest guys I knew. He would never hurt anyone on purpose, despite his enormous size.

Still gazing at his hand as though wondering whose it was, Isaac dropped the knife. It bounced with an ominously loud thud on my name, then tumbled to the floor. Before anyone could say anything, Mr. Gonzales picked up the knife with his thumb and index finger, handling it like a crime scene investigator might, then took Isaac by the arm and led him out the door.

"Everyone stay quiet and seated. I'll be right back."

But the moment the door closed, the room burst into an uproar of conversation. Half the room was asking me what happened, and the other half had rushed over to see the desk.

Brooklyn shooed them all away and led me back to my own desk, saying, "Boy, Syd wasn't kidding about her boyfriend acting strange."

Honestly, I wondered if this day could get any stranger?

Little did I know . . .

After ending up in the nurse's office again, this time selecting a stylish blue cold pack for my wrist, Brooke and I headed to the last class of the day, grateful that the end was nigh. Luckily, Foods and Nutrition was usually a very low-stress class. Even so, a part of me was hoping Ms. Phipps would have another hangover. Sadly, she wasn't quite the lush we'd hoped she would be. Instead, she gave us a quiz on the video we saw the day before. If I'd actually paid attention, I might have passed it.

But Brooke, dang her, knew every single answer. It was at that moment, at that pivotal turning point in our relationship, that I realized she'd sold her soul to the devil. No way could she have aced that quiz when neither of us paid any attention.

"It's an absorption thing," she said. We'd stayed behind to clean the kitchen for extra credit, so the halls were almost empty when we left class. "I just absorb information. I'm like a sponge."

"You're like a sphincter." I said it before I thought. And yet, didn't regret it. Clearly, I needed to work on a few issues. Resentment was never the answer.

She raised a superior brow, mocking my insolence, but her gaze quickly slid past me. "Jared's coming."

I whirled around. Fast. Too fast. So fast, I lost my balance and had to grab on to Brooke's jacket.

And the world was depending on me.

We were in so much trouble.

Jared smiled as he walked toward us, but it was different—he was different, harder. His gaze was cavalier. His walk was more arrogant than confident. His gait almost taunting.

He strolled up to me. "I've actually stumbled upon you without your bodyguard. That's not an easy thing to do."

I glanced around, looking for Cameron. He was always right outside my classroom or waiting just down the hall. Brooke stepped to the side to check her phone. Mine beeped too. I ignored it.

"Is there a reason you wanted to catch me without Cameron around?"

The grin that slid across his handsome face was more like a leer. He hooked his thumbs on the pockets of his jeans and leaned against the wall. Most of the students had vacated the premises. We were alone except for a couple of stragglers at the lockers down the hall.

Brooklyn tapped on my arm. "You should check your phone," she said. When I looked at her, she'd placed a wary expression on Jared, her brows crinkled in distrust.

Jared noticed. His mouth tilted as I took out my phone. Just as it lit up, I heard a clicking of heels and turned to see Tabitha walking toward us, her blond head bouncing, her white teeth visible from a hundred yards.

Then I felt Jared tug at my shirt. I backed away. He'd pulled my neckline and, I could've sworn, looked down my shirt. I clasped it to me with one hand. "Did you just look down my shirt?" I couldn't decide if I should be flattered or offended.

"Ever the good girl." His grin was gone and he stood eyeing me from underneath hooded lids. No expression on his face. No emotion. "Did you know there were seraphim, sons of God, who came to Earth to marry the daughters of man?"

I blinked at the abrupt change in subject and glanced at my phone. It had a text from Cameron. One word. *Run.*

"Well, yes," I said, frowning in confusion. Run? Run where?

"They had children who were called nephilim, right? Like what Cameron is."

His gaze traveled down again, paused on my hips.

I stuffed my phone back into my bag. "Jared, I don't understand—"

"You don't understand what I am," he said, his voice as sharp as steel with a razor's edge. He tilted his head, his eyes sparkling darkly underneath his lashes. "Did you know that I took the firstborn from ten thousand families in a single night, because one man, one human man, refused to submit to a power greater than his own?"

I tried to step back, but he curled the tail of my shirt into his fingers and held me to him. "The Pharaoh of Egypt," I said. I'd heard the story dozens of times, of how Moses had warned him. Of how he lost his own son that night.

"I have killed princes and paupers, kings and slaves, all upon a word. An order. And I could kill every person in this town without a second thought." He leaned closer and whispered in my ear. "I've done it. So many times, I lost count."

I really should have run. I could see that now.

"And in all that time, I never understood the allure. The desire inside my brethren to give up everything to be with a human." His expression hardened. "Until you." His hand slid around to the small of my back and he pulled me even closer.

I placed my hands on his chest and tried to speak with calm authority. "Jared, let me go."

He looked up as Tabitha walked past. "Then again, maybe any human will do."

Tabitha, seeing our position, had turned up her nose and clearly had every intention of walking on. He looked back at me, the smirk on his face cruel, punishing. Without taking his eyes off me, he whispered, "Come here."

And she obeyed. Tabitha stopped, turned toward us, and walked forward until she was on his other side.

"Maybe even this human will do."

He took hold of her jaw and dipped his head to place his mouth on hers.

And the world fell out from under my feet.

I couldn't believe what I saw. Not that I could blame him. He was stunning. And I was . . . well, I was not. If I defined any adjective in the English language, it would not be "stunning." I wasn't tall or gorgeous or a blonde or brunette. I was a short, redheaded pixie stick with curly hair and freckles. Truth be told, Jared deserved someone just as stunning as he.

But to see that. To have reality slap me in the face with the truth was a bit much to bear at the moment. Was he just doing it to be cruel? If so, why? What had I done?

I tried to tear my eyes away when his mouth slanted onto hers. Tried to disengage myself when she melted against him. Against us. Tears burned the backs of my eyes. I pushed against his rock-solid hold in vain.

"Going dark side on us, Azrael?"

I stopped and turned to Cameron, my humiliation complete.

"Why doesn't that surprise me?" he asked.

Before I could blink, Cameron crashed into the wall opposite us. I didn't even see Jared move. The Sheetrock cracked as the two-by-fours holding the wall up bent beneath the force. The moment Cameron started to catch himself, Jared was in front of him, a hand around his throat. He slammed Cameron into the wall again, his head making an indentation.

But Cameron was just as fast and just as strong. In a movement too quick for my mind to register, he broke Jared's hold, grabbed him by the throat, and smashed him to the ground. It shook the floor and rattled the windows. I heard a scream from Tabitha as she stumbled back, and I realized I had fallen as well. Then I felt Brooklyn by my side, tugging me to my feet, trying to pull me out of harm's way.

I had seen them fight before. I had seen the devastation left in the wake of their aggression. And the trauma of it had sent me into a state of shock. This time, I was already in shock. I was confused and hurt and frustrated.

Then a male voice, loud and threatening, boomed from down the hall. "What is going on?"

I looked over and saw Mr. Davis rushing forward. If he saw them, if he saw how fierce they were, how inhuman, he would have one more piece to add to his puzzle. One more link that would place Jared in his past.

"Lusk!" he yelled when Cameron picked Jared up and slammed him to the ground again.

A part of me began to worry for Jared. He wasn't himself, and beating him to death would not right it. I started forward, but something stopped me. Something dark. That's when I saw it. The grin on Jared's face. The smirk of satisfaction.

He glanced over at me and winked a microsecond before reversing their positions. He knocked Cameron to the ground and crushed him with the force of his body landing with a knee to his throat. I didn't care what Cameron was made of; there was no way he could survive a pulverizing blow like that. Then Jared dropped and rolled, taking Cameron with him and literally throwing him down the hall.

The fight was like before. Supernatural. Otherworldly. Impossible for mere mortals. But last time I had been the only one to witness it. Jared had stopped time. This time, those who were still around saw everything, including Mr. Davis.

Tabitha sat sprawled on the floor, petrified. I couldn't blame her. After Cameron once again crashed into a wall at the other end of the hall, Jared turned on Mr. Davis. The contempt sparkling in his eyes was primal. He was a predator now. And he was angry. There was nothing controlled or sane about his actions.

I broke free from Brooke and ran to intervene, taking a position between Jared and Mr. Davis. Jared smiled, but the gesture held no warmth, no hint of affection. Before I knew it, Brooke was beside me again, clinging to me, her eyes like saucers.

"Stay back, Jared," she said.

A whisper of a laugh escaped him and he took a calculated step forward, mocking her.

I tried to push her behind me as I glared up at him. "Stop."

His dark gaze landed on me, and he showed his palms in surrender. "I just want him to be with his brother," he said.

Slowly, and with deliberate care, Mr. Davis wrapped his arms around us and pulled us back with him. As we inched away, Jared watched, his expression humorous. We were mice and he was the jaguar, playing with his meal before he devoured us.

Just as he started to step forward, a sharp crack echoed down the hall and Jared spun around, jerking what looked like a tranquilizer dart out of his shoulder. Before he could do anything, another loud crack sounded. And another. He pulled out two more darts, one from his chest and one from his upper arm; then Cameron was on him. With a rifle in both hands, he whipped the butt of it across Jared's jaw. I was sure he would go down. Instead, he shook his head, then refocused on Cameron, his stance fierce, his expression so full of venom, I wondered who he was.

He took a step forward, then stopped and fell to one knee. When he looked down at his hands as though he'd never seen them before in his life, Cameron struck again.

I squelched the scream inside my throat with both hands as Jared went down. Cameron yelled over his shoulder, "Hurry, he won't be out long!"

That's when I noticed Sheriff Villanueva running toward us, carrying chains and shackles. Real shackles. Jared moaned.

"Hurry," Cameron repeated. He tossed the rifle to the sheriff and grabbed the chains. As the sheriff reloaded the rifle, Cameron went to work. "I can't believe it took that long to take effect. He should have gone down instantly."

Mr. Davis was standing there wide eyed, not quite sure what to think.

Cameron spared him a quick glance, then said through clenched teeth, "Get them out of here." When Mr. Davis didn't move, Cameron yelled, "Davis! Get Lorelei and Brooklyn to your car."

Mr. Davis snapped to attention and, oddly enough, followed Cameron's orders. He motioned us forward. I stopped to drag Tabitha to her feet; then we followed Mr. Davis out the back entrance to the faculty parking lot.

"Wait," I said once Tabitha was sitting safely on the steps. "I have to go back."

Brooke grabbed me, her nails biting into my already sore wrist. We were going to have a serious talk about her nails. "Absolutely not. Something is wrong, Lor. It's not him."

Mr. Davis grabbed me and I grabbed Tabitha again. He seemed more than happy to get the heck out of Dodge, and Tabitha was in a complete state of shock. We climbed into his SUV and tore out of the parking lot.

Mr. Davis fished out his phone and was calling someone, probably the police.

Tears blurred my vision. I wanted to call my grandmother, but didn't dare. Then my phone rang. It was her.

"Lorelei," she said when I picked up, "are you okay?"

I wasn't sure why I confided in her. It just kind of came out. "Cameron and Sheriff Villanueva have Jared."

"I know, sweetheart. Where are you?"

"You know?" How did she know?

"Honey, where are you?"

"Brooke and I are with Mr. Davis."

A relieved sigh slipped from her mouth. "Thank God. Have him bring you to the Sanctuary. We're getting everything ready."

"Everything ready for what?" I asked, growing warier with every breath. What were they going to do?

"We just figured it out a little while ago, hon. We had to act fast. I'm so sorry we couldn't get word to you, but we didn't know where Jared was, if he would hear us or read a text if I sent one. There was just no way to know."

"Well, he's not here now." Resentment hit and hit hard. I was out of the loop yet again. "What is going on?"

"Can Mr. Davis hear me?" she asked, and I glanced over at him. He was ordering someone to pull the fire alarm so the building would be evacuated completely.

"I don't think so."

"I can't take the chance. I'll explain everything when you get here, but for now, tell him you don't know what's going on."

At least I wouldn't be lying. I took in a deep breath that caught in my chest. "Fine." I hung up. "Grandma wants you to take us to the church."

He looked at me, surprised. "I was thinking the sheriff's station."

"The sheriff is going to meet us there," I said. He was confused and I was right there with him.

"Of course he is." He worked his jaw. I could almost hear his teeth grinding from where I sat. "A tranquilizer dart? They shot him with a tranquilizer dart? Who does that?"

I looked back, scanning the area for signs of Cameron and the sheriff. "I don't know."

"Of course you don't."

He was angry. And worried. I could see it in his eyes. That, and fear. When Jared mentioned his brother, I sensed a jolt of fear rush through him. Not that I could blame him. From what Jared told us before, Mr. Davis had looked right into his eyes that day as he was taking Mr. Davis's brother. And he had never forgotten him.

Just as we pulled into the church parking lot, I spotted Cameron and the sheriff coming up from a back road. They pulled around the side entrance, their tires kicking up dirt when they skidded to a stop. Several members of the Order were waiting, and I wondered how many were in on this.

When we pulled up, I climbed out of the SUV and headed to the side entrance with Brooke right behind me. Tabitha was in the backseat, staring, while Grandma rushed out the front door. She headed off Mr. Davis as he tried to follow us. I heard her talking to him, but didn't stick around to find out what she said.

Out of sight of the main road, Cameron, Sheriff Villanueva, Granddad, and Mr. Walsh, one of the elders, carried Jared into the Sanctuary, down the stairs, and past the anterooms to the main rooms in the back of the massive underground structure. Jared was bleeding from the last blow Cameron had given him. He was bound from neck to ankles in industrial-strength chains with metal shackles that looked like something from a horror movie.

"Granddad, what is going on?"

"Lorelei," he said, surprised, "get back. Are you crazy?" He looked around and spotted another member just coming into the anterooms. "Get her back!"

Betty Jo, Grandma's best friend, rushed forward, took me by the shoulders, and started to drag me away.

"Wait," I said, but Brooke, having caught on, was helping Betty Jo. I fought them both. I wasn't stupid. I knew to keep my distance, but I wanted some answers. "Wait, Granddad, what are you doing with him?"

I heard a sound come from Jared, deep and guttural like a growl, and saw Granddad take out a syringe. "Hold him if you can." He plunged the needle into Jared's leg. In return, Jared offered him a look I could only describe as pure, seething hatred.

Then he bucked under their grip. They lost their hold and he fell to the ground with a thud. He tried to roll onto his knees, but he overshot the move and almost toppled over. Shaking his head as though disoriented, he tensed, panting and gasping as the drug took effect. Then he collapsed, the chains rattling as he hit the floor.

"Get him in there," Granddad said. "Quickly, before it wears off."

They took him into the archive room. It was more like a vault than like a room, created to protect the ancient documents that had been passed down. But why there?

"Hurry, close the door." Granddad rushed out.

Jared was already regaining consciousness and the men were struggling to close a door I had never even paid attention to. It was behind stacks of boxes and filing cabinets that had to be cleared before they could close it.

"Bill, hurry!" Grandma yelled. She must have gotten rid of Mr. Davis. She stood behind me, her eyes glued to Jared.

I turned back to him as he shook his head again and rolled onto his knees once more.

"Bill," she whispered, her voice faint with fear.

I didn't like seeing her afraid. I stepped to her, took her arm into mine as Jared watched me from underneath his lashes, the same arrogant smile sliding across his face, the same taunting air. In one concentrated effort, he forced his arms apart, broke the chains. They slipped from his body like satin falling to the floor.

"Bill, please."

His hands were still shackled behind his back, and with the force it might have taken me to break a silk thread, he pulled them apart.

In a breathy whisper I barely heard, Grandma tried one more time. "Bill," she said, and the hopelessness in her voice broke my heart.

NIGHT VISION

"Push!" Granddad said, straining under the weight of steel. Just as the huge door swung shut, Jared rushed forward, his eyes locked on to mine until the thick, metal door separated us.

He slammed into it with all his might, and the six men who were trying to shut it skidded back, losing valuable ground. Two actually fell. But before Jared could take another run at it, Cameron pushed it shut, his teeth clenched with the effort, his face red as he pushed with every ounce of strength he possessed.

Another loud thud echoed in the room, but the door barely gave that time. Granddad rushed forward and spun the vault handle to lock it. Cameron collapsed and slid to the ground, holding his abused throat and coughing. Brooke hurried to him.

He looked up at the sheriff. "Took you long enough to get there."

"Sorry. I couldn't find the right tranquilizer darts. We only had the ones for small bears."

I gasped. "What did you use on Jared?"

The sheriff turned to me. "The ones strong enough to bring down an elephant. Since we don't have many pachyderms in these parts, took me a while to find them."

Cameron grinned at Granddad. "We totally need to oil that door."

Granddad stood and nodded in agreement, winded from the effort it took to get the massive thing closed. Then he turned on Betty Jo. "What part of 'get her out of here' didn't you understand?"

I had never in my life heard him talk to anyone that way. Especially not to Grandma's best friend.

"Do you know what he could have done to her? Do you understand the consequences?"

"I'm sorry," she said, then added, "She's stronger than she looks."

Granddad was in her face before I could blink, and I jumped to her defense. "Granddad, this isn't her fault."

"You're right," he said, turning his anger on me. "It's yours." He pointed to the door we'd come in through. "When I tell you to get away—"

"What?" I asked, interrupting his tirade. "Are you going to tell me how right you were to insist Jared stay away from me? Are you going to keep more secrets from me until I'm in another perilous situation where that information would have come in handy? Are you going to send me away?"

Both Grandma and Granddad stilled.

"Bill," Grandma said as another thud echoed around us. She squeezed his arm to calm him.

But my own anger refused to be squelched. It spread like a nuclear blast. "Just so I have this straight, you guys get to keep things from me again and again, treat me like I'm an idiot, and I'm just supposed to obey your every order like a robot?"

Granddad seemed to snap to his senses. He stepped back as though appalled at his own behavior. "I'm sorry, pix."

The thought of being sent away caused a hollow pain to well up inside me. My chin wrinkled as I tried not to cry. Did they really think so little of me? To decide my future without even talking with me about it?

I stood there, accusing them with my stare. I was six again and my parents had just disappeared and I had no control over my life whatsoever. No direction other than certain doom.

"We just want to keep you safe."

"Then stop lying to me. Stop keeping things from me."

He wanted to talk more. I could see it in his eyes, but he cleared his throat and dropped it for now. Turning to Betty Jo, he said, "Betty, I am so sorry. I—"

"No," she interrupted. "You're right. I risked everything by not following your orders. I was just . . . I was so scared."

That made Granddad feel worse. He pressed his lips together and put a hand on her shoulder. "No, this is my fault. I should have caught on to this sooner, when Cameron first felt it."

"Felt what?" I asked, questioning Cameron, but he didn't have time to answer before another thud echoed in the room. "This won't hold him," I said, my tone worried. "It doesn't matter what you put him in, he can dematerialize and pass through anything. I've seen him do it."

"Not in there, pix," Granddad said. "That room was built to hold anything supernatural. Do you remember the symbols on the walls?"

I thought back and nodded. There were hundreds of symbols carved into the metal walls. I just thought it was decoration.

"Those are impenetrable bars to supernatural entities, like a steel cage would be to us. Nothing preternatural can get past it. It will hold him."

I was shocked. "You built this room to hold Jared?"

Exhausted, Granddad stepped to a folding chair and lowered himself into it. Grandma knelt beside him. He squeezed the hand on his arm, then said, "No, hon. We built this room to hold you."

I glanced at the vault, at the thick metallic walls and steel door. "Does the word 'overkill' mean anything? Because I'm pretty sure a small closet would suffice. And what did I do to deserve imprisonment anyway?"

He smiled sadly. "We built it after you were taken. After you were possessed. We thought that if we managed to exorcise the demon, we would need a place to hold it. Otherwise, he could just jump into someone else. And, we just didn't know what you would do with it inside you. If you would try to kill us. We had to plan."

"Oh. And I love that you never told me that either." Now I was just being childish. What were they supposed to do? I had a demon inside me. They had little choice.

"You're right. I'm so sorry, pix. You're getting old enough to be able to handle all this. We won't keep anything else from you."

For some reason, I seriously doubted that.

"I think it's going to hold," Mr. Walsh said. He'd been inspecting the room, walking around it and checking for faults in the metal. Brooke was sitting against the vault door with Cameron, and for the first time, I realized she was shaking uncontrollably. I was about to step to her but was blindsided.

"It's up!"

We all turned to Glitch as he beckoned us from the doorway.

"Glitch?" Brooklyn asked, surprised. "What are you doing here?"

He winked at her, then turned back to my grandparents. "We have audio and video out. Nothing in. Didn't have time."

After another thud that sounded like the earth beneath us was giving way, Brooke and Cameron stood. We followed Glitch as he led the way to yet another outer room, a small supply closet on the other side of the vault. There was a monitor set up, along with other technical equipment.

"Did you do all this?" I asked him.

"With the help of Mr. Lusk, Cameron's dad, yes."

Mr. Lusk popped up from underneath the desk and nodded a hello. "Cameron, how are you?"

Cameron massaged his throat. "I might need a beer, but I'm okay."

Mr. Lusk cast him a dubious frown.

I frowned at him too. "I thought beer didn't do anything for you."

"Okay, an aspirin, then."

I looked closely at the monitor, at the green glow of a night-vision camera projected onto the screen. It was Jared. I sank into a chair and watched as he paced like a caged animal, his shoulders hunched, his movements sharp and calculating.

Glitch reached over and turned a knob on a speaker. "It would be better if I'd had more time, but it should work."

That's when I heard Jared's breaths, his whispery curses, his soft footsteps.

"We can hear him, but he can't hear us. I didn't have enough—"

"Are you sure?" Brooke asked, interrupting. She'd come in behind me and noticed the same thing I did. "Because the minute you said that, he turned."

Jared had spun around when Glitch spoke, looking up at the

camera in the corner, his eyes bright, his stare hard and intentional.

I decided to test it. I leaned forward and asked, "Can you hear me, Jared?"

A slow, purposeful smile spread across his face, one that I was getting used to. One that held no humor whatsoever, no warmth, nothing but scorn and indifference.

"What happened to you?" I asked him.

He took a step forward. "Open the door and I'll tell you."

"I can't do that."

"I'll take you quick, Lorelei, painlessly, if you open it now."

Grandma gasped and put a hand to her mouth. Granddad draped an arm over her shoulders.

"Why do you want me dead?" I asked.

His head tilted to one side. "It's what I do."

My chest squeezed painfully around my heart, hitching my breath, stinging my eyes. Was it all just a game? From the beginning to the times that we'd kissed, was he just playing with me?

"Come on, pix," Granddad said as he took my arm to lift me out of the seat. "No good can come of this."

"Stay," Jared said, his voice calm, threatening. I stood to leave the room and he stepped closer to the camera. "Stay or they all die."

I hesitated, then sank back down into the seat. Grandma kneeled next to me. "If he gets out of there, hon, we're all dead anyway. He's just taunting you, baiting you." I suddenly understood why everyone was so afraid of Jared when they had found out what he was. I could now empathize on a level I didn't want to.

"No," Cameron said, bending to the monitor. "He probably does want her to stay, so he's making empty threats."

"And the hybrid speaks," Jared said.

"How is he hearing us?" Glitch asked, checking wire after wire. "That room is encased in steel ten inches thick. And there is no audio in. I guarantee it."

Cameron reproached him with a baleful look. "He's an archangel, Glitch-head. He can do things like that."

Glitch flipped him off, but Cameron paid no attention.

"Why would he want her to stay?" Grandma asked, and Cameron offered her a much softer version of his reproach.

"Because he really is in love with her."

My grandparents bristled, but I didn't believe him. This wasn't love. This was hatred. Contempt. Blind rage.

"Then, then I don't understand," she said.

"He's an archangel, a messenger. He doesn't kill for the sake of killing. He kills because he's been ordered to. But there's a balance." Cameron sat beside me. "You remember what I told you? About how he is made of light and darkness, right?"

I nodded, trying to understand, but sinking deeper and deeper into a state of despair.

"Something has shifted, has caused the darkness to overtake the light."

"What?" I asked in helplessness. "What could do that?"

Before Cameron could answer, Jared took another run at the door. He was still strong, still ridiculously fast, but he apparently couldn't dematerialize. Granddad was right.

When he failed again, Jared gazed into the camera. His expression was filled with so much hatred, so much apathy, I took a mental step back. Then he turned away, and the strangest thing happened. When he spun back around, he became a blur. He did dematerialize, became a mass of smoke and fog that spun and swirled like a whirlwind.

As though proving he still could.

As though he'd heard my thoughts.

The camera shook, vibrating until the room went completely

black and only sound was left. And the sound we heard was like the fluttering of a thousand birds. It grew louder and louder, feathers brushing against the speakers, wings rustling against one another in a chaotic frenzy until, in an instant, it stopped. Silence, abrupt and surreal, settled in the room like a blanket.

I gazed into the monitor, searching the blackness. "Jared?" I whispered. When I received no answer, I asked, "Is he still in there?"

Granddad looked worried too, but Cameron nodded and said, "Parlor tricks. He can't get past those walls. I guarantee it."

After another minute of waiting and watching, Granddad took me by the shoulders and lifted me out of the chair. He set guards on the vault and one at the monitor while the rest of us went back to the house to regroup. I just wanted an explanation. Something to help me understand what was happening. Before Jared escaped and killed us all.

My grandparents had been right all along.

"How did this happen?" I asked as we sat around our kitchen table. Betty Jo was making coffee and Glitch was setting out sandwich meat and bread at the behest of my grandmother. She sat in the chair beside me, so tired and so scared, she seemed to have aged right before my eyes. A sadness had consumed me as well, along with a genuine desire to die. I'd never been particularly suicidal, but would death be so bad? On the plus side, the pressure to save the world would end.

"I don't know how they did it," Cameron said, "but somehow, when the descendants got a hold of Jared, they branded him with some kind of symbol."

"They branded him?" I asked, appalled. "Do you mean they burned him?"

"Yes. I saw the scar on his back when we were restraining him."

I closed my eyes. Starving for answers, I asked, "What kind of symbol? What does it do?"

"I don't know. I'm not into that voodoo-hoodoo stuff. But, for lack of a better phrase, it seems to be blocking the light. All I see when I look at him now is darkness. And not a normal darkness. Comparing the color black to what he is encased in is like comparing a picture of the Grand Canyon to actually standing on its edge and looking down. It's so deep, it's disorienting. That's what looking at Jared is like. An endless darkness that is just as frightening as it is deep."

"Can you draw it?" Grandma asked. "The symbol. Do you remember what it looks like?"

He shrugged. "I can try."

She stood to scrounge up a pen and a piece of paper and handed them to Cameron.

"So, it's a symbol, right? It's sending a signal," Glitch said. "Then why don't we just disrupt the signal?"

Glitch, ever the techie, but he did seem to have a point.

Cameron sat with head bowed in thought. "There's something even more strange about this."

How could this get any stranger?

"It'll heal," he continued. "They're descendants of nephilim. They had to know that. They have to know how fast he heals. And when he heals, whatever power that binding spell had over him will cease to exist. Or are they too stupid to realize that once that scar heals and the light resurfaces, he'll kill them all?"

"You're right," Granddad said. "Branding Jared was like putting duct tape on a collapsing dam. It might hold for a little while, but when that dam breaks, nothing will stop it."

"Absolutely nothing," Cameron agreed.

"I think they are very aware of that fact," Granddad continued. "But it was obviously a risk they were willing to take."

"So why now? Binding Jared can't last more than a few days."

Grandma looked at him. "He could kill us all in the flash of a moment. Can you imagine what he could do in a few days?"

"That's true," Brooke said. "But maybe they know something we don't. You guys keep talking about a war. Maybe it's coming now and they wanted him out of the way."

"But why?" I asked, no closer to understanding. "What would they have to gain? This a war that has nothing to do with them."

"It has everything to do with every human being on Earth," Cameron said, "so that's a definite possibility. Whatever the case, we need to reverse the spell. We need him on our side." He glanced at Granddad, a worried expression drawing his brows together. "We can't fight what's coming alone. If we're going to have even the slightest chance, we need him."

"But what if that's not it?" the sheriff asked. "What other motive could they possibly have?"

"A pretty simple one, actually." Cameron stopped drawing the symbol. "They needed him out of the way for another reason." He nodded toward me. "Just long enough to take out the prophet."

I straightened when the focus shifted my way. "You still think they're after me?"

Granddad put a hand over mine. I saw for the first time the sadness that pressed on his shoulders. They didn't seem quite so broad as usual. Quite so strong. "Either way, this needs to be dealt with now."

Cameron placed a hard gaze on Granddad. "I have an idea, but you aren't going to like it."

"There's nothing about this I do like. What are you thinking?"

"I'm thinking Glitch-head is right."

"Can you not call me that?"

Cameron ignored him. "We need to disrupt the signal. We need to distort the symbol somehow."

"Of course," Grandma said. "We need to break the lines, to make it not mean what it means."

"And how do we do that?" the sheriff asked. "It took three tranquilizer darts and a nephilim just to get him to the ground."

"Then we'll use four this time," Cameron said.

The sheriff seemed doubtful. "He'll see that coming."

Cameron looked at me, his eyes suddenly glistening with hope. "Maybe not."

BARGAINING CHIP

I tiptoed into the room where the monitor was set up. The screen was still black, no signal whatsoever, but the audio was on. I heard a sound here and there. A tap. A scrape.

Filtering as much hope as I could into my voice, I whispered, "Jared?" The sounds stopped. I waited a full minute, gathering my courage, before asking, "Can you hear me?"

After a long moment, he said, "Yes."

My eyes slammed shut. I turned up the audio so I could hear from a distance, then walked to the vault door. "If I let you out, will you take only me and spare my family and friends?"

He waited again before asking, "Bargaining now?"

I looked over at Cameron. His mouth formed a grim line as he beckoned me to continue with a nod. I took a steadying breath, looked behind me into the dark anteroom of the bunker, knowing an army stood behind me, and said, "I'm going to open the door now."

After another long pause, he said, "I wouldn't."

With a hard swallow, I ignored him. "The door is heavy. You'll have to push from your side."

Never taking Cameron for the Catholic type, I was surprised when he did the sign of the cross. He bowed his head, took a deep breath of his own, then turned the huge locking mechanism.

I hurried forward and helped him pull. It opened far easier than it had closed. When the breadth spanned about three feet, I stepped around and expected to see Jared there helping, but he was standing back, his arms folded over his chest. I had also expected to see wings, huge and black and all consuming, but he was in his torn T-shirt and jeans, both bloodied from the fight.

"You're taking a huge chance," he said.

"We made a deal, though, right?" My body shook so uncontrollably, I felt like I was having a seizure, but I couldn't stop it. No matter how much I tried to force myself to calm, I couldn't stop the shaking. I stepped close to him. "Just me, and you leave Riley's Switch."

Without moving, he graced me with another of his smiles, this one all too knowing. "So all those people in the other room are just there to make sure you opened the door correctly."

I put a shaking hand on his chest, fear consuming me to such a degree, the edges of my vision darkened. "Jared, please."

Then I was airborne. I flew straight out of the vault and skidded into the wall, the air knocked out of my lungs. And the fighting began anew. Jared was ready for Cameron this time. He didn't stand still long enough to be shot with the dart gun.

The sheriff kneeled and took aim, but he was helpless. They moved at inhuman speeds. Blurs of color and light. At one point Jared was on the ground. The next, Cameron was on the ceiling, their strength and agility incredible.

No one could help. Granddad pulled me to my feet and we just stood there, watching with our mouths hanging open. Sheriff Villanueva's finger stayed wrapped around the trigger, waiting for the opportunity to tranq Jared. But it just didn't come. The second one of them would get the upper hand, the other would employ some technique to reverse the odds.

Grandma had pulled me back and was holding on to me for dear life.

A group of men hurried to the vault door, prepared to close it again, to lock Cameron in there with the Angel of Death.

I tugged at Grandma's arm. "I want to try something."

Her eyes rounded. "No, pix."

"Grandma, you said it yourself: If he gets out of there, we're all dead anyway. Whether from Jared or from this war, it doesn't matter." A sickly kind of despair had taken over. A desperation. "The end results will be the same."

She couldn't argue that point, and she knew it. With fear and sadness stiffening her expression, she let go.

I walked past Granddad. "Pix," he said, reaching out for me, but I ducked under his arm and sprinted into the vault. Jared had Cameron in a choke hold, and for a second, I thought Cameron might lose consciousness, but he elbowed Jared in the gut and wrenched himself free.

"Jared," I said, holding out my hand to him.

His gaze snapped up for a split second. Barely enough time to blink. And Cameron took advantage. While I thought he would score the skin where the brand was inlaid, just enough to disfigure the symbol, he snatched the knife from his waistband and plunged the blade into Jared's back.

Without thought, I ran to him, but Cameron tackled me down. By the time we turned back, Jared was holding the knife.

Cameron's eyes widened. "There it is. Do you see it? That spark of light?"

Jared looked down at the knife in his hands, at the blood dripping from his fingers, and he stumbled back. He leaned against the metal wall, his breaths raspy and spent, then slid down it, falling onto all fours.

"Crap," Cameron said. He was shielding his face with both hands, squeezing his eyes shut as though a bright light were saturating the room. "I can't see," he said, struggling to his feet.

Everyone glanced around, clearly unable to see what he was seeing. He fell onto his knees and cradled his head. His father ran to him and covered his head with his body. Cameron groaned through gritted teeth. And Jared was doing the same. Cradling his own head, fighting something deep inside.

Then they both collapsed onto the floor in choreographed unison. I ran to Jared as Brooke did the same for Cameron.

Jared was completely unconscious, his solid body impossible for me to move. I looked at his face, ran my fingers over his strong jaw.

"Pix," Granddad said, rushing toward me. "We don't know if it worked."

"It worked," Cameron said, taking in huge gulps of air. "It worked."

They picked Jared up and placed him with great care onto a table they brought in. His T-shirt, torn and bloody, hung off him like an overused rag. Granddad turned him over as Mrs. Strom stepped cautiously inside. She worked at the hospital and was the closest thing we had to a doctor in the Order. Jared's limbs hung limp, as though all the energy they'd once contained had evaporated. And yet, even unconscious, he looked powerful, like a sleeping panther. No one could deny the omnipotence of such a lethal animal.

I stripped off my jacket and placed it under his head as Granddad examined the knife wound. "The scar was healing fast. It probably would have been gone in a matter of days."

"And that would have been too long." Cameron joined us, his face swollen, his eyes bloodshot. "Whatever they had planned is going to happen soon."

"What did you see?" I asked him, relieved that Jared would be okay and wouldn't kill everyone I'd ever loved. Instead of waiting for an answer, however, I touched his arm.

And the nuclear flash that hit me almost knocked me off my feet. The moment the knife plunged into Jared's back, it started. A tiny spark became a beam, then a flood, then—in one massive burst—Jared's essence infused the room in a blinding light.

It was similar to how Cameron had explained the darkness, only with light. It was so deep, so forever, an infusion of warmth, genuine and radiant, I doubted I would ever be the same again. Knowing that such a love existed. Knowing that such affection was out there. And then slowly a balance began to settle around him. The darkness and the light merged to become the essence of Jared, of Azrael the archangel, the supreme being who may have been created for one specific reason, but could choose his path.

I blinked back to the present and gazed at Cameron.

"Isn't that cheating?" he asked me.

"You saw?" Brooke asked, astonished. "You have to tell me everything."

"Okay," I promised.

"That's definitely cheating."

Brooke and I both gave Cameron a grateful hug, each of us on either side of him. He hugged us back.

"Should we break more of the lines?" Granddad asked him. "The knife wound is already healing. What if—?"

"It won't," Cameron and I said in unison. I smiled up at him, having caught a glimpse of his world, now knowing a miniscule amount of what he knew. The things he must have seen. The miracles he must have witnessed his whole life. I almost envied his heritage at that moment before I realized what lay on his shoulders. It was bad enough being the prophet that was supposedly going to stop the coming war. I hated war. I hated even worse that so much was riding on my paltry abilities. But to have to be responsible for so many, to have been created for such a specific purpose.

"It's okay," Cameron said to Granddad. "Whatever kept the light at bay is gone. But it took a lot out of him. The repercussions of such a trip into darkness could very well be long and lasting. It may take him a while to come back to us. I just hope he hurries. We clearly don't have much time."

With Cameron's assurance that Jared would be back to normal when he woke up, we moved him to the spare bedroom on the first floor of our house. Mrs. Strom came over to clean and bandage Jared's wound, while Grandma and I bathed him with cool washcloths.

"You were amazing," Grandma said.

I let a breathy laugh escape me. "Cameron was more amazing."

"But he couldn't have done it without you. I just—" Her eyes watered as she glanced down, embarrassed.

"Grandma," I said in surprise, "I—I wish you would trust me more."

"I'm so sorry, pix." She hugged me to her and I let her, even though I still wanted answers.

"My turn," Granddad said from beside us.

I smiled and let him hug me, too.

"We're so proud of you, pix. What you did—"

"Was probably stupid. I'm sure I'll look back on it and cringe."

He chuckled and set me back from him. The sheriff came in then, regarded Jared a moment, then placed a hand on my shoulder. "That was kind of magnificent."

"Hey, why is she getting all the attention?" Glitch said, frowning as he brought in more water. "She always gets all the attention."

"She does," Brooke agreed, following him in with an armful of towels. "I think we should strike."

"I think you should get to bed," Brooke's mom said. Her parents had stuck around the church to help clean up the mess compliments of one Jared Kovach. Man, he could tear stuff up. The archive room would never be the same. Then they came over to check on things here.

Mrs. Prather had gathered bedding and was slipping a pillow under Jared's head. She handed me back the jacket I'd left at the church. "He's something, isn't he?" she said, eyeing Jared with both reverence and appreciation. "What happened was not his fault, Lorelei. I hope you know that."

I thought back to the picture, the one of Brooke's seventh birthday party. She had hardly changed at all. I wished I could tell her where her brother was. I wished something good would come of my visions instead of just darkness and fear and impending doom. I hated impending doom.

"I do. Whoever did this is very powerful."

"Yes, but so are you," Grandma said, and my reservations came crashing to the surface again. They had such hope. Dang it.

Still, there was something in her eyes. In Granddad's, too. A fear. An apprehension. They were still planning on sending me away. The first chance they got. I could see it. Feel it. And I didn't trust them as far as I could throw them.

"Can we have a note excusing us from homework tomorrow?" Brooklyn asked.

I laughed softly. She had a good point.

"I think you kids should stay home from school until we know exactly what is going on," Mrs. Prather said.

At first, the thought gave me a snuggly, happy feeling. We could sleep late and drink hot chocolate and I could pet Jared. Then Brooke and I glanced at each other, a knowing expression on each of our faces.

"We can't," Brooke said.

"Not now." I sat on the bed beside Jared. "With Jared out of the picture for goodness knows how long, we have to try to figure out what is going on. Why some of the kids at school are acting so strange. What is going to happen that required Jared be taken out of the picture. We need to know."

Cameron nodded from his seat in the corner. Brooke kneeled beside him to administer first aid to him. He had some nasty cuts and bruises as a result of the most recent smack-down. "She's right. We need to get back in the thick of it all."

"I don't know," Grandma said, a worried expression lining her face. "Don't you think today was enough? We need to lie low awhile."

Lie low? First texting and now lie low? Who was this woman?

"I agree with Cameron," Sheriff Villanueva said. "These kids are our best shot at figuring this out."

"I like the lie-low idea," Glitch said, casting his vote.

"Bill," Grandma said, fixing a beseeching expression on him. "We can't just send them back out there."

"No, we can't, but pix doesn't seem to care what we can and can't do." He turned to look at Brooke's parents. "Maybe you'll have better luck with Brooklyn."

"I'm going," Brooke said, a hand on her hip. "I'm in this,

Mom. You guys keep saying that if this war is what we think it is, we're all dead anyway. So what does it matter?"

The Prathers supported the Order of Sanctity and its mission 100 percent, so I wasn't terribly surprised when Brooke's mom gave in with a nod. "Okay, but you kids need to get some rest."

"I think we need to get some pizza," Glitch said.

Cameron brightened with the thought.

Mrs. Prather turned to the sheriff. "I need some kind of guarantee Cameron can stay with them all day."

"I'll see to it."

I wondered just how he was going to manage that, but the last thing I wanted to do was leave Jared. "Can I stay down here with him?" I asked Granddad, taking a long, meandering gaze at Jared.

He bit down, clearly not wanting me near him even now. "For now, until we get something warm inside you kids."

"Like pizza?" Glitch asked.

Mrs. Prather smiled. "I was thinking soup, but pizza it is."

"Sweet," Glitch said.

Soon, all the adults were gone and we sat in the room in relative silence. I had the sudden urge to collapse into a heap that may or may not have resembled a washed-up, redheaded jellyfish.

I couldn't stop staring at Jared. Sometimes it was so hard to remember he was a supreme being. And that he had just tried to kill me. He looked like a little boy. His breathing was deep and rhythmic. His face softened by the solace of sleep.

I leaned in and whispered into his ear. "I really like you, Azrael."

"You realize he kissed Tabitha Sind," Brooke said.

With a satisfied smirk, I said, "But he was under a spell of darkness. Why else would anyone kiss her?" I gave her my best look of bravado even though I couldn't help the niggling in the back of my mind, the one that said she was better for Jared than I was.

Brooklyn, who was sitting on the arm of the chair Cameron was reclining in, holding an ice pack to the back of his head, asked him, "Would you kiss Tabitha Sind if you were under a dark spell?"

I looked back at him, my brows raised in interest.

He cleared his throat. "No. No way. Tabitha who?"

We chuckled and Brooke socked him on the arm. He feigned injury, rubbing it.

Glitch rose to his feet, averting his gaze. "I'm going to check on the pizza."

As Glitch left, Brooke leaned over and kissed Cameron on the cheek. "That's for saving all our lives."

When she went to pull away, he wrapped a hand around her neck and placed his mouth on hers. I was a little shocked, but she let him.

And let him.

And let him.

It was getting embarrassing. And rather tongue-y.

"Brooke, have a little self-respect," I said, trying really hard not to giggle.

She pulled back, her breaths a little fast.

With a grin, he said, "I figured I deserved more than just a peck on the cheek for saving your life."

"You figured that, huh?"

"Pretty much."

"So, I'm all paid up." She scooted out of the seat and went to the attached bathroom to put away the ice pack, humor playing about her mouth.

He threw a towel at her as she walked away. "Actually, you

still owe me for saving everyone else's lives. I'll put it on your tab."

She stuck out her tongue.

"You guys make such a disturbing couple," I said.

"This coming from the girl dating the Angel of Death."

I glanced down, remembering the kiss he gave Tabitha again. "We're not dating, in case you forgot." Seeing Jared kiss her had been painful, no matter how I played it in front of the others. I'd never felt pain like that. Now I knew what all those country songs were talking about.

Of course, he did try to kill me. That was pretty painful, too.

SHADOWS IN THE BASEMENT

"So, what do you think is really going on?" Brooke asked me as she took her turn to wash her face and get ready for bed. We'd left the boys downstairs on guard duty.

"I think there's a stupid war coming and everybody thinks I am somehow going to stop it. How can we do anything without Jared?"

"That was amazingly brave what you did in the vault. Which, by the way—" She stepped out of the bathroom, her face white with soap. "—did you know that was an actual vault?"

"I had no idea."

"And they made it for you." Brooke shivered. "That's just eerie."

"We have to figure out what's going on and we have to do it fast. And I think I might know who can help."

Intrigued, she rinsed her face, then came back while drying it with a towel. "Who?"

"My grandpa Mac."

"Grandpa Mac?" she asked.

I shrugged. "I had to call him something besides 'paternal grandfather.' But he grew up with this stuff. He might know something we don't."

"If he is actually alive, he probably knows a lot of somethings we don't."

"Agreed."

After I took my turn at guard duty while Cameron took a shower in my bathroom, Glitch, Brooklyn, and I went back upstairs to review Plan A. Then we waited for everyone to go to bed.

"Okay, you ready?" I whispered to Brooke, cracking open my bedroom door.

"Yes, but I'm still not sure how we are going to get down to the basement without alarming Cameron or waking your grandfather. He is the lightest sleeper on planet Earth, as evidenced by the night we tried to sneak out your window to go to a frat party in Albuquerque."

I cringed at the memory. "That was awful."

"I was surprised at how red his face could get."

"I know, right? But I sneaked out the other night and he didn't know a thing about it. I think on that particular night, he knew we were up to something."

Glitch snorted. "You guys are always up to something."

With a chuckle, I led the way downstairs. Each step creaked. Each door squeaked. It was like we were living in a haunted house, it was so loud. I had never noticed before. But we managed to make it to the basement without anyone the wiser, including Cameron.

When we got to the basement steps that, I didn't mind admitting, creeped me out, Glitch closed the door and turned on the single lightbulb overhead. The one that created more shadows than light.

"Okay, this is creepy," Brooke said.

"Right? And my grandparents wonder what's wrong with me. Why I don't like going into the basement. Have they even looked in their basement?"

"I don't think it's that bad."

Like when the victim in a horror movie stalks slowly forward and opens a cabinet only to have a cat jump out at her, the three of us jumped about ten feet in the air. Brooklyn squealed and Glitch let loose a string of curses any tattoo artist would be proud of. And I knew enough to slap my hands over my mouth to suffocate a scream before it left my throat.

We turned in unison to Cameron, who stood behind us, casual as could be.

"What are you doing here?" Brooklyn asked, her hands over her chest as she tried to catch her breath.

"I wondered where you guys were sneaking off to, so I followed."

"You heard us?"

"The entire neighborhood heard you."

"Cameron, you can just admit it," I said. "You like hanging out with us."

"Can't."

Brooklyn frowned at him. "Why not?"

"You guys are weird. Bad for the rep."

She scoffed. "You have to have a good rep to be worried about anything bad happening to it."

"True. So, what are we doing?"

"Nothing," I said, a little too fast and a little too aggressively.

His brows shot up. "Okay, count me in."

Glitch sighed and walked down the stairs past us.

"Who's watching Jared?" I asked.

"Your grandfather's asleep in the recliner."

"Poor guy," Brooke said.

We crept down the eerie stairs and past jars of canned vegetables, an old typewriter that fascinated me as a child, and a box of collectible snow globes until we came to the shelf with an ancient trunk stuffed underneath. I knew from previous explorations that it contained my parents' personal items. Things they had saved. Things of no importance to anyone but me. Every time I rummaged through the trunk, a nostalgic sense of pleasure washed over me. I knew what was inside. The dress I'd worn home from the hospital. My favorite blanket I'd practically eaten as a child. A teddy bear named Garth.

But I'd never paid much attention to the documents inside. They were mostly things like receipts and travel logs and such. And how could I forget the awards certificate for my Best of Show in Finger Painting? The more important documents like birth and marriage certificates were kept upstairs in my grandma's file cabinet. But these were from my dad's personal effects. If there was anything about his father, surely it would be in here.

As I rummaged through the trunk, Cameron asked, "So, what are we doing again?"

"Nothing you'd be interested in," Glitch said.

"Sure I would." Cameron's voice held a hint of humor. He seemed to love nothing more than baiting Glitch. Then again, Glitch did start it. And yet he knew better than anyone what Cameron was capable of. Glitch had gone crazy.

After practically emptying the chest, I came across a manila envelope I hadn't noticed before. I opened it and thumbed through the papers inside. They weren't my father's but Mac McAlister's. My grandfather's. My pulse quickened.

"Oh," Glitch said, reading over my shoulder. "I thought Mac was short for McAlister. But it was actually his name. Then it makes sense that they called him Mac."

"Yeah."

"Your grandfather on your dad's side?" Cameron asked.

"Yep."

Brooklyn pushed past Glitch to point at the paper I was holding. "What is that?"

"It's a license of some kind. A pilot's license. And here is a receipt with his name on it."

"But there's nothing here to indicate that he might still be alive," she said.

"You think your paternal grandfather is still alive?" Cameron asked.

Crap. I didn't want him to know why I thought that quite yet. My new ability was just that. Shiny and new. I wanted to explore it further before announcing it to the world. "I have my suspicions."

"Why?"

Brooke and I looked at each other. At least, I was pretty sure it was Brooke. In the low light, it could have been Elvis.

"It's a long story." I stopped on the last page of documents and read. "But it's what's not here that's interesting. These are my dad's papers, but there's no death certificate for my grandfather."

"There's not one for your grandmother either."

"No, but there is an autopsy report." I held up the paper for a better look and startled.

"What?" Brooklyn asked.

Cameron leaned down and saw it immediately. "Wow."

"According to this report," I said, my voice suddenly hoarse, "my grandmother died the day I was born."

I took the contents of the envelope up to my room for a better look and to study the report. Cameron said he had to do a perimeter check, so we hurried upstairs to learn what we could while he was gone. I didn't want to slip and say anything about the magic picture trick. Not just yet.

The description of my grandmother's death made me ill. I had to stop reading because I thought I'd be sick. According to the report, my grandmother died while being tortured. And the report, while very cold and technical, listed the multiple lacerations and contusions consistent with a person suffering from traumatic physical abuse and/or torture, and it did so in great and explicit detail.

My stomach turned. Why would anyone torture her?

And crazy thing was, my grandparents knew.

"Do you think your grandmother's death was what your parents were talking about when you were born?"

"No. I don't. They said he was still alive. *He.*"

"Lor," Brooke said, placing a hand on my arm to draw me back to her, "do you think your grandfather killed your grandmother?"

"No!" Glitch shouted.

We jumped and turned to him. He was busy doing a search on my computer for my grandfather's name.

"No, he didn't," he repeated. "But he is in prison for voluntary manslaughter."

"What?" I practically flew across the room to get a good look at the screen. "He *is* alive?"

"Well, he was fourteen years ago. Okay," Glitch said, semi-reading aloud, "'Frustrated with the authorities' reluctance to pursue an anonymous tip, Mac McAlister tracked down the people whom he believed had kidnapped his wife.'"

Brooke was glued to Glitch's other side and even Cameron

was vying for some space to see what was going on. She pointed to the screen farther down the article. "'In the gunfight that ensued, McAlister killed . . .' Oh my gosh, twelve people."

"'He was shot numerous times,'" Glitch continued, "'yet continued to search for his wife when the firing ceased.'"

Brooke interrupted again. "'After the smoke had settled, twelve people lay dead with McAlister not far behind, but a passing vehicle heard the gunfire and called the police.'"

Glitch read, "'Authorities arrived on the scene to find several dead bodies and McAlister unconscious and barely breathing. He had his wife cradled in his arms. She had been dead for hours.'"

I covered my mouth with my hands, the image the article evoked so heartbreaking, so agonizing.

Brooke looked at me, searching my reaction, her eyes wet with emotion. "I'm so sorry, Lor."

"'One thing the investigators noted as an anomaly was that every member of the group that neighbors referred to as a cult was unusually tall,'" said Glitch.

Brooke jumped to read. "'Unusually tall.'" She looked back at me. "Do you think they were descendants?"

"Maybe," I said, still stuck on the image of my grandfather holding my grandmother's dead body in his arms.

"If so, Lor, we need to bring this up to your grandparents."

"Wait a minute," Glitch said, reading on. "It happened in northern New Mexico. Your grandfather is in prison here." He looked at me, stunned. "He's been here this whole time."

I awoke to the sound of my own labored breathing as I tried to catch my breath. Fire had consumed my lungs as they begged for air. With dry gasps, I fought to provide it. It was the usual, of course. And yet, the dynamics of the dream were changing. I was beginning to welcome the demon inside. To swallow him with pleasure, his presence both strange and familiar at once. The thought of the demon inside me becoming a welcomed guest disturbed me on several levels.

"You do that a lot," Cameron said, straightening up from his perch on the window seat. I'd forgotten to turn off the lamp on my desk and I could see his shadowy figure clearly. His eyes were hooded with weariness, making him look like he'd just woken up, which was good. Maybe he'd actually slept.

"I know." I placed a hand over my chest and tried to slow my breathing. "I've been having nightmares."

"Me too. Mostly about short chicks ordering me around like they own the world."

I couldn't help but chuckle. "You can't be talking about me. I hardly ever order you around, and I don't own even an inch of this world."

He grinned and cast a quick glance toward the bossy short chick who was blinking awake as we spoke.

"Are you awake?" Brooklyn asked me through a yawn.

"No."

"Me neither. Did you get any sleep?"

"No."

"Me neither. I am just so floored by everything," she said, sitting up in her bed. She looked over at Cameron as he sat on the window seat, gazing out the window.

I glanced at the digits glowing atop my nightstand. Three o'clock. In the morning. I didn't even know three o'clock in the morning existed. I thought it was a myth. Like mermaids and snowballs in hell.

"You snore," Cameron said to Brooke without turning around.

"Okay, I may have slept a little, but I don't snore. And how can you just sit there all night without crashing?" she asked him.

He finally turned to her. "I slept a little too, but I don't need as much sleep as you do."

"Oh, right. I keep forgetting. Well, I'm okay now. It's your turn for the bed. I'll take watch."

With a soft smile, he said, "I'd feel a bit safer with me on point, but thanks."

"Suit yourself."

A thought occurred to me as I sat hallucinating due to lack of oxygen in my dream. "I wonder how Mr. Davis is doing after today. And the creature whose name shall not be spoken aloud."

"No kidding," Brooke said. With everything that had happened, those two must have slipped her mind as well. "What do you suppose he thinks?"

"Do we care?" Cameron asked.

I shrugged. "Sure. Well, about Mr. Davis anyway. But Tabitha did seem pretty freaked out."

"Thank goodness her parents are with the Order," Brooke said. "They'll know how to help her, what to tell her."

I nodded. "Right. She's been through a lot."

Brooklyn gaped at me.

"Well, you know, what with Jared making out with her, then trying to kill us all. But what about Mr. Davis? He already suspects Jared."

"Suspects him for what?" Cameron said. "For killing his brother a thousand years ago? Whoever that was would have aged. He can't possibly know anything."

Crossing my arms over my chest, I scrutinized him with a dubious expression. "You mean besides the fact that both you and Jared have superhuman abilities? He was there, Cameron. He saw what I saw."

"His mind will create a scenario that'll fit with his interpretation of events. Most likely, we were both on some mind-altering drug that gave us super strength."

I had serious doubts it would be that easy this time, but who was I to argue?

"What is that sound?" Brooke asked, squinting into the darkness outside.

"It's rain," I said. "And wind. Again." I sat up and placed my back against the headboard. "So, what is going on, Cameron? I mean, really? Too many strange things are happening at once. Like a convergence of bizarre activities."

"I think it's beginning."

"What?" Brooke asked. "That war thing you guys keep talking about?"

My stomach lurched just thinking about it. I didn't want a war. Especially not one that relied heavily on my abilities to stop it. Unless I could convince the invading army to stand still long enough for me to get a vision off it, we were toast. Whole wheat. Extra crunchy.

Then again, what good would a vision do us? I was no Joan of Arc, that was for sure. She may have led men into battle, but I was more of a "lead the school choir in a moving rendition of 'One Hundred Bottles of Beer on the Wall'" kind of girl.

"If you weren't stuck guarding me," I said to Cameron, "you could hunt down that new kid, Vincent, and find out what's going on."

"I don't believe in that game," he said.

I frowned. "What game?"

"The what-if game. There only is."

"Okay, Mr. Miyagi," Brooke said. She sank back into her blankets. "I still think you should get some rest and let me take point for a while."

The expression on his face turned to one of horror. "And just what would you do if something happened? Moon the enemy?"

"What enemy, exactly?" I asked.

"What do you mean?"

I had a feeling he knew precisely what I was asking, but I

humored him anyway. "I mean, you and Jared keep watch all the time. For weeks now. Against what? What are we supposed to be on the lookout for?"

"Anything unusual."

"Like, every single thing that has happened this week? Unusual like that?"

After drawing in a deep breath, he said, "Yeah. Pretty much."

"And then what?" I asked, pushing for more intel. "You guys get to go do cool guy stuff while I sit here and be all protected, but from what, exactly? From whom? Don't think I haven't noticed how much my hours at the store have dropped. How often my grandparents send Brooke and me to the church to study the documents of the Order. Funny how there's always someone there. Always someone on guard duty. It's suffocating."

"What's suffocating," he said, turning to me with purpose, "is when your enemy has you by the throat and squeezes until the blood stops flowing to your brain, until your lungs feel like they are filled with acid because they can't get oxygen, until your head feels like it's going to explode." He turned back to the window. "But, yeah, I can see where being protected would be suffocating."

I ground my teeth. "That was uncalled for. I was just trying to make a point."

"Well, then, I suggest you keep trying," he said with a soft grin.

I burrowed under my covers again and glared at him. Brooke did the same.

"Glaring doesn't really affect me, but you can keep at it if it makes you feel better."

"I'm sorry I woke you up," I said to him as my lids drifted down.

"You didn't." He looked out into the darkness. "Something else did."

GHOSTLY

I sneaked down to Jared's room about an hour later, unable to sleep when I found out something was out there. Cameron could feel it, sense it, as he had for days now. Were they taunting him? Trying to get him to come after them as they had Jared? Either way, the realization was enough to push away all thoughts of sleep.

I tiptoed into the room. Granddad lay in the recliner, snoring, and Mrs. Strom sat in a chair by Jared's bed. She had hooked up an IV and a monitor, probably *borrowed* from the hospital.

I sat on the bed next to Jared, stroked his hair, ran my fingers along his full mouth.

"Hey, pix," Grandma said. She'd apparently come in to check on things too.

I tried to bite back the disappointment. "Hey, Grandma." I wondered how much she knew about my paternal grandparents. Did she know my grandmother was tortured? But, wait. What if she did know? What if she took that very thing into consideration when she took on all that was me after my parents disappeared? What if it kept her awake nights, knowing she could suffer the same fate?

She looked over at Granddad. "First time in years I've slept without that buzz saw going, and I can't sleep. Guess I'm used to it."

With a smile, I said, "You must be." I noticed Cameron sitting at the kitchen table in the dark. My constant shadow. "Cameron, you can come in here."

"I'm good. And there's a fridge in this room." He stood and went to raid it.

Grandma insisted on making him breakfast. I had no idea people actually ate breakfast this early. Since I was up already, I headed for the shower. The wind had died down, but the frigid morning had left a sheet of ice on the window. It sparkled in the moonlight, the night still thick and black. I was tired just thinking about it.

All the events of the last few days were like a weight. I was moving through water instead of air. And my appearance left much to be desired. Was my skin actually paler? My eyes darker? My hair brighter? I looked ghostly. Maybe I was turning into a vampire. No, I couldn't be that lucky. At least then I'd stand a chance of helping in this war we had yet to check off our to-do list. Maybe it could be rescheduled. A war would be really inconvenient at the moment.

First Jared being attacked. Then the picture thing. Then Isaac Johnson's whittling skills and dire warning, which, better a warning be dire than realized. But still. Then Jared's make-out session with a girl at least six inches taller than me, and his attacking us. Then the tragic story of my paternal grandparents, only to find out my grandfather had been alive all this time. Or, well, quite possibly.

This had been one messed-up week.

And so far today, I couldn't quite get enough air in my lungs. My eyes stung like there was no tomorrow. And I was certain my wisdom teeth were growing in. Surely my cheeks weren't usually that puffy.

"This humidity is not helping my hair," I said to Brooke as we vied for the mirror.

"It's funny, my hair looks fantastic."

I gritted my teeth, but she was right. Her hair, thick and black and straight as an honor student, looked amazing.

She eyed me a long moment. "You look like you caught a tropical disease or something. Are you okay?"

"After the last few days, no."

"Oh, right. Good point. So what are you going to do about your grandfather?"

"I have an idea, but you aren't going to like it."

She pursed her lips. "I love your ideas." When I cast a doubtful gaze at her, she said, "Well, I love some of your ideas. That one that involved ice cream and coffee was amazing."

"True. That was one of my better ones. But this one requires deception. And possibly skipping school."

"Sweet. We can always say you got a vision or something. And we have the sheriff on our side. Oh, my gosh, we can get away with anything now. I love being in this gang."

I chuckled and looked in the mirror. I thought about taunting Mal some more, maybe poking him with a stick, but I didn't want to risk his wrath. The way my luck had gone, he'd answer this time. I leaned forward to rate the redness level of my eyes on a scale of one to ten, but they weren't mine. The eyes looking back at me were blue and full of hatred.

Then I heard a voice. "Ready for round two?"

I jolted back and almost fell as Brooke tried to put the blow dryer away. "Did you see that?" I asked, and she glanced around, suddenly wary.

"What? What did you see?"

"In the mirror."

Brooke stood to look into it. "I don't see anything."

I leaned forward, gazed into the mirror again. Nothing.

"Did you have a vision?" she asked, her voice infused with hope. That girl loved my visions.

"No. I don't think so."

I couldn't get out of my room fast enough. I went down to check on Jared. Still asleep. Still angelic. Which, since he was an angel, made sense. I kissed his cheek and promised him that I'd kiss more than that if he'd wake up. And not try to kill everyone when he did.

Cameron had warmed the truck and was waiting for me to finish my make-out session with an unconscious archangel. He clearly did not understand Jared's allure. After offering my grandparents a solemn good-bye, Brooke and I hurried to the truck and snuggled together as Cameron drove out of the parking lot. That was about the time Glitch decided to stick his head through the sliding glass window in Cameron's truck, the one that led to the camper.

"Hi," he said.

His voice wasn't particularly loud nor was his tone particularly threatening, but for some reason, the surprise struck a chord. I shrieked like a doomed chick in a horror movie. For, like, a minute. In my frazzled state of mind, I went for the door handle but couldn't quite get a grip. Luckily, Cameron put the truck back into park to wait out my panic attack. If I were really in a horror movie, I'd be so dead.

Brooke put some distance between us, and Glitch sat there, eyeing me like I'd lost my marbles.

Maybe I had. After taking several deep breaths, I looked back at them. "What?" I said, suddenly defensive, placing a hand over my palpitating heart. "He scared me."

"Sorry," Glitch said. "My car won't start. Cameron said I had to sit back here."

"Cameron." Brooke admonished him with her surly tone. "He would have fit up here."

A sly grin slid over his face.

"I'm fine," Glitch said, opening his jaw and rubbing his ears. "My eardrums burst all the time."

"Sorry." I crossed my arms and pretended to be repentant, perhaps lay off the caffeine. But I'd gotten very little sleep. How would I make it through the day without caffeine?

I thought about it. Contemplated the pros and cons.

Nope. Not possible.

I leaned over to Cameron. "I might need to stop at the Java Loft on the way."

Brooke brightened and nodded in agreement.

"Because that's what you need," Glitch said. "Something to put the edge on."

I completely ignored him, and three mocha lattes and a whipped almond toffee cappuccino with nonfat milk later, we headed to school.

The minute we entered the building, a supercharged drink with chocolate warming our hands, Brooke nudged me with her elbow. "Check it out." She pointed across the hall into Mr. Davis's office. "Sheriff Villanueva is talking to Mr. D."

Cameron was right behind me as usual, making me wonder

why I didn't have bruises on my heels. "He did say he was going to make sure I could stay with you all day."

As if on cue, they both turned and spotted us. Mr. Davis summoned Cameron into his office with an index finger, his movements sharp.

"Crap," Brooke said. "That was weird. It's like they knew we were talking about them."

"I'm out of here," Glitch said. He ducked down the hall while we shuffled forward and into the main office.

"Hi, Mrs. Gutierrez," I said to the school secretary.

"What can I do you girls for?" she asked. She was so nice. She was older but looked young because of her dark bob and huge brown eyes.

I was about to tell her when Mr. Davis barked, "In here, Lusk," in that gruff voice of his.

Everyone jumped. Including Mrs. Gutierrez. She turned a sympathetic expression on Cameron as he walked into the principal's office. We sat in the outer office as Mr. Davis and Sheriff Villanueva talked to him. Moments later, he came out with a grin and a note.

"I have to admit," I said as we walked to first hour. "I love having the sheriff on our side."

"Me too," Brooke said.

We walked into Ms. Mullins's classroom armed and ready. Cameron handed her the note. She took about two seconds to look it over, then scanned the classroom, completely unsurprised. Which left me completely surprised. I mean why would another student be joining her class for the day? It made no sense. I had serious doubts the rest of my teachers would be so obliging, but at least for the next fifty minutes, things would go smoothly.

"I don't have an empty chair this hour, so we'll have to wait and see who's absent."

"I'd like near the back, if that's okay, close to Lorelei."

She nodded, as though strategizing a stakeout were an everyday thing for her. "Okay, you know what? Just take Nathan's desk right there." She pointed. "I'll put him somewhere else."

"Thank you. And I'm supposed to let you know—" He stuffed his hands into his pockets as though he felt bad about what he was going to say. "—you've been summoned."

Her lips thinned and she bit down, reprimanding herself. Without taking her eyes off me, she asked Cameron, "I've been found out, haven't I?"

He grinned and leaned down to her. "Like a thief in a cop bar."

With a sigh, she bowed her head in resignation. Cameron tipped an invisible hat, then strolled to a middle desk closest to the door. Like a guard, or a barrier.

"I just wanted to apologize," she said to me, her voice soft so no one would overhear. "For all the secrecy. I couldn't tell you who I was."

"Ms. Mullins, how long have you been the observer?"

She smiled. "For as long as you've been alive, sweetheart. I was friends with your mother and couldn't even tell her. And we certainly can't talk about it here, but I just wanted to apologize. I wanted you to know, I wasn't purposely trying to keep a secret from you."

That meant a lot. "Thank you."

Brooke leaned in. "Since we've been under all this stress with visions and prophecies and all, can we get extra credit on the upcoming test?"

"No." Her eyes sparkled with humor. "And you always pass my tests with flying colors. Why do you want extra credit?"

Brooke shrugged. "There is one thing better than an A."

"And what's that?" she asked.

"An A-plus."

"Ah, got it."

"Nathan," Ms. Mullins said when he walked into the room and noticed Cameron in his chair. "Take Michelle's desk for today. She's out sick." She glanced down at the messages on her desk. "Lots of kids are out sick today, actually."

For a moment, Nathan looked like he was going to argue, but when Cameron glowered at him, he quickly conceded. Cameron had such a way with people.

The minute we stepped out of first hour, Ashlee Southern rushed up to us, her eyes like saucers. Glitch met up with us too. Her gaze darted to him, then back to me. "Isaac tried to commit suicide last night."

"What?" Brooke and I said in unison.

"When? What happened?" Brooke asked.

"He called Syd and—" She glanced around to make sure no one was listening. "—and said he couldn't do it. He couldn't kill the prophet. Syd tried to find out more, who he was talking about, but he hung up. Next thing we know, his parents are calling from the hospital. He'd taken his dad's gun." Her voice broke, so we gave her a minute. She swallowed hard and continued. "His dad walked in on him just as he was about to pull the trigger. They fought for the gun, it went off, and that's all we know."

I looked around. "Where's Syd now?"

"At the hospital. They have Isaac sedated, but she's sitting with him."

Our hospital was more like an urgent care center with a couple of beds for overnight observation. "We have to go," I said to Brooke, who agreed with a hearty nod.

But Cameron was less enthusiastic. He seemed a tad perturbed, actually. "What do you mean, he couldn't kill the prophet?"

"Oops," I said, realizing I'd never told him or anyone about what Isaac did the day before. "I meant to tell you, but everything that happened with Jared, I just—"

When he leveled an astonished gaze on me, I got defensive again. "You have to admit, we had a busy afternoon yesterday."

"Fine. What happened, exactly?"

"Isaac carved my name into a desk really creepy-like and told me they wanted me dead."

Ash gaped at me. "He did what?"

"I know, right?" Brooke said.

"You knew about this?" Cameron asked her.

"Hey, Mr. Sensitive, we forgot. We were *busy.*" She got in his face. Or tried to, since he was over a foot taller. It was kind of funny.

"I need to touch him," I said. "I might be able to see exactly what's out there."

"I'll drive," Cameron said, fishing his keys out of his pocket.

"Maybe we should call your grandparents," Brooke said. "Let them know what's going on."

"Are you kidding? We have Static Cling here if anything goes wrong." I grinned when Cameron scowled at me.

"Can I get a ride with you?" Ashlee asked. "Syd has our car."

"Sure," Brooke said, "if you don't mind riding in the back with Glitch."

Ash lifted one shoulder, her gaze landing on an oblivious Glitch. "I don't mind if you don't."

"Suit yourself, but it's not very comfortable."

"That's okay," she said with a shy smile.

"I get the left wheel well," he said, walking off. Still oblivious.

I so wanted to head-butt him.

VINCENT

When we got to the hospital, we went straight to Isaac's room. He was surrounded by his family, Sydnee, and a nurse who was checking his vitals. I started to back out again when I heard him talk.

"I'm so sorry, Dad. I just don't remember what happened."

I took a cautious step inside and Isaac looked over at me. "Lorelei?"

Everyone turned. "Sorry," I said, backing out again. But Brooke was right on my heels, trying to peek over my shoulder. "I'll leave you alone."

"No." Isaac looked at his family apologetically. "Can I have a minute with Lorelei?"

"Sure, son." His mother leaned over for a kiss. The image was adorable. A huge, scruffy football player being kissed by his mom.

His dad patted his shoulder. "We'll be right outside."

After his family stepped outside, the whole gang stepped in, including me, Brooke, Cameron, Glitch, and Ash. Sydnee had stayed, and we waited until the nurse left before starting our conversation.

"Thank you for coming," Syd said.

Isaac looked at me with those big brown eyes of his, and all I could see was the teddy bear I'd grown up with. The one who picked me up and dusted me off when Joss Duffy knocked me off the monkey bars. The one who, soon afterwards, had a talk with said Joss Duffy, and oddly enough, said Joss Duffy never bothered me again. "Lorelei, I'm so sorry. Whatever I did—"

"What exactly *did* you do?" Cameron asked, his voice razor sharp.

I cringed. "It's okay, Cameron. Nothing happened."

"I'd like to hear Isaac's side of it."

I realized Isaac had become anxious. His expression was wary when he looked at Cameron. I'd heard that pretty much everyone in school was afraid of him, but it was just so hard to believe this huge guy would be afraid of anyone. "From what I've been told," he said to Cameron, "I threatened her with a knife."

Cameron bit down and he turned a heated gaze my way. "Did we forget to mention that?" He stepped closer to the bed, making his own threat with the set of his shoulders.

"And here we go," Glitch said. He sat on a heating unit by the window to watch the show.

Sydnee stood protectively at the other side of the bed, and I stepped to intervene. "I can toss you out of here, Cameron, if you don't behave."

He placed the most cavalier expression on me I'd ever seen. "You can try."

"Cameron," Brooke said, tugging his arm. She laughed softly, as though trying to excuse Cameron for his bad manners. "Lor has this. Really."

I decided to ignore him. "I'm sorry, Isaac. Just pretend he's not here. Do you remember what happened at all?"

He shook his head as Sydnee took his hand, her face lined with worry. "I can't seem to recall the last few days, in fact. But some of the guys told me I'd threatened you. That I carved your name into a desk and said I was going to kill you or something."

The heat from Cameron's gaze intensified. He so wasn't helping.

"You didn't threaten to kill me, Isaac. You said they want me dead."

"Who?" Cameron asked.

"I don't know." He plastered his palms over his eyes.

Cameron leaned closer. "Would it help if we went outside?"

I'd had it. I pointed to the door. "You can leave now. Isaac is the victim here, Cameron. Just like Jared was."

"I just find it really interesting that nobody thought to mention this before."

"I had a few things on my plate. You can't expect me to remember every little death threat."

"Yes," he said, his voice frighteningly calm, "I can. This changes everything."

I frowned. "How does this change anything?"

He stepped closer to me. "Now we know for certain they simply wanted Jared out of the way. They want you dead, Lor. *They*."

"Oh." He had a good point. "Then let me do my thing, yeah? Maybe I can get something."

Cameron stepped back but still kept up the menacing act. Brooklyn nudged me and nodded toward Isaac's shoulder. When I looked at Syd, she gave an approving nod.

I leaned in and placed a hand on his arm. "I'm so sorry about all of this. You'll be fine," I said, patting his arm before resting a hand on it. Brooke said something in the background to keep his attention while I concentrated.

Blue eyes, sharp and crystal clear, appeared underneath a mop of sandy brown hair. "Ready for round two?" a boy asked.

"Do I know you?" Isaac asked him.

He was tall, his face somehow disproportioned. It was the new guy, Vincent.

He said something. A word I didn't understand, and Isaac's vision blurred. The scene was hard to make out, but I saw a hand, two fingers red, dripping with blood. Vincent lifted them, rubbed them across Isaac's forehead. "This is the most powerful blood available on Earth, big guy. You'll either do what we ask, or you'll die. *Comprende?*"

When he'd finished, he slipped his fingers into his mouth and licked off the remaining blood. His eyes drifted shut as he let a feeling of ecstasy overtake him. After a moment, he blinked back to Isaac, his expression blissful, intoxicated. But he stopped and leaned in closer. "Who's in there?" he asked, squinting. Then a seedy smile slid across his face. "Is that you, Lorelei?"

I gasped and jerked back. Cameron caught me before I slammed into something important, like a heart monitor.

"Are you okay?" Isaac asked.

I coughed to cover my spaz attack and said, "Yes. I'm fine."

"Isaac was just telling us about the knife he had," Brooke said to me.

"Right," he said. "I don't even own a knife. I remember images, like blurry snapshots of the last few days, and I remember being in Mr. D's office, him opening a drawer and dropping a knife into it. That's the first I remember seeing a knife. It struck me as odd because I got the impression he thought it was mine." Isaac gazed at me, pleading with me to believe him. "It wasn't mine, Lor. I swear."

I patted his arm again, this time for real. "I believe you, Isaac. I know you would never hurt me."

"Or stab her repeatedly," Brooke offered. "Or strangle her with your bare hands."

Turning to her, I slid a finger across my throat giving her the *cut* signal. I'd covered all that with the you-would-never-hurt-me line. At least she had my back. In a morbid, sadistic kind of way.

Isaac turned to Syd, his expression sad, full of regret. "I could have killed my dad last night. What is wrong with me?"

"Lorelei will figure it out," Syd said, her faith startlingly humbling.

Isaac turned to me in question, and I had no idea what to say to that.

"But we should leave so you can rest."

"Thanks for stopping by," Syd said, her eyes questioning.

I nodded to her. "He's going to be fine."

A relieved smile spread across her face.

We thanked the Johnsons for allowing us some time with their son. They were happy he was okay and yet worried about why he'd tried to kill himself in the first place.

I would've loved to reassure them, but what did I know? Whatever Vincent did to him, it seemed to be over. But who could say for certain?

We stepped into the morning sun. The day was chilly despite the brightness around us. Typical winter weather in New Mexico. Sunny and brisk.

"What did you see?" Brooke asked.

They all stopped and gathered around me. While I hesitated to say anything in front of Ashlee, it wasn't because I didn't trust her. Far from it. She'd kept my secret for weeks now. I was more worried for her safety. Then again, my touching Isaac to try to get a vision was hers and Sydnee's idea. I at least owed her an explanation.

"I saw the new kid," I said, looking up at Cameron. "He spread something across Isaac's forehead. Blood. He said a word and Isaac seemed to come under a spell. Then he told Isaac to either do what they asked or die. Right before he licked the blood off his fingers." I shivered in revulsion. "It was like a drug to him."

Cameron seemed to pale before my eyes. "Did he say whose blood it was?"

I shook my head. "No. But he did say it was the most powerful blood available on Earth."

He cursed softly under his breath and turned from me. "You should have told me about Isaac yesterday."

"I was going to," I said, my defenses rising. "But you were busy with that whole beating-the-crap-out-of-Jared thing. I'll just walk back to school."

I stepped around him, but for every step he took, I took three. Outwalking him would be impossible. And he would never leave me anyway. I wasn't sure why I was suddenly behaving like an impetuous child.

"You realize this changes everything," he said, keeping step with me.

"You said that before."

"They wanted him out of the way to take you out. Plain and simple."

I stopped and looked up at him. "You said that before too. But accepting it is not going to be easy. I plan to fight it tooth and nail. Pretend it isn't real. Give me my fantasy, will ya?"

"And with his blood, they have the means."

"With his blood?" I asked, a noxious dread creeping over me.

Cameron looked away, lost in thought. "They must have harvested his blood when they took him down. I have yet to figure out how they managed to do that, by the way."

"Can we get back to his blood?"

The others stepped close again.

"As far as I know, Jared is the only archangel stuck on Earth. There would be no blood more powerful than his. It would make for a great elixir." He bowed his head, his brows drawn in a sharp line. "They could get anyone to do anything they wanted with it."

"With Jared's blood?" Brooke asked, her nose crinkling in distaste.

When he didn't answer, I stated the obvious. "But Isaac didn't do what they wanted."

"His size," he said with a nod, "his personality, his faith. Any number of things could've given him the will to stop himself from killing you. If they'd chosen any other student."

"But they have," Brooke said. "There are others. So many kids have been acting strange for a few days now. Have you noticed how many kids are out sick?"

"Ever since that party Friday night," Ash said.

Glitch nodded. "And there was blood by the campfire at the clearing."

"If they were made to ingest it . . ." Cameron's voice trailed off.

"The new kid was there," Ash said.

That surprised me. "I didn't see him."

"It was late. Isaac told Syd that the new kid showed up after almost everyone had gone home. He was there just long enough to meet a few of the guys. Said he was interested in playing football next year. Then he left."

Cameron breathed out a frustrated sigh. "Vincent could have harvested Jared's blood earlier, then performed the ceremony there. Got them to ingest the blood, especially if they were drunk."

"Ew," Brooke said. "That is so wrong."

"I need to know who was there late," Cameron continued. "If he got to anyone with a weak constitution, Lorelei is still in great danger."

Ash gave an uncertain shrug. "I can try. I'm not sure Isaac will remember."

"That's okay," he said. "Just try." He looked down at me. "We need to know who that shooter is from your vision."

I nodded and started toward Cameron's truck. "Our conversations are so uplifting anymore. So full of hope and promise."

Glitch followed and wrapped an arm over my shoulder. "We'll figure this out, Lor."

Brooke hurried to my side too. "That's right. Don't you worry about a thing. We have Cameron on our side. And an unconscious archangel who apparently has ecstasy for blood."

"Actually," Cameron said, looking up in thought, "it's probably more like heroin."

I sighed softly. In the long run, this wasn't about me. None of it was. It was about this war. It was about my grandparents and the Order of Sanctity. The people of Riley's Switch. The entire human race, if the documents of the Order were to be believed. Which, I had seen enough strange events in the last few weeks to believe anything those documents had to offer a thousand times over.

We rode back to school in silence, all of us stewing in our own thoughts. Add some potatoes to us, and we'd be a meal.

The rest of the morning progressed relatively smoothly. Besides the plethora of odd looks. I hoped the looks meant they were curious about how I got my hair so healthy-looking and not about how they'd been programmed by an evil nephilim descendant to kill me. Either way, the looks were odd. And there were a lot of them.

I broke down and texted Grandma for a status update on Jared. No change. Cameron was starting to get worried. I could tell. He didn't want to tackle this alone. Facing nephilim hopped up on the blood of an archangel was a lot to put on a guy.

We realized pretty quickly the creature whose name shall not be spoken aloud wasn't in school. So that was a bummer. Then I had the bizarre impression that she was at the house with Jared. Alone. While I was at school. I had to call Grandma between fourth and fifth to make sure she wasn't.

Which, she wasn't. So, I was good.

Hopefully, she was in therapy. She'd probably need it after what she saw.

We heard more kids were getting sick, having to go home left and right. One even had a seizure in the gym. The paramedics had to be called.

"Okay, there has got to be something in the water," I said.

"Like your boyfriend's blood?" Brooke asked, crinkling her nose again.

By lunch, over 25 percent of the student body was out sick. It got to the point where parents were picking up their kids for no reason other than to avoid whatever unexplainable ailment was going around. I could hardly blame them. It was all over town. My grandmother texted me, asking me if I was ready to go home yet. I told her no. We were no closer to finding out what was going on, who was behind the shooting in my vision. I couldn't give up now.

As Brooke and I walked to lunch, Cameron close on my heels, I had the distinct feeling I knew how the presidents' daughters felt over the years. Always watched. Every move scrutinized. I thought about trying to outrun him for a few glorious seconds of freedom, but the run probably wouldn't last even that long. I might get a couple of feet. A yard if I were lucky. Sadly, nobody had ever accused me of being lucky, so I didn't risk it. The failure would be humiliating.

As I fished through my bag for my cell phone, Cruz de los Santos, a Riley High basketball player who had the height to prove it, brushed past me close enough to send my book flying.

"Hey," I said when he kept walking.

Cameron was there at once. He picked up my book and handed it back. "Did he hurt you?"

"No. The punk."

"That was so rude," Brooke said, looking back at Cruz. "He didn't even apologize."

"How much you want to bet he was at the party?" Cameron asked.

I sighed loudly. "You know what? I'm not even hungry. I just want to sit outside in the open air while you guys eat."

"No," he said.

"I'll sit on that bench on the other side of the cafeteria. You'll still be able to see me."

"Just eat fast," Brooke said. "I'll take watch."

"I thought we'd discussed my level of comfort with you taking watch."

"Fine," she said, putting an arm in mine and dragging me off, "just get something to eat and come sit with us. You'll be two minutes."

Left with a growling stomach and no choice, Cameron led us to the bench, then hurried inside to grab a tray.

After the huge, four-o'clock-in-the-morning breakfast and all the coffee I could drink afterwards, I didn't mind skipping lunch. Or skipping the odd looks that surely awaited me in the cafeteria. Brooke stuck by my side the whole time, offering her support, her shoulder, and her complaints.

It was too cold to be outside. She was hungry. She felt like a sticky bun. Not sure on that one.

She draped herself across the bench melodramatically. "I'm going to starve before the day is over."

"Dude, go eat."

"I don't want to be disloyal."

I stopped rummaging through my backpack. My lip gloss was gone. No doubt about it. "How is your eating disloyal?"

"Because then I would sit with all those people who want to kill you. It would look bad."

"Oh, good point. I wonder what's keeping Cameron."

She tried to raise her head off the bench but couldn't manage it. "I don't know."

"For heaven's sake, I'll go hit the vending machine."

She bolted upright. "Sweet. Bring me something colorful."

With a chuckle, I headed out in search of sustenance. My leaving the bench was hardly dangerous. There was absolutely no one crazy enough to be outside in the cold. Of course, I thought, halfway to the building, nephilim don't feel the cold. I wondered if the *descendants* of nephilim felt the cold.

I glanced around and decided to hurry. The vending machines lined the back wall of the main building. After picking an array of colorful foods, I started to head out—when the hairs on the back of my neck stood up. No way. I kept walking. Better to ignore the hairs on the back of my neck than invite trouble.

A male voice echoed down the empty hall. "Hi."

I whirled around, but no one was there. Without looking away, I started backing toward the doors. Toward Brooke. Toward safety.

Or, well, toward a short chick with a killer glare.

"Is your name Lorelei?"

A yelp escaped me as I whirled around again, dropping a MoonPie and Brooke's chocolate milk.

The kid in front of me caught them both, one in each hand, then straightened to face me. I recognized the army jacket that was three sizes too big. It was the kid from the Clearing the other day, the one hiding in the trees. He looked about thirteen, with matted black hair under his hoodie and bloodshot eyes. Though he wasn't that tall, he seemed to tower over me. Perhaps it was the curious look in his gaze that held something corrupt, something dark.

"You should be careful." He stepped forward.

I stepped back. "I saw you at the Clearing the other day. Do you live here?" I took the milk and pie-ish-like substance from him. When he didn't say anything, I asked, "Are you hitting the vending machines too?" If he was programmed to kill me, best to play dumb. Pretend like all was right with the world and run the microsecond I got the chance.

"No. I just wanted to see you. Alone."

That sounded bad. "Um, okay." Speaking of alone, where the heck was Static Cling when I needed him? Easing toward the door, I asked, "So, what's your name?"

He fell in step beside me and grabbed the door when we reached it. "Noah."

I started to say it was nice to meet him, but he didn't open the door. He was actually holding it closed. Why did I get myself into these situations? I couldn't even go for a MoonPie alone? I smiled the most nonthreatening smile I could conjure. "Can you open the door, Noah?"

"No." The expression on his face startled me. It was almost apologetic. His hand around my throat startled me more. I dropped the contents in my arms and pushed, but he was much stronger than he looked. "You have to help me," he said.

"Okay," I squeaked out.

The door jerked open. I watched as Cameron grabbed Noah by the shirt collar and tossed him roughly outside. Noah rolled, but before he could even think about getting to his feet, Cameron slammed him against the brick wall. The few kids that were outside started to gather instantly.

Noah's eyes didn't register fear as he struggled against Cameron's rock-solid hold, but sadness.

I hurried to Cameron's side. "This is the kid from the Clearing the other day." Then I looked at Noah. "Noah, why did you grab me?"

"I—I need your help," he said.

"That's not a very nice way to ask for it," I said.

"Lor, really?" Cameron said.

"What?"

"Can you let me handle this?"

"Cameron, he's a kid."

Cameron looked back at him. "You're not a kid, are you?"

Noah's mouth thinned. "No. I just want to talk to Lorelei. She's in danger."

"And you came to warn her by grabbing her throat?"

I stepped closer. "What do you mean, you're not a kid? Are you a descendant?"

"A descendant?" He seemed almost repulsed by the idea. "No. I just want your help."

"Cameron," I said, "this is ridiculous. Let him go."

"What do you think, Noah? Should I let you go?"

He went still and a smile drifted across his handsome face. "Probably not."

"Why did you risk coming here?" Cameron asked him.

"To warn you," he said. "If you don't stop them, we're all going to die."

"Hey!" Coach Chavez was walking toward us, his strides aggressive.

"Damn it," Cameron said. He looked at Noah hurriedly. "Do you know when?"

"Let go, Lusk." The coach pushed Cameron off him.

"He was threatening Lorelei," Cameron said as he let go, and Coach Chavez seemed to calm.

He looked at me. "Did he touch you?"

"No, he just got mad at me."

"Then you need to file a statement with the counselor. She'll know what to do from there. You," he said, looking at Noah, "need to be someplace else." Thankfully, he didn't realize Noah wasn't a student.

Noah headed off, but he turned back and said, "Soon."

Coach Chavez offered him a warning expression, then pointed in the opposite direction of the school. "You too. Go."

"Can I get my things?" I pointed inside.

"Hurry."

I rushed in and gathered the snacks I'd bought, then burst out the door and hurried away. While Cameron's walk was more like a saunter, unhurried, thoughtful, he caught up to me in only a few steps.

"What was that about?" I asked, looking over my shoulder to make sure Coach Chavez was leaving.

Cameron plucked the MoonPie out of my hands. Then he went for the chocolate milk, and I yanked it back from him.

"Dude, Brooke likes her chocolate milk. Take it and you're risking my life. Just where the heck have you been?"

He stuffed half the MoonPie in his mouth. "I was eating. I thought you were supposed to stay on the bench. You said you weren't hungry."

"I wasn't." When he looked at the contents of my arms doubtfully, I added, "I am now. What was that about? Who was that?"

"Noah, apparently."

"You don't know him?" When he shook his head, I asked, "Then what is going on?"

"He's possessed."

I stopped and stared up at him. "What? You mean, like, with a demon?"

He put his free hand in a pocket. "No, Lor. Not like you. He's possessed like Brooke was when her parents first brought her to Riley's Switch, to your grandparents. He's possessed by a rogue spirit. And he must know things if he came here seeking our help."

I started forward again. "Then we have to help him. That poor kid."

"That's just it," Cameron said. "I don't think we were talking to the kid."

DETENTION

"Nutrition bars?" Brooke moaned as I walked up to her. "Granola? What the heck is up with that?" She grabbed one out of my hand and pointed accusingly. "That machine has Cheetos. I've seen them. Orange. Crunchy. How am I supposed to live on this stuff?" I plopped down beside her and let her get it out of her system. After a rant that lasted two whole minutes, she opened the nutrition bar and took a bite. "Strawberry. Yum."

I sat on the bench beside her in a trance. "You will not believe what just happened."

"Is that a MoonPie wrapper?" She finally spotted the evidence in Cameron's hand.

"N-no."

I handed over her milk before Cameron lost a leg.

"Oh, yes. Milk from my favorite color of cows: brown."

"Brooke, seriously, you will not believe—"

"I was starving," she said. "I'm surprised you didn't have to revive me. You took, like, forever."

Ashlee and Glitch walked up then, Ash's eyes darting around furtively. "Did that kid try to hurt you?"

"What?" Brooke's gaze bounced back and forth between Ashlee and me. "Who? What happened?" She finally realized I was taken aback. "Lor," she said, putting a hand on mine, "what happened?"

"That boy from the Clearing. He's possessed."

"What boy?" she asked. "That kid in the army jacket?"

I nodded and told her the whole story of what just happened.

"So, what does that mean?" she asked, as clearly disturbed by the idea as I. "Cameron?"

"It means he won't live much longer with that thing inside him."

I gasped.

"And it means he knows something. I'll have to see if the sheriff can find him. Before Vincent does."

I glanced up in surprise. "Vincent?"

"Did you see his reaction when you mentioned the descendants? There's no love lost. Did you find an address on Vincent?" he asked Ashlee.

"I'm sorry," she said, clearly disappointed. "I couldn't get his file. The cabinets were locked today because Mrs. Terry is out sick."

"Oh, crap." I stuffed wrappers in my pockets when I saw Mr. Davis walking toward us. I had no idea why. It just seemed like the right thing to do.

I was so hoping this day would be incident-free.

He turned his big mustache-covered head toward Ashlee. "Ms. Southern, would you mind giving us a minute?"

"Oh," she said in surprise. "Not at all. I'll see you later," she said to Glitch.

He eyed her a long moment. "Oh-kay."

Maybe he was getting a clue. He turned back to us and shrugged.

"We can do this out here, or I can take you into my office one by one," Mr. Davis said, his expression grave. "I'm fine with either, but I want to know what happened yesterday."

Brooke said, "Didn't the sheriff talk to you?"

His mouth formed a solemn smile, and while it wasn't actually out of appreciation or humor, it wasn't harsh or derisive either. It was almost sad. "You kids did a lot of damage yesterday. I don't even know what to say to the superintendent. To the school board. But one thing I can't tell them is that you went completely unpunished. One month of after-school detention for all of you, starting today. And that includes Kovach when he comes back."

"Oh, man," Glitch said, kicking up dirt.

Brooke stood, indignant. "What? That's—that's—"

When Mr. Davis leveled a challenging stare on her, she caved. "That's more than fair, Mr. Davis."

"I don't think that's a good idea," Cameron said to him. He wasn't so much challenging Mr. Davis as—and I could hardly believe it—as confiding in him. "And I'm certain Lorelei's grandparents won't think so either."

Mr. Davis stepped forward menacingly. Or at least he menaced me. "Then when you can explain to me what happened, we'll talk about it. I'll be in my office." He glanced at each of us. "If any of you would like out of ASD."

After he left, Glitch scoffed at Cameron. "You couldn't have taken Jared outside where your little wrestling match wouldn't have caused so much damage?"

Cameron looked down at him. "Why don't you take some Midol, little man?"

To everyone's utter surprise, Glitch actually took a swing at Cameron. A swing! Cameron easily sidestepped it, his brows raised as though impressed. But I was not. I ran forward and got in between them. Unfortunately, Glitch was already in the process of trying again. Noble but suicidal.

His fist struck me on the temple, and unlike Cameron, I ate dirt.

In an instant, Cameron had Glitch by the throat and pressed against the wall in a chokehold that was more choke than hold. Brooke and I both ran to him, pulling on his arms.

"Are you psychotic?" Cameron asked him.

But Glitch was just making these gurgling sounds.

"Cameron," I said in a loud whisper, worried Mr. Davis was still around.

But he didn't listen to me. Not really a surprise. What did surprise me was when Brooke took her turn at him. "Cameron Lusk, drop him this minute."

He did. Glitch went down hard. He grabbed his throat and coughed a full minute.

"What are you thinking?" I asked him.

He pushed my hands away, stood, and strode off.

"What has gotten into him?" I asked.

"What has gotten into you?" Brooke asked Cameron.

"He took a swing at me. What did you want me to do?"

"Cameron, you know he can't hurt you."

I put a hand on Brooke's shoulder. "I think that might be the problem." I strolled to the trash can and started emptying my pockets of trash. "But this is just not the time for these kinds of antics. I'm worried about Glitch."

"Me too." She turned and watched him disappear behind the building. "Me too."

Maybe I had been accosted one too many times lately. School was beginning to feel more and more like a prison where I didn't know whom to trust or whom to fear. When I scanned the faces around me, I saw anger. Envy. Excitement. Despair. Jealousy. Distrust. Euphoria. Boredom. All the emotions that ran rampant every minute of every day at every high school across the country—and yet suddenly, I didn't know anyone. Every emotion was directed at me. Every look of distrust, of anger and jealousy. And I realized I might be a tad egocentric at the moment.

"Okay, I cannot be trusted," I said as we headed to detention after our last class.

Brooke stopped chewing the granola bar she'd saved and nodded. "Got it," she said, her words muffled. "Don't trust you. These things are fantastic."

By the time we got to detention, all I wanted to do was get back and check on Jared. Instead, I was stuck at school even longer.

Turned out, detention was like prison too, only without uniforms or the constant threat of being shanked. Though Hector Salazar—math geek, chess champion, and all-around overachiever—sat on the opposite side of the room, wearing the angriest scowl on his face I'd ever seen. Maybe shanking was a real possibility after all. He didn't want to be there any more than I did.

Brooke and I had never been in detention, so we had no idea what to do. Thank goodness Cameron and Glitch had the routine down. They sat at one of the many desks that lined the walls, leaving a space only where the door was and the warden's desk. Each desk was enclosed on three sides so the students' backs were to the warden, but allowing the warden to see what the students were doing. That would certainly cut down on note passing.

"I hope I'm not claustrophobic," Brooke said, sitting at a carrel next to me.

Due to the partition between us, we could see each other only if we leaned back. So, naturally, we leaned back.

"Me too. Now what?"

The moment the words left my mouth, the warden walked in. No, Ms. Mullins walked in. Humiliation burned my cheeks. She now knew my dark secret. My time in the big house was not going as unnoticed as I'd hoped.

"Okay," she said, her voice a little sharper than usual, "Mr. Gonzales has been detained. Until he gets here, you got me. So get out your homework and get busy." I figured she had to become a bit harder with us problem students. We were being locked up for a reason.

"You girls better hop to it," she said to Brooke and me. Pointing us out. Drawing attention our way. We'd be labeled do-gooders in no time. Or worse, snitches. I'd seen enough prison movies to know that was bad.

"Detention or not," Brooke said, "I have to go to the bathroom."

"Didn't you go before we left?"

She ignored me and walked to Ms. Mullins. They spoke for a moment, then Brooke headed out.

"Two minutes," Ms. Mullins said, her tone edged with warning. She was taking her job as prison warden very seriously.

I dragged out my homework.

"This is ridiculous," I heard a voice say from the hall. A female voice with a distinctive nasally twang. It was her. The creature.

But . . .

She walked in accompanied by the saucy click of her heels, clearly appalled at having to be in detention. I couldn't help but wonder what she did to end up there. What dark path she'd taken, what bad hand fate had dealt her.

But . . .

She stopped at the warden's desk. "I was tardy. I'd been at the dentist. Really? That requires after-school detention?"

But she didn't even come to school this morning. She must have shown up that afternoon. This day just got better and better.

"No, but the five tardy slips before today does. Take a seat, Tabitha, and get out something to work on. You aren't going anywhere for the next hour."

After exhaling a sigh that lasted longer than my attention span, she headed to a seat with all the fuss and flourish of a Hollywood starlet. It was the most dramatic entrance I'd seen since the Riley's Switch rendition of *Cat on a Hot Tin Roof.*

I couldn't help but notice the look of horror on Cameron's face as he watched her settle in. He wasn't good with people. If he were, he'd realize his look of horror would be wasted on Tabitha. No look, horrific or otherwise, would faze the creature whose name shall not be spoken aloud.

But she glanced over at us, like she'd been ignoring us but just couldn't manage it anymore. Her cheeks turned pink. Just barely before she looked away. And in that instant, I felt bad for her.

Not bad enough to offer her solace, but bad.

Glitch leaned over to me. "We can pass notes underneath the partitions." He wiggled his brows, and I realized he was right. The partitions were just sitting on the desks. Sweet.

Just when I was about to write him, ask him how he'd been since sixth hour, Brooke came back. But not just back. She tore into the room and skidded to a halt by my chair.

"Brooklyn," Ms. Mullins said, her tone admonishing, but Brooke didn't seem to notice.

She stood panting with a hand on her chest. "Mr. Davis must have spilled something," she said before swallowing and trying again. "He's coming." The fact that she was out of breath didn't alarm me. Brooke could be just as melodramatic as Tabitha when she put her crazy little mind to it. It was the look of sheer terror on her face. The genuine fear in her eyes.

A feeling of dread crept over me.

Cameron knelt beside my chair and looked up at her. Glitch cast a quick glance toward Ms. Mullins, then leaned over to listen.

Brooke stopped, forced herself to slow down, and leveled a panicked gaze on me. "Mr. Davis changed ties."

"What?" I asked, wondering what that had to do with anything.

"It's red. He's wearing his red tie."

Then her meaning sank in. No. That was impossible. It was Wednesday. He only wore his red tie on Fridays. It was tradition, practically an unwritten law. As sure as the sun rose each morning, Mr. Davis wore his red tie on Fridays. And then I remembered there were no desks in the middle of the room in my vision. Nothing we could use for cover. All four of us turned to look around the room.

Everyone was staring at us. Ms. Mullins stood and started toward us when Hector stood, turned, and raised a gun. His expression turned into a sneer. I almost fell back in my chair, but Ms. Mullins stepped between us.

Time slowed. I tried to say something, to warn her, but it all happened so fast, I froze, my mind not quite able to absorb the truth of what was happening. My vision was coming true right before my eyes. And I was back in the dream. Shocked and catatonic like a deer in headlights.

But something had changed. Cameron was there, and he hadn't been in my vision. And unlike me, he did not freeze. He reacted with the decisive speed of a cobra. Before Hector could pull the trigger, Cameron had shoved Ms. Mullins out of the way, but that's as far as he got before the gun went off.

The sonic boom of gunfire ripped through me, startling me into action. It did the same for Glitch. We both tackled poor Ms. Mullins to the ground as another round was fired. We tumbled to the floor, the eerie sound causing bile to surge hotly into my throat.

While screams of terror filled the room, Brooke rushed toward Cameron. Glitch reached out to grab her but missed. With a curse, he covered Ms. Mullins protectively. I turned to help Cameron as well, and my heart sank when I realized where the bullets were landing. Into Cameron's chest. Point-blank. One shot after another. Before I could get to my feet, a third shot hit its mark. The blast echoed against the walls as Cameron finally stumbled back, grabbing his chest in pain.

Hector walked forward, each step full of purpose, full of malicious intent, the gun held steady, a smirk in place. He clearly thought he had Cameron beat. He clearly didn't know Cameron.

Another shot. This time, Cameron didn't stumble. With a speed too quick for my eyes to register, in a single movement too smooth for my mind to comprehend, Cameron lunged forward, knocked the gun aside, and twisted the boy's head around. The next sound to meet my ears was the sharp crack of a neck being broken, and Hector slumped to the ground in a heap of torso and limbs.

In the next instant, Brooke was on Cameron. He caught her to him, used her for support as he fell to his knees first. But she was little use when he collapsed all the way to the floor. I got to them as quickly as I could. He groaned with the pain that etched his face, that welded his teeth shut.

Mr. Davis ran into the room, weaving his way around terrified students scrambling to safety.

It happened so fast. So impossibly, impossibly fast.

Had I just traded Cameron's life for mine? For Ms. Mullins's or Mr. Davis's? He wasn't even in my original vision. What had happened to change the events?

I blinked and Glitch was there, kneeling, putting pressure where Mr. Davis instructed. His hands were covered in blood faster than I thought possible. I heard Ms. Mullins as though from a distance calling for an ambulance. I heard Brooklyn screaming Cameron's name, tears running in thick rivulets down her dark cheeks. I couldn't focus on any one thing. It all hit me like a hurricane, strong and fast and overwhelming.

Cameron grabbed Glitch's collar and jerked him forward. "This is what they want," he said, his voice hoarse as he spoke through clenched teeth. "They got us out of the way. She's vulnerable now. Get her to the Sanctuary." Then he pushed. Hard.

Glitch pitched back and looked at me, his gaze frozen behind a shocked expression. I took over for him. I put pressure on one of the bullet wounds. The thick, warm blood seeped through my fingers.

"Glitch, damn it!" Cameron ground out between labored breaths. Now that he'd put Glitch in charge of my well-being, Cameron's expression was murderous.

Glitch started forward slowly. He didn't seem to want the job, and I could hardly blame him—but no way was I leaving Cameron like that. When Glitch took my arm to pull me away, I shook him off.

"We have to stop the bleeding," I said to Cameron. Then, despite the fact that Mr. Davis was right there, I added, "*You* have to stop the bleeding. You're different, Cameron. You heal really fast. Can't you do something?"

He raised a bloodied hand from around Brooklyn and placed

it on my cheek. "Not that fast, shortstop. And if I have to say it one more time, Blue-Spider, the last thing you will ever see will be the satisfied smile on my face as I snap your neck."

Glitch took my arm again just as Sheriff Villanueva ran into the room. I looked up, relief flooding every cell in my body. Surely he would know what to do, how to help Cameron. But he barely spared Cameron a glance. He took my other arm as Mr. Davis gaped in confusion. When I fought to stay by Cameron's side, the sheriff wrapped an arm around my waist and hoisted me off my feet.

"What are you doing?" Mr. Davis asked, appalled.

But the sheriff ignored him. He pulled his gun, handed it grip-first to Glitch, and said, "Shoot anything that gets close to us."

Glitch nodded; then the sheriff whisked me out the door with him right behind us.

Before I could even protest, we were out the side doors.

Thank goodness the final bell rang twenty minutes earlier. The last of the kids to be bused were on the other side, and there were only a couple of stragglers leaning against the building on this side. They straightened when we passed them, startled.

This being dragged away from school was becoming a habit. I just wanted to get back to Cameron, to Brooklyn and Ms. Mullins.

"Stop!" I yelled, but the sheriff thrust me onto my feet, then dragged me to his car.

An ambulance pulled into the parking lot, lights flashing and sirens blaring. Right behind it was another patrol car, then another, all with lights flashing and sirens blaring.

"Glitch, we have to go back," I said, pleading with him. He was scared. I could tell. He kept the gun pointed down and close to his body like a real professional.

When the sheriff stuffed me into his cruiser, I pushed his

hands away. In one movement, he twisted my thumb back and had my face against the dashboard before I knew what was happening.

"I *will* cuff you," he said, the warning edge in his tone unmistakable. He let go, but he'd gotten his point across. I was not going anywhere except with him.

Glitch pushed me over and sat next to the door as the sheriff went around. Only then did I see the blood smears on his neck and shirt where Cameron had grabbed him.

We flew out of the parking lot, and somewhere in the back of my mind I realized I'd lost track of Tabitha. She was so going to need therapy.

My vision blurred as hot tears pooled between my lashes. I gazed straight ahead. "I don't want to do this anymore," I whispered to myself.

MAC WITHOUT THE CHEESE

Sheriff Villanueva drove straight to the Sanctuary like everything behind us was on fire. By the time we got there, I was little more than a basket case.

Granddad ran out the side door of the church to intercept us.

The sheriff helped me out his side. "They've taken both Jared and Cameron out." He looked down at me, his eyes soft with concern. "They'll be coming after her next."

Granddad rushed me into the church and down the steps to the headquarters. The archive room was on the other end, and I sat staring at it as members of the Order filed in. Some hugged me in assurance. But they were worried. I could see it in their eyes. We'd failed. That stupid war was going to happen, and we didn't have Jared or Cameron to fight. We had me.

We were all dead.

I listened to the members of the Order for two hours. Well, kind of. My mind wandered to Jared. To Cameron. To Brooke and Glitch.

Glitch was with me. He watched as Grandma cleaned the blood off my hands and went for a change of clothing. Even though his clothes were just as bloody, he stayed. And sat. We both stared at the archive room, our backs to the proceedings.

I just wanted answers.

"We're just sitting here," I said to no one in particular, but the entire council quieted. "We're just sitting here waiting for something to happen. For someone else to get hurt." I offered my grandparents a thoughtful look. I wondered if they were going to ship me off now. They'd stood by me, by the teachings of my father, through thick and thin and everything in between, and I could never repay them. Not in a thousand years. But they'd kept so much from me, and I wanted answers. For that, I needed an expert. Someone who grew up with the knowledge of the Order. With its teachings.

I bowed my head, almost ashamed of what I was about to say. "I want to see my paternal grandfather."

Because we had lost our supernatural advantage, I was ordered to sleep in the vault in case of an attack. It was huge and had plenty of air through a venting system. They could watch from the monitor, make sure I was okay. If I needed out for the bathroom, I could call out to whoever was monitoring me. This was getting ridiculous.

Brooke stayed at the hospital with Cameron, and Grandma was at home with Jared. Glitch was allowed to stay with me under one condition, that his father stay as well, so among our guards was Glitch's dad. Granddad had assigned two rotating guards on two-hour shifts. If there was even the slightest hint of trouble, they were supposed to ring the church bells, which was actually an electronic bell that just took the press of a button to ring.

They brought in two cots for Glitch and me. We had a restless night, but that was to be expected. I felt raw. Dry. Like the slightest touch would cause excruciating pain. Would crack open my skin. All I could do was hope my paternal grandfather would have some answers, and pray that Cameron lived.

The next day, I found out he'd made it through the night. He would make it. I knew he would.

Thanks to our connections with the sheriff, we were able to get a visitation scheduled with my paternal grandfather on short notice. He grew up with the prophecies. And he was the only one who might actually know what was going on. He was in the prison in Los Lunas, about an hour away from us. All these years, an hour away.

The prison was minimum security and had been built for two reasons: for intake and diagnostics of new inmates and to house inmates with either a medical or mental condition. I wondered which one my grandfather had.

After we got through the check-in, Granddad let me go into visitation alone. I sat down at window 4. It was strangely like the desks in detention, only with glass separating an identical desk on the other side.

An older man stepped into sight, and the breath in my lungs stilled. I recognized him. He looked so much like my father, I wanted to cry. A lump formed in my throat. Average height. Thick, solid build. Graying red hair with about a week's worth of scruff on his chin. He looked rugged and kind at the same time.

When his gaze settled on mine, he looked confused. His brows slid together—first in puzzlement, then in recognition. My identity dawned and the shock on his face gave irrefutable evidence that he was not expecting to see me. Possibly ever. I couldn't decide if I should be hurt or appreciative.

After he regarded me a long, long moment, he sank into the chair behind the glass and picked up the receiver with lengthy, strong fingers. I did the same, but the act did us little good. All we could do was stare. He had the same gray eyes as both my father and I. The same chin dotted with a soft cleft. The same squared-off nose and wide mouth.

His eyes followed every line of my face, every curve, a combination of disbelief and admiration in their shimmering depths. "Lorelei," he whispered at last.

"Mr. McAlister," I said, not sure what to call him.

A crooked smile appeared, and my heart leapt in response. I remembered that smile. Though I was only six when my parents disappeared, I remembered that smile like I'd seen it yesterday. My father's had the same tilt, the same sparkle that made me feel like love had manifested into a facial expression.

"Why don't you call me Mac?"

I could tell he'd started to say something else, perhaps Granddad, but changed his mind. Maybe he didn't want to push things too fast. I could understand that. I nodded. "Okay."

"They told you about me?"

"No," I said, jumping to my grandparents' defense. "No, I found out on my own. Kind of on accident."

"I should've known you would." He glanced around, then back up at me. "You shouldn't be here. It's too dangerous."

"I need some answers, and everyone I know is getting hurt." My breath caught in my throat, and my vision grew blurry.

"Oh, sweetheart." His eyes watered as he watched me.

"I need to know, did the descendants kill my grandmother?"

The question threw him. He sat so long I thought he wouldn't answer, then nodded as though unable to believe I knew.

"They're here," I said, and a hand shot to his mouth. I leaned forward. "I need to know how to kill them."

He had to stop. He laid the phone on the desk as sobs shook his shoulders, and I could hardly contain my composure. I cried. He put his hand on the glass, and my innate reaction was to reciprocate. I was so sorry for what he'd gone through. For what my grandmother went through. But placing my hand against his might not have been the right thing to do. Even through the glass, a vision hit me like a freight train. The prison disappeared in a flash and I stood in an abandoned house. No real furniture, just a mattress here, a broken chair there.

Darkness filtered through the house like an animal waiting to pounce, and I was scared. No, Mac was scared, his breathing the only sound I could hear besides the rush of blood in his ears. His heart crashed against the walls of his chest.

He stepped forward. Knowing they were there. Waiting. It took him two days to find her. He would not be stopped now. Even when the first bullet ripped through his leg, he would not be stopped.

He shot a gun into the darkness. Was hit again. Shot again. Over and over. He pushed forward. Searching. Vowing to kill them all if it was the last thing he did. He ran out of bullets three times, dropping guns as he went and lifting others to replace them. The satisfaction he felt when a bullet hit home lasted only a microsecond before he would feel the heat of their return. Each round that slashed through him was a new kind of excruciating. A new kind of pain he'd never imagined existed.

Then there was just smoke and silence. He tore through the house and found her in the last bedroom. The only piece of furniture it could lay claim to was a chair, and she was in it. Olivia Marie McAlister. The most beautiful woman he'd ever seen. Tied up and slumped over.

Before he even got to her, he knew. She was just a shell. He knew that, but he couldn't help but feel sorry for the universe at the loss of such a bright star. The world would be a lesser place without Olivia McAlister in it.

He sank to his knees, took out his knife, and cut the ropes. When she fell into his arms, all he could do was apologize for being late. He was always late, even to his own wedding, so he apologized. Over and over until the encroaching darkness swallowed him whole.

I bolted back to awareness and slammed my hands over my face, sorry beyond comprehension for what my grandfather went through. Such agonizing sorrow. Such needless devastation.

Mac paused and looked up at me; then understanding dawned on his face. He picked up the receiver again. When I put my handset to my ear, he asked, "Did you just see that?"

He clearly knew what I was. I nodded and swiped at the wetness on my face.

"Why did they do that to her?" I asked.

He wiped his eyes with a handkerchief and regretted what he was about to say; I could see it in his expression. "They wanted you, Lorelei. Your parents went into hiding when they found out they were having a girl, and your grandmother knew where they were, so they tortured her for information." He fought another sob, gathered himself, then said, "She never told them a thing."

I covered my eyes with one hand. The flow of tears seemed endless.

"When the smoke had settled, we thought the entire sect was gone, so your parents came out of hiding."

After a moment, I took in a cool ration of air, then said, "She died on the day I was born."

A sad smile settled on his handsome face. "A bright star to replace the one lost."

I shook my head emphatically. "But I'm not," I said, pleading with him to understand. "I'm not anybody. Everyone thinks I'm this person that's going to stop some stupid war. And our best defenses are either hurt or unconscious or possessed."

"Lorelei," he said, his voice calming. "You are the last prophet of Arabeth."

"That's right. The *last*. What does that say about my chances of stopping this war?"

He chuckled then, his eyes glittering with appreciation. "What that means is that there will be no more female descendants of Arabeth. You are the last one. In other words," he added, leaning toward me, "you're going to have sons."

I sat back, took another deep breath. Somehow his words gave me hope.

"But first," he continued, "we have to keep you alive."

I sniffed into my sleeve. "That's a good plan."

"The initial faction that wanted you dead is dead themselves. I saw to that. It took a new generation of descendants to come after you again. Sixteen years of grooming and priming for this one kill. Make no mistake, Lorelei, they want you gone. Period."

"I don't understand. Why would they *not* want me to stop this war like I'm supposed to?"

"They feel like we humans have an unfair advantage. Like we're cheating. They're descendants of true nephilim, and they consider themselves a balancing force between the human and supernatural realms. Like supernatural cops." He looked at me. "They're actually nothing more than cult members who believe they are better than the rest of humanity. And they are absolutely psychotic, one and all."

"An unfair advantage? That's what this is about?"

"Basically. They feel that by having you on our side, we're tipping the scales, disrupting the natural balance."

"What about war is natural? What about the deaths of millions of innocent people is balanced?"

"Exactly. I'm not sure what their endgame is, be it power or just revenge against humanity."

"This doesn't even make sense," I said, tumbling into despair.

"Lorelei," he said, drawing me back, "they're psychotic, remember?" He tapped his head. "It doesn't have to make sense to us. It makes sense to them."

I straightened. "Okay, what do we do?"

"You saw it yourself. They're watered-down versions of nephilim. They can be killed much easier than an original nephilim." He leaned even closer. "They're arrogant and callous, and that makes them vulnerable. And they bleed just like you and I."

By the time I met my grandparents and Brooke in the front waiting area, Mac and I had a plan. He'd described in detail their habits, their weaknesses. He said the Order would have to hunt them down, but the descendants would not be hard to find. They nested together, and we were to look for an abandoned house or building that looked like squatters had been there. We would find them there.

I figured the sheriff and a couple members of the Order could handle that part. The other part, I didn't like so much. He told me I had to go into hiding until they were found. It was the only way I would survive.

"It isn't fair that Mac is in prison. None of this is fair," I said to my grandparents as we drove home, fighting to block the images I'd gleaned off my new grandfather. Of his horrible ordeal.

"Life isn't always about what's fair and what's not, pix,"

Granddad said. "It's about doing the right thing, no matter the risks. No matter the consequences."

If the consequences meant the suffering of the people I loved most, I wasn't sure I agreed.

That night, I slept alone in the vault. The door sat open with one soft light filtering in from the next room. Glitch and his father were out helping the sheriff and other members with the search. He promised to come back as soon as they'd checked out a couple of abandoned houses in Abo Canyon. Granddad took point in the Sanctuary along with Delores, a girl who believed very much in the mission of the Order of Sanctity and moved to Riley's Switch a few years ago just to be a member. She worked at the library with Betty Jo, Grandma's best friend. Brooklyn was at the hospital with Cameron, her phone set to speed-dial the sheriff if anyone came after him. He was vulnerable now, and the descendants would know that.

Granddad wouldn't let me go see him. Said it was too dangerous. He wouldn't even let me go back to the house to see Jared. I was to sleep in the vault tonight; then Granddad, Glitch, and Cameron's dad, Mr. Lusk, were going to take me into hiding. For how long, I had no idea. It looked like my grandparents were getting their wish after all. Sending me away. I realized they were still afraid of Jared. Of what he would be like when he woke up. Granddad warned me he could have amnesia when he did regain consciousness, or some other mental condition. Like he could still want us all dead.

I hoped not. The thought of Jared killing me with his bare hands made me sad. The thought of anyone killing me with his bare hands made me sad. Being a target sucked.

The heat in the vault had me tossing and turning. The crisp winter air didn't reach the cavernous basement. I wasn't sure if someone had turned up the heat or what, but it was hot. Of course, it could have been the fuzzy pajamas I was wearing with long bottoms and sleeves. Then again, I'd been having trouble sleeping for days. If I wasn't waking from the fits of a nightmare, I was hearing the wind or feeling something on my skin. But this was different. The stillness woke me. The absolute calm. Basements were creepy enough without being so motionless. So dark.

I checked my phone. It was almost six. Brooke and I had texted until well past midnight. She told me Cameron was coming around and would probably be a horrid patient. I didn't envy her. I glanced at Brooke's last text. She was wondering where she could get some sedatives because Cameron was much easier to deal with doped.

Then I noticed Grandma had sent me a text at around two. Grandma never stayed up until two. She was going to be exhausted today, but she had to let me know that Granddad was coming home for a shower and breakfast around five and that he would bring me something to eat and some fresh clothes for the road after that. He'd left Delores and Mr. Walsh in the Sanctuary and Harlan in the basement with me.

Then she went on about how much she loved me and how she knew I was going to be okay because she couldn't live knowing I wasn't. With my heart breaking, I exited the text before reading on. Her sadness caused a pain deep inside me.

I rose and exited the vault in search of hydration. While an orange soda would be preferable, water would do in a pinch.

"Hello?" I called out.

No answer. I figured Harlan must have been sleeping. I could hardly blame him. It was hot and dark. Not much else to do.

I took the stairs all the way up to the Sanctuary where Mr. Walsh and Delores—who, while working at the library, was taking online classes to learn to be a paralegal—had volunteered to keep watch on the doors. Through the old stained glass windows, I could see the sun peeking over the horizon when I topped the stairs.

I wondered if Brooke was going to school today. I wondered if anyone was going to school today. Surely they'd closed it after the shooting. There were probably reporters camped out there.

"Delores?" I said into the darkness.

"We sent her home."

I turned to the male voice coming from the back of the church. I didn't recognize it, but I knew it wasn't Mr. Walsh's. It sounded young, perhaps someone my age, but no one my age was in the Order, besides me and my closest friends, of course.

I couldn't see him, so I started for the back of the church. "Did Granddad send you? Sorry about the odd hours."

"Not a problem. I like the dark. Makes killing humans so much easier."

THE DESCENDANT

I stopped.

"You seem surprised, Lorelei." When I started to back up, he said, "I wouldn't bother. You won't get far."

"What do you want?" I asked, looking around for a weapon. Churches were so lacking in that area. I fought the paralyzing effects of fear as I inched back.

"I just wanted to see you. In person. Not through someone else's eyes."

In that instant, I realized who stood in the shadows. Vincent. The new guy. The descendant. He'd seen me through Isaac's eyes.

"Killing you has become quite the challenge. First the truck. Then that useless football kid. Then the chess nerd whose aim is shit."

I took another step back, wondering where everyone was.

"What do you mean, the truck?"

"You're Lorelei. You're in every prophecy ever written about this new war. Hell, Nostradamus himself prophesied about the last descendant of the first witch, the girl who saves the world. This was going to be the end of humanity as we know it. But you, the prophet, are supposed to do something completely stupid and figure out how to stop it before it even starts. You don't honestly think you were supposed to die before that time came, do you?"

I stopped and gaped into the darkness. "You . . . you sent that truck?"

"Gosh, you're quick."

I heard a swishing sound and he was in front of me. I tried to back away but he caught me around the neck and pulled me forward until our faces were mere inches apart. His sandy brown hair hung messy over his brow and he still wore that same tweed coat, long and loose.

"No wonder you make good grades." Turning my face to inspect it, he said, "Did you know that in Germanic mythology, Lorelei was a siren who lured men to their destruction?" He ran his thumb along my jaw. "Fitting, don't you think? Though I've never heard of an archangel being brought to his knees by a human girl." With a hoarse laugh, he shoved me away from him. I tripped and stumbled to the ground. "I thought you'd be prettier."

I looked at what I'd tripped on and almost screamed. It was an arm. Delores's arm. She lay sprawled between two pews. I couldn't see her face, but I'd tripped on her arm and she didn't move an inch.

"The truck thing was a big disappointment," Vincent continued, unmindful of Delores. "All that work. Do you have any idea how hard it was to get that timing down? Having that kid shove you into the street at exactly the same time that truck sped through town? That took crazy planning. And then the freaking Angel of Death shows up?" He scoffed. "What are the odds?"

"Did you kill her?"

He finally looked at Delores. "Unless her head has the natural ability to turn counterclockwise three hundred sixty degrees, then probably yes."

My hands shot to my mouth. What was it with supernatural beings and the breaking of necks? "What did you do to Jared?"

"Jared? Ah, yes, Azrael." Vincent was enjoying this cat and mouse play. Jumping on a pew, he sat on the back and looked down at me as I lay sprawled in the aisle, inching away from him. "Did you know that the most powerful psychotropic in existence is the blood of an archangel?" When I didn't say anything, he continued. "No? That's understandable. Not many people do. But lo and behold, Riley's Switch just happened to have one. How else do you think we were able to control so many students at your high school?"

He seemed to pause for an answer, but I couldn't imagine he actually wanted one.

"Convincing a high school student to try to kill a perfectly innocent girl is not as easy as it might sound. But with the blood of an arch—" He spread his arms wide and looked toward the heavens. "—all things are possible." Laughing at his own joke, he hopped to the ground and straddled me, looking down from his tremendous height to intimidate. "Let's face it, shortstop, blasphemy is fun."

I bristled at the use of my nickname and continued to inch away, holding out hope someone would show up. Someone with an Uzi and lots of ammo. How could it end now? Just when my grandfather Mac had convinced me I was the right girl for the job? What would happen with the war?

"And yet," he said, shaking his head in astonishment, "here you are. Just goes to show, if you want to do something right, you've got to do it yourself."

I shook my head too, still unable to believe he could hurt Jared. "But Jared's strong and really fast."

He leaned toward me. "Yeah, well, so is a .50-caliber at a hundred yards."

"You shot him?" I asked, appalled.

"Lot of good it did us." He turned away and hopped back onto the pew. Stepping lightly onto the back, he walked it like one would a balance beam: one foot in front of the other, his arms out. He was like a kid. Like a really big kid who was psychotic and hard on the furniture.

He glanced over his shoulder. "What would have ripped another man to shreds simply wounded him, but he was out long enough for us to harvest his blood and do a small but effective binding spell to block out his light. We were hoping he would do the job for us, that he would take both you and the nephilim out." He spun and maneuvered his way back along the pew. "But when the nephilim actually got the better of Azrael—*the* Azrael—with a freaking dart gun? Made me proud to be what I am." He shook a finger at me. "We nephilim are not to be messed with, I can tell you that."

"You're controlling the kids from high school with Jared's blood."

"That I am." He fished in his pocket and brought out a metal vial. Lifting it for me to get a better look, he said, "Tell you what: I'll give you a taste right before I kill you." The smile that crept across his face was the most evil thing I'd ever seen. He jumped down and kneeled close. "You'll die happy, I promise you that."

Even knowing how futile the effort would be, I scurried away from him and ran. If nothing else, it would make him laugh and give me valuable seconds to get away. My bare feet padded across the tiled church and I burst out the side door. I could hardly believe I'd made it that far, but when I hit the outside, a frigid blast of wind hit me and my feet crunched across freshly fallen snow. Feeling like I'd just dived into a lake of ice, I sucked in a sharp breath. It took about two seconds for me to feel the pain from the frozen ground, but adrenaline pushed me forward.

Though the sun had managed to make it over the horizon, it was still lazing low in the distance, making my trek through the trees dark and dangerous.

At first, I headed for the safety of home. Then I thought about Delores and probably Mr. Walsh as well. Maybe even Harlan. If I led this guy to my house, what would happen to Grandma and Granddad? I quickly turned south into the trees and toward the canyon. The ground, frozen and unforgiving, cut into my feet with every step, the snow excruciating, but the adrenaline pumping through my veins kept me running at full speed ahead.

I looked back but didn't see Vincent. Did something happen? Did someone show up at the church? I stopped and waited, my lungs burning as I gasped for air. Then I saw a figure walking toward me. Casually, like he was taking a stroll in a garden. And he wore a smile on his face.

With feet numb now, I turned and ran up the mountainside some more. I had no idea why. I had no plan other than to lead Vincent away from my family and friends. Maybe I'd be enough. Maybe he'd stop with me.

He caught up to me a few minutes later. I had a feeling he appreciated my running so far. It would be harder for them to find my body. But I had to stop. I'd come to the canyon, a deep drop that ended below with a shallow river and lots of body-breaking rocks.

"There you are," he said, laughing. "You little minx. Never figured you'd get this far." He strolled a few feet from me as I looked down the canyon wall, frozen, shivering, and paralyzed with fear.

I wish I had gotten to know Mac better. I wish I could have seen Jared one more time. And thanked Cameron. And hugged my grandparents. And kissed Brooke and Glitch. Surely they knew how I felt about them. Surely they would understand.

"Thanks for running, by the way." He brushed some snow off his shoulder. "Couldn't kill a prophet in the church. Hallowed ground and all. Bad for the karma."

I turned toward him, tears blurring my vision and freezing on my skin.

"By all rights, I should be able to just kill you right here and now. I'm a descendant. I'm stronger than most humans. Faster."

I inched away from the edge of the canyon. If he was going to kill me, he was not going to do it by throwing me off a cliff. He would have to do it with his own hands. He would have to work for it.

He stepped forward and captured my jaw in a firm grip that had pain shooting through it. "I should just be able to break that scrawny neck of yours. To reach into your chest and rip out your heart." He closed the distance between us until his mouth was almost touching mine. "And yet every single time we try to kill you, you survive for one reason or another. So this time, I brought help."

He nodded over his shoulder, indicating the others who had come up behind him. Over a dozen boys, some no older than me, and others who looked well over twenty, stood scattered around us. All of them tall. All of them not quite right, disproportioned somehow. Their gazes were both threatening and blank. White fog drifted from their mouths like animals as they watched. But that wasn't the scary part. The scary part was what they were carrying. Each held a weapon. A machete here. An axe there. Blades so sharp, the sunlight reflected off the edges.

"Never send a human to do a nephilim's work." Vincent's expression changed, turned sadistic. "This time, there'll be no coming back."

With a shove that had me seeing stars, he pushed me to the ground.

I grabbed my throat, coughing and choking, and looked up at him. "Why?"

"Because you will be chopped into little pieces," he said, looking at me like I was an imbecile. "There's really no coming back from that."

"No, why do you want this war?" I asked between coughs. "What does it have to do with you?"

"Nothing. It has to do with humans and their arrogance and angels and their supremacy. We're the bastards of two worlds. Outcasts. Unable to enter heaven because of our ancestry. Discriminated against by humans because we're different."

"What does that have to do with the war? Why would you want demons to rule the earth?"

"We don't necessarily. We just think they deserve a fighting chance. Because of you, humans have an unfair advantage. By eliminating you, we're evening out the odds. Leveling the playing field, if you will."

I scooted back, trying to get out from under him, so I was a little surprised when I heard a thud and he went flying back to slam into a tree, the impact so hard, his body broke under the pressure.

I gasped and looked up into the smiling face of an angel. Literally.

Jared was standing over me, positioned so that from my

vantage, he looked upside down. He grinned. "You get into more trouble when I'm not around," he said.

With a cry of delight and relief, I scrambled to my feet and flung myself into his arms. He wrapped them tight, buried his face in my hair. Which must look horrid. He felt like heaven with central heating, warm and safe.

"Where are your shoes?"

I pulled back to look at his face. His perfect, beautiful face with the rich brown eyes and a full sexy mouth. He had a bluish tint under his eyes that blended into reds and purples. He was still recovering.

One corner of his mouth tilted up teasingly. "No, really. Your feet are blue."

Vincent interrupted. "We thought you might show up." A pained smile slid across his face as he tried to stand upright. "In fact, we were counting on it." He lifted a hand and before I knew what was happening, I was back in the snow. So fast, I barely registered the movement. So hard, the breath was knocked from my lungs.

Then the sound registered. A splintering blast of gunfire that ricocheted off the trees as the bullet tore through the forest.

With a growl, Jared turned on Vincent. Blood dripped down his arm from his shoulder. The bullet had grazed him. But he was smiling right back.

"Thank you," he said. Standing again, he looked past Vincent into the trees. "I was wondering where he might be." Then he fired off a rock he'd been holding. It shot out like a cannonball and hit something with a sharp thud, the sound quickly followed by a groan.

I looked around, wide eyed, but saw nothing. No one. Did he just hit the gunman?

"That was for shooting me the first time."

Vincent looked back slack jawed, then caught himself. "Get him!" he yelled, his voice full of anger, his face twisted with rage, and the descendants started forward en masse.

Jared couldn't fight them. He had no weapon, and there were simply too many. He picked me up and pulled me to him.

"You're back," I said, my voice hoarse.

"I'm so sorry, Lorelei."

"No, please." He had risked his life for my own, had given up everything for me. "There's nothing to be sorry for."

The descendants were getting closer. We had mere seconds before the first strike.

"So, when I tried to kill you and your friends and your family? I'm still forgiven?"

I threw my arms around him. If he was the last thing I saw on this Earth, I'd die happy. That I knew for certain.

"I'll take that as a yes."

I laughed. Despite the circumstances, which mostly consisted of our impending doom, Jared had me laughing. I heard sirens in the distance. They must have found Delores. They must have realized I was gone. My grandparents would be worried and they'd have no idea where to look. My heart broke for what they would go through when they found our bodies.

"Do you trust me?" Jared asked.

He'd asked me that before. Once when I had a grand piano about to crush me. I leaned back and looked up at him. The descendant with the axe was barely three feet away. He readied it, taking his time to aim, to get it just right.

"Of course."

"Then jump."

I looked over the side of the canyon, disbelief in my eyes. I stepped out of his arms and away from the edge. "I—I don't think—"

"Lorelei," he said, the grin sliding back into place like a favorite pair of jeans. He lifted my chin and placed the most understanding smile on me. "Jump."

Just as an axe arced toward us, I ran through the snow, closed my eyes, and jumped over the canyon wall.

FUZZY BOTTOMS

I wasn't the first. Two people had jumped off that same cliff before, both of them alleged suicides. I hardly had time to think, to gather my thoughts before the ground came barreling toward me. A split second before I hit, I heard two words, like a whisper of wind through the trees.

"Be still."

And I stopped in one breathtaking jerk.

My eyes flew open and I looked at the ground below me. The one that was just sitting there, being all groundlike. I gasped and craned my neck to see a pair of feet planted before me. They were followed by two long legs. Then hands, strong and scuffed with fresh blood. Forearms, the muscles that corded around them flexed and ready. A lean stomach with an open wound on one side, blood spreading across a white T-shirt. Wide shoulders and the most amused smile I'd ever seen.

"I'm—I'm flying," I said, my voice high with astonishment.

He laughed softly. "Actually, you're hovering." He reached toward me and took one of my hands and like magic I fell into his arms. My favorite place to be.

"How—? What did you—?" I looked up the side of the cliff, then back to him. He waited patiently, letting me absorb what had just happened. "How did you—? I don't—" I stopped, assessed the situation, then looked back up at him. "I think I peed my pants."

He tightened his hold. "You aren't wearing pants."

"I think I peed my fuzzy bottoms."

Jared arched his brows, but I had a thought.

"If we live through this, Brooke and Glitch have got to try that."

Throwing his head back, he laughed out loud, the sound rich and luxurious and welcome. It caused a fluttering sensation to rush over me, like butterflies, like warm water.

After a moment, he sobered and leveled a reluctant stare on me. "They're coming."

I turned and saw the descendants scrambling down the face of the cliff like monkeys, strong and sure-footed. The sight was disturbing on about seven thousand levels. While there were fewer of them now, only six or seven left, they were still coming, still hunting.

Loosening his hold, Jared lowered me to the ground.

I pulled on his bloodied shirt. "Run!"

He looked back at the advancing enemy.

How had he taken out at least half a dozen nephilim and

managed to beat me to the canyon floor? But he'd paid a price. He was hurt. Blood was oozing from between his ribs and down the side of his head, a crimson river trailing under his collar.

Someday, I would get used to seeing him beat to heck. It was a day I looked forward to. Actually, I looked forward to any day that did not end here and now, making this one my last.

I pulled again. "Jared, we have to run."

"What?" he said, sharing another teasing grin. "Leave now? When I have them right where I want them?"

They jumped down from an impossible distance, landing one by one in front of us. I toppled back, but Jared caught me to him. Then Vincent was there, still holding his stomach. Jared had hurt him, and that made me happy inside.

Jared pushed me behind him protectively. I latched on to his arm as he draped it across my body.

"This is where you wanted them?" I asked in a whisper.

"Those were some very good friends of mine," Vincent said, planting his feet and glaring. "The men you just killed."

"You'll see them again. Very soon, in fact."

He scoffed. "I told you, it doesn't work like that for us. We're bastards, remember? When your kind decided to go rogue and join the gang down here, God was not happy." He pointed to the heavens. "He kept the one thing from nephilim that he gave every full-blooded human on Earth. Souls. So, no. I won't be seeing them anytime soon. They're gone. Just like you're about to be."

He started forward, but Jared stopped him when he said, "I am the last being you should challenge."

"Why?" he asked, his tone full of contempt. "Because you're an arch? You archs are all alike. So supreme. So powerful. But you." He spit at Jared's feet and I couldn't help but notice there was more blood than saliva. "You are the worst. You were given a power far beyond anything the others have, the power of life and death over humans. You could kill them all with a wave of your hand. With a thought."

That was disturbing.

"And yet you've squandered that power as callously as humans squander the lives they've been given. They appreciate nothing. They worship food and drugs and movie stars."

"What do you hope to gain by tipping the scales?" Jared asked.

"No, no, no," Vincent said, wagging an index finger at us. "Balancing the scales. Thanks to the carrot stick, they've already been tipped."

Did he just call me a carrot stick?

"Do you have any idea what will happen if the darkness of hell is unleashed on Earth?" Jared asked.

He tried to laugh but grimaced instead, a tight expression full of pain. Blood had pooled between his teeth and dripped down one corner of his mouth. "A darkness that cannot enter us? A hell that cannot destroy us? By the time the fallen are done with this world, there won't be enough humans left to run a convenience store. And it will become ours. We'll rule like kings."

"Or fools," Jared said. "Just because you can't be possessed doesn't mean the darkness can't affect you. There'll be nothing left to rule."

"Mr. Dyson has a plan."

"Mr. Dyson? Is that the man who opened the gates of hell ten years ago?"

"The one and only. Let's just say he's the architect and we're the contractors. We don't ask for much. Just a little corner of the world to call our own without the interference of human overpopulation. I mean, six billion? Really? We're just hoping for the extermination of a few billion, just enough to restore the balance."

As they spoke, the descendants circled us, their blades at the ready, yet I couldn't help but notice their bravado had vanished. They were scared of Jared. It showed in the circular shape of their eyes, in the slight parting of their lips.

"He has forsaken us. Why should I worry about what happens to his world? To his pets?" He glanced around at his cohorts, then back to us. "Get them," he ordered. "Only this time do it right."

But before the descendants could move, Jared spoke, his voice calm, his manner unhurried. And he said only one word: "Cameron."

The next instant, something landed solidly beside us. I jumped back and watched as Cameron unfolded to his full height. He paused to wink at me before turning toward the advancing crazy people. I looked toward the sky, wondering where he'd come from. Was he in the trees? Then I remembered what happened to him.

"Cameron," I said, worried about his injuries. He'd been shot. Four times. And now he was running through the forest and jumping out of trees? "Are you crazy?"

"Shhh." He shushed me like he didn't want his secret getting out, a mischievous glint in his eyes.

"I'm a little surprised," Vincent said, but Jared had pushed me farther behind him, and I couldn't really make out whom he was talking to.

"Oh, yeah?" Cameron said, his voice a little too joyous. That boy loved to fight.

I peeked around Jared's arm.

"You're one of us. You're nephilim. Why are you fighting with that thing?"

"I'm not one of you." Cameron raked a cold gaze over him. "You're a copy of a copy of a copy." He threw back his shoulders. "I'm the real deal, bitch."

And he liked using the word "bitch." A lot. How was he even here? He'd been shot. A lot.

"Take her," Jared said to him without looking away from Vincent.

"What? No, wait."

Cameron started to pull me away, but I was tired of being manhandled, of decisions being made for me. Before I could make my case—which could be seen as either noble or psychotic, due to our current circumstances—the descendants rushed Cameron. He had no choice but to shove me out of the way. So he shoved. Really hard.

I felt oddly airborne for a brief moment before crashing and skidding across the forest floor to slam against a fallen log. Things like this seemed to be happening a lot to me lately.

The air rushed out of my lungs with the impact. And my hair caught in some twigs. I looked back just in time to see Jared stop an axe from plummeting into his neck, but the length of a machete sliced across his back as another descendant attacked him from behind. A scream escaped before I could stop it. I slapped my hands over my mouth, trying not to draw Jared's attention from the task at hand: surviving.

I caught sight of Cameron. He ducked, barely escaping an axe aimed at his temple, before he swung around and smashed a fist into the culprit's jaw. It broke under the pressure of Cameron's punch.

In seconds, the descendants had been downed. It was hardly a match. Though both Cameron and Jared had been hurt, the descendants would be lucky if they were still breathing after today. So it was too bad when Vincent walked me forward, one arm locked around my throat, the other wrapped tightly around my head. I was clutching on to his wrists, my toes barely touching the rocky ground as he stopped some distance away from the two victors.

The slightest effort on his part would snap my neck. I knew it. Cameron knew it. And Jared knew it.

Jared stopped what he was doing—namely delivering one last blow to his adversary—and turned on us, still crouched from his most recent effort, still panting from the adrenaline coursing through his veins.

He lowered his head even farther as he eyed Vincent from under his dark lashes. I'd seen that look before. I knew what he was capable of. Vincent was a fool. He may succeed in killing me, but he'd never make it out of this forest alive. He would never see the fruit of his delusional endeavors.

I expected him to say something smart-alecky. He loved to talk. But apparently, he'd learned not to give an archangel a chance to recover. Without further ado, he tightened the muscles in his arms, and I felt my head being jerked to the side.

Knowing I was taking my last breath was not as scary as I'd thought. I had resigned myself to dying a few moments earlier. I felt bad, though. For my grandparents, mostly. And for Brooke and Glitch. I knew how I would feel if they'd had their necks broken in a forest. I even felt bad for Cameron. He had literally been created to protect me, the prophet. How would he feel about my death? It was hardly his fault, but Cameron was so male. He'd blame himself. I was sure of it.

But out of everyone I felt bad for, I mostly felt bad for myself. As selfish as it sounded, I would never get to see Jared again. That thought alone was enough to make me angry.

I had put up with this guy's crap for long enough. I saw Jared start forward. Cameron right on his heels. They would never get to Vincent in time. My vision was already darkening and pain rocketed down my spine. Vincent may take my life, but he was going to take something else with him today. A really bad scar.

Adrenaline surged through me at the speed of light, liquid and red and hot. I lifted my feet off the ground and used Vincent's own arms as leverage. Pushing up on his elbows with all the strength I could conjure, I forced my weight down and slid out from under his grip. Without taking the time to blink, I spun around and lashed out at him, raking my nails across his face and neck in one vicious swipe.

Then I wobbled back, waited for his final blow, the one that would end my life.

But he just stood there. Looking at me. All surprised.

I blinked and glanced at Jared when he slid to a stop behind me. He pulled me back against him, his gaze fixed as we watched Vincent. He had five huge gashes on his face and neck. Exactly where I'd struck. But my fingernails couldn't have made anything that deep.

It took a long moment for him to react. He reached up, dazed, and felt the fissures in his neck. Blood pumped through his fingers, flowing out of him like a floodgate had opened. I looked down at my hands. Not an ounce of blood, not even a trickle. Not a mark or a scratch or even a broken nail.

I looked back up as Vincent fell to his knees. Blood flowed in rivulets over his hand and down his arm, draining the life out of his eyes in seconds. He fell forward onto his face, and I covered my mouth, dumbfounded.

"How did you do that?" Cameron asked, clearly as surprised as I.

The only answer I could manage was a stunned shake of my head. Because I had no idea. Then an inkling of an idea surfaced. One I dared not acknowledge.

There was no way. I looked down at my hands again. They were shaking to the point of convulsions. But there was no way. Simply no way the demon inside could have somehow manifested through me, through my actions. Did Malak-Tuke kill Vincent? Those gashes were made by something long and sharp, and I remembered exactly what Malak-Tuke's claws were like. It was the only explanation, but how?

Jared took my hands into his, drawing my attention. "Lorelei, it's okay. You're going to be okay."

"They're here!"

Someone called from a distance.

"They're over here!"

"Did I just take someone's life?"

Without answering, Jared scooped me into his arms. I felt his steps as we trekked over the uneven terrain. I felt cool air as he laid me on a stretcher. I felt weightless as they lifted me and carried me to an ambulance. Jared was beside me, holding my hand. Grandma was there too, crying and fussing. Cameron was talking to the sheriff, pointing to the top of the ridge where the authorities would find more bodies.

Then sounds blurred and bled together. Images faded and receded into darkness. And I drifted inside myself.

Are you in here?

My voice echoed in the darkness but received no answer.

Have you been here this whole time?

I heard a shift. Felt a stir of air.

I know you're here. Inside.

A fine edge grazed across my ankle, like the tip of a very sharp claw.

There you are.

I knelt beside the sleeping dragon, folded myself into its wings, and slept.

NOAH

Hypothermia. That's what they called it. I called it being freaking alive, and I couldn't have been more grateful. After a group of crazy people tried to kill me, I got to miss another week of school beyond the week it was closed due to the shooting. I felt the absences justified. And I spent that week with one Mr. Jared Kovach. And Cameron, of course, who was becoming a permanent window fixture. And Brooke, who practically lived at our house anyway. And, naturally, Glitch.

I was never lonely, though privacy was quickly becoming an issue. There were just certain things boys didn't need to know.

Luckily, Cameron and Jared had enough injuries to back up the we-were-attacked story. Lots of investigators were brought in, and we were questioned for days. Sadly, the descendants had killed Delores. Harlan, who had been in the basement, really did just fall asleep, and Mr. Walsh suffered a concussion when they knocked him out. The whole town showed up for Delores's funeral. The guilt that gripped me that day was overwhelming, knowing she believed in what we were doing so vividly that she died to protect me.

Not so many showed up at Hector's funeral, and I felt just as bad. He'd been programmed to do that shooting. But Cameron said that stuff worked only so far. That if he hadn't wanted to do it, he could have fought it. I wasn't so sure, especially after what Vincent said about Jared's blood. My heart broke for his parents. I couldn't imagine what they were going through.

With the sheriff backing everything we told the police and the district attorney, the authorities weren't really questioning the whats. They seemed more concerned with the hows. How did the three of us defeat a dozen axe-wielding, machete-swinging cult members? Especially after one of us, namely Cameron, had been almost fatally wounded two days before?

If they dug very deep, they would find a connection to a similar *cult* catastrophe and my paternal grandfather. It would raise some brows for sure. I hoped they wouldn't dig. But until then, we were just basking in the fact that none of us were in jail. And we were freaking alive.

I was still floored that Cameron was able to show up in the forest at all. His and Jared's ability to heal was unfathomable. And very much appreciated.

I was still sore a week later. Being shoved, thrown, tossed, and dragged by the head wreaked havoc on us mere mortals. Not to mention almost frozen to death. So while Cameron was out playing tag football after receiving four gunshot wounds to the chest, and Jared was giving him a run for his money after getting shot with a .50-caliber sniper rifle only days earlier, I was sitting on the parking lot sidelines—aka, the sidewalk—trying not to grimace too hard when they dented a fender here, crumbled a brick house there.

"They need help," Brooke said, sitting beside me and holding out a hot chocolate.

I took it with an oddly elated sense of glee. Hot chocolate. How would I be able to live without hot chocolate for all eternity when I finally did bite the dirt?

"Do you want to talk about what happened?" Brooke asked me as we watched Jared put Cameron in a choke hold.

"Are those even legal?" Glitch asked from my other side. He sat drinking his usual whipped almond toffee cappuccino with nonfat milk.

We enjoyed watching them play, then cringed when Cameron flipped Jared over his shoulder and slammed him onto the ground.

"Lots of things happened," I said to Brooke. "Which part?" I knew which part, of course, but a part of me, a big part of me, like my entire torso, was hoping she'd blow it off.

"The part where you ripped a guy's throat out with your nails."

Nope.

"I didn't rip a guy's throat out with my nails."

"I just didn't realize your nails were that strong."

"They're not."

"Do you eat a lot of gelatin?"

"No."

"Do you sharpen your nails with a whetting stone?"

"Not usually."

"Hey," Jared said, jogging up to us, the grin on his face causing little quakes to shiver through me. He did human so well.

"Hey." I offered him my hot chocolate. He took a swig, winking at me from behind the cup, then handed it back just as Cameron tackled him, ramming him into the back wall of our house.

"Cameron, we totally need that wall," I said, suddenly annoyed. "If I didn't know any better, I'd say Cameron was genuinely trying to hurt him."

"He might be," Brooke said. She bowed her head. "He was really scared."

I looked over in surprise. "For Jared?"

"For you. He didn't think he could do his job without Jared. He was worried he'd fail, and he believes by getting shot he did."

"He told you that?"

She shook her head. "No, but I'm beginning to read him pretty well now."

"Like, when his tongue is down your throat?" I asked. "Can you read him pretty well then?"

She gaped at me, appalled, and I laughed the evilest laugh I could. Which wasn't so much evil as sad. I couldn't help but notice Glitch turn away. I felt so bad for him, but he would have to face Brooke's affection for Cameron sooner or later. Fortunately, I had a Plan B, and she was walking up as we spoke. *Un*fortunately, Glitch chose that exact moment to confront his archnemesis.

He stood and pushed Cameron as he tossed the ball. "She's too good for you," he said, matter-of-fact. "She is better than you will ever be."

Brooke and I hurried over before Cameron could grab him by the throat again. You'd think Glitch would learn.

Cameron turned a humble expression on him. "You think I don't know that?" he said softly, as though embarrassed. Then he looked over at Ashlee Southern. Who'd just walked up because I'd invited her over. Yep, Glitch just pretty much blew Plan B.

"Oh," Ashlee said when we all turned in unison to look at her, "I'm sorry. I didn't know, Glitch."

"Didn't know what?" he asked.

"That you . . . I'm sorry." She hurried away.

"What was that about?"

"Glitch," Brooke said, rolling her eyes. "Oh, my gawd, she likes you, you idiot."

"Really?" He looked at Ash's retreating form. "Me?"

"Yes, you," I said. "I'm getting really sick of you pining after our best friend. We're best friends! It's like having a crush on your sister."

Everyone cringed just a little at that thought.

Glitch had yet to take his eyes off Ashlee. She was getting in her car. "So, Ashlee Southern likes me?"

I stepped next to him. "Yes. Dork."

"Okay, well, I'll be right back." He took off as Ashlee was backing out of her parking space. She stopped and rolled down her window.

"Wow," I said to Brooke, more than a little shocked, "he got over you really fast."

"He did, didn't he?"

Cameron and Jared went back to playing football. Or, well, their violent, bloodthirsty version of football. And Brooke and I went back to our parking lot seats.

"Hey, you guys," Ashlee said as she walked back up with Glitch. "Sorry about that." She was embarrassed now, but not enough to leave, which boded well for Plan B.

I grinned. "Hey, Ashlee. How's Isaac?"

"Much better. Thank you so much."

"Oh, no, I didn't do a thing."

She glanced around at Jared, Cameron, Brooke, and then Glitch. "I'm pretty sure you guys did a lot more than you're letting on."

Glitch shifted, suddenly uncomfortable. "Lor did all the hard work."

"I'm glad you're okay," she said, looking at me before turning back to Glitch. "All of you."

"Thanks," he said. "Want to sit down?"

They sat beside us, and Brooke and I exchanged high-five glances.

Jared called a time-out and plopped down beside me, stealing my hot chocolate in the process. We'd done a lot of talking over the past week. About the attack. About the darkness and where it came from. He remembered everything like it was a dream, overcome by a great and terrible black, a cloud so thick and choking, he felt he could hardly see right from wrong. Like they were tangible things just out of his reach.

Then he explained where it came from. Deep within his core, within his makeup was a darkness of unspeakable cruelty. But the light that surrounded it kept it at bay. Somehow the symbol the descendants had branded on him had blocked the light and let the dark loose.

"That's what'll happen to the world if we don't stop the war," he'd said. "A darkness that will block the light, that will bring out the evil, and millions will fall victim to its force."

No pressure.

I wrapped my arm in his and snuggled up against him. Storm clouds were rolling in and the wind was picking up. Cameron ran up to him, nudged him with his foot.

"I'm taking a break," he said, looking up with a challenging sparkle in his eyes.

"Breaks are for wusses," Cameron said.

"I hope Tabitha's okay," Brooke said out of the blue, and we all gaped at her. "You know, after that kiss, the girl might think you two are an item." She grinned at Jared.

"Kiss?" Ashlee asked, suddenly very interested.

Jared ducked his head in embarrassment. "I still think you guys are lying about that part."

We laughed, but with everything that had happened, that kiss still stung me. I was pathetic.

"Speaking of kisses," he said, turning his beautiful gaze on me, "I seem to remember a promise about kissing me somewhere other than my cheek."

"What?" I asked, a microsecond before his meaning dawned. A heat spread up my neck and over my jaw. "I have no idea what you're talking about and you were unconscious. How could you possibly know that?"

"It's all coming back to me in pieces. And I distinctly remember a promise you made. But if you're the kind of girl who doesn't keep her promises . . ."

He let his meaning hang in the air, studied me with his incredible eyes. I lifted his hand, turned it over, and kissed the inside of his palm.

"There," I said, wrapping my hand in his. "I've kept my promise."

But all the humor had fled from his face. He looked down at my lips, and I could feel the heat of his gaze. Everywhere it touched, it left a trail of warmth. His tongue slid out to wet his own lips; then one corner slid up and he asked, "Are you getting anything?"

I gasped. "How do you know every single time?" I asked, appalled.

I dropped his hand in disgust at having been caught trying to get a vision off him again, but he continued to gaze at me, his expression serious. "You can ask me anything, Lorelei. I'll answer truthfully. You know that, right?"

"Of course." But just to test out that theory, I asked, "So, is your blood really like heroin?"

He pressed his lips together and sighed. "Yes."

"Can I try some?" Brooke asked.

Cameron pulled her to her feet, took aim across the lot with the football, and told her to go long.

"What the heck does that even mean?" she asked. "And these boots have heels. I'm not going anywhere, especially long."

He scooped her off her feet and spun her as she squealed.

"Can I try it?" I asked Jared.

He placed an appreciative look on me. "No."

I crossed my arms over my chest. "You said I could ask you anything."

"And I answered truthfully."

"So, what? Would I get addicted?" I asked, kidding around.

"Yes."

"Oh." That put an abrupt end to that. "Okay, then how did you beat me to the canyon floor?"

He grinned. "I stopped time, how else? But one of them knocked me senseless for a moment, and time restarted. I was worried I'd be late."

"That would have ended badly," I said.

"Yes, it would have." He wound his fingers into mine and placed them against his heart. "I wouldn't have let that happen."

The conversation he'd had with my grandparents seemed to be forgotten. He was back to his old, charming self, and I wondered what that meant.

"Your grandparents were right, Lorelei," he said, holding my hand steadfast when I tried to pull away. He always seemed to know exactly where my thoughts were. "I'm not worthy of you," he continued. "I never will be. But I *am* in love with you, and if wanting you makes me selfish, then so be it."

His words caused a hopeful warmth to rush through me. It

mingled with the heat radiating off him, soaked into my skin, and in turn caused a heat of a different nature. A spark flared to life inside me and spread from my abdomen to the tips of my toes.

Jared's face went blank. Then he leaned back and gazed at me wide eyed, as though I'd surprised him somehow. "That— That was amazing."

I blinked to attention and looked around, completely confused. "What?"

"You. Your aura." He leaned close again, still holding my hand. "It's like the smoldering embers of a fire. But just now, it flared to life, its flames roiling softly over your skin, bathing you in a soft, glowing light. I've never seen anything so beautiful."

His description stole my breath. His eyes, sparkling with something more than just mere interest, made my heart shudder to life, like it had been lying dormant before, waiting.

"Your Grace!" Grandma cried from the back door.

Her summons startled me out of my stupor, mostly because she sounded alarmed. When we turned around, I realized she wasn't looking at Jared, but was looking inside the house, her back to us.

Jared was beside her in a flash. Cameron was next; he had farther to run. And the rest of us followed eons later, even though we were hurrying. Jared pushed past her and into the house. We shuffled inside and gathered around one end of the breakfast bar. There was a kid on the other side, wearing an army jacket three sizes too big.

"Noah," I said, starting forward, but Jared stopped me. "Noah, it's okay. You can put down the knife."

He had drawn one of Grandma's kitchen knives and was holding it at his side, staring blankly at Jared.

"We won't hurt you."

"You're not with the descendants," Jared said.

He scoffed, and yet never blinked, never took his eyes off

Jared. "The descendants are bottom-feeders. They have no real power without chants and incantations and blood rites. Always trying to hold on to their heritage, but they lost it centuries ago. Half of them aren't even real descendants. They just believe they are, like people who believe they've been abducted by aliens."

"Can you help him?" A woman was inching inside our house from the store. It was locked. Noah must have broken in.

The woman was so frail looking, so fragile, shaking with fear and cold. She had a bruise on her cheek and the remains of a black eye. "Can you help my son?" she said through a breathy sob. "He said to come here. That you could help him."

"What's your name?" Jared asked him.

"Noah."

He glared at him from underneath his lashes. "Lie to me again, and I'll make sure you suffer."

"That's his name," the woman said. She eased closer but kept her distance from her son.

"What is your name?" Jared asked again.

The woman seemed confused. She looked at Noah.

"Atherol," he said with a smile. "I seek Azrael."

"You've found him," Jared said. "What do you want?"

"Out."

"Then leave him."

"To have you come after me?" he asked. "To wait for the war? I can't go back. And you are the only way out."

Jared was in front of him in that faster-than-the-eye-can-see way of his. Cameron was beside me, doing his static-cling thing he did so well.

Jared tossed the boy onto the island like a sack of potatoes, oddly enough, knocking over a sack of potatoes. Noah started to struggle, but it was short-lived. Jared relieved him of the knife and tossed it to Cameron before refocusing on him.

He held him down, his brows drawn in question. "You'll cease to exist."

Noah's gaze slid back to him. "Better here with you than face what is to come."

"So be it."

The thing inside the boy finally spared me an angry glance. Like this was somehow my fault. "They'll never stop," he said, his words venomous. "And everyone close to you will die."

"That's enough." Jared leaned over him, almost touching his mouth to his like he was about to give mouth-to-mouth, but Noah kept his gaze locked with mine.

"More are coming," he said. He refocused on Jared. "So many more."

"I know." Locking his hand around Noah's throat, Jared opened his mouth and breathed in the evil spirit that had been consuming him. A dark fog left one mouth and entered the other, and I jerked forward in reflex, my only thought that Jared would be possessed.

Cameron caught me to him. "It can't live inside him," he said. "The spirit is essentially committing suicide."

"Why?" Brooke asked, her eyes glued to the scene.

"It's jumping ship. Like a rat does before it sinks. It wants out before the war begins."

Jared rose up, looked toward the ceiling, and filled his lungs as though absorbing the spirit. Noah grew limp and the woman ran to him, her eyes pleading with Jared, hopeful.

"It's done," Jared said. "The spirit's out."

"Thank you," she said, sobbing and holding an unconscious Noah to her.

"Do we need to call an ambulance?" I asked Jared.

"Wouldn't hurt."

Grandma went for her phone just as an older man rushed

into the store. "I'm looking for someone named Azrael," he said, glancing around, his expression panicked. "My granddaughter. There's something wrong."

"Where is she?" Cameron asked.

"In the car. Out here. Please, hurry."

We hurried outside, leaving Grandma inside to help with Noah. I was right behind Jared and slid to a stop when I saw the little girl.

"Please," the man said.

Glitch took over. He went to the man's car and lifted her out, so tiny and frail, no more than five.

"Jared," I said, my voice a soft whisper. He wrapped an arm around me and looked up at the sky. The clouds were dark and low, rolling over us in waves.

"It has begun," he said, words I never wanted to hear. Words I feared more than anything.

I felt a sprinkle then, a drop of rain, and I knew everything I'd ever known was about to change.

THE LIGHTS OF RILEY'S SWITCH

Everyone close to me is going to die.

Those words reverberated in my head over and over as I gathered my belongings by candlelight. After the incident with Noah, I realized my presence was the problem. *I* was the problem. I was the reason bad people were coming to Riley's Switch and I was responsible for all the horrible things that were happening to everyone around me. So I did the unthinkable. I bent to my grandparents' wishes. I went to them and agreed to be secreted away, thus the 5 A.M. wake-up call. I'd packed that evening while everyone was at church so no one would know what

I was doing and then hid the bags in my closet until Brooke and Glitch went home.

"Don't forget your pillow," Grandma said, holding the candle up high to give me more light. "You'll need it."

Her voice trembled like china during an earthquake, and I understood at last how hard this was for her. For both of them. They were doing this to keep me safe. I was doing this to keep them safe. If my presence was going to get everyone close to me killed, then surely my absence would keep them alive.

But sneaking out of town with two supernatural beings on full alert was not as easy as it sounded. Granddad sent Jared back to the Clearing with the sheriff to investigate some mysterious anomaly he'd made up. Then he sent Cameron to the church to check the munitions supply. There was about to be a war, after all. We had to prepare.

Even with those precautions, we didn't want to turn on any lights. It might alert them to our plan. We had a very small window of opportunity in which I could sneak out of town. If we were successful, I would be handed off to another set of believers. Then another and another until we got to the boarding school in the Northeast where I was registered under the name Lorraine Pratt. Granddad had papers, a birth certificate, a student ID from a school in Arizona . . . everything a girl needed to start a new life. A new existence.

They drove me to the edge of town, where an SUV sat idling on the side of the road, its parking lights on. We climbed out and Granddad grabbed my bags. He handed them to a man in his early thirties. I had never seen him or the woman with him before. These were complete strangers to me, and I was about to be wrapped in a bow and handed over to them.

But this was my choice. The only way I could keep everyone safe.

"Pix," Grandma said, and the pain in her voice brought tears to my eyes. Before she could say more, she pulled me into a hug, and I realized she couldn't have said more if she'd wanted to.

Granddad patted her back as she hugged me to her. "Vera, we don't have much time. Cameron's going to figure this out sooner than we want him to if we don't get back."

Her breath hitched and she held me at arm's length. "You know how to contact us if anything goes wrong."

I nodded and bit my trembling lip, afraid to say anything. Granddad hugged me then, and his shoulders shook with emotion. Emotion that almost crushed me into dust. When he let go, I hurried to the SUV and slammed the door shut. I hugged my pillow to me as the couple got in. They introduced themselves, but I didn't hear a word they said. They smiled nervously, and I got the feeling they thought I was something special. It made me dislike them. Just a little.

I was going to be in one car or another for two days straight. Four legs of the journey. Four different vehicles. Trying to keep supernatural entities off my trail was going to prove tricky, but Jared and Cameron had been through enough. They had both been shot because of me. And they would both give their lives for me because they also thought I was something special. No one understood I didn't know a thing about war, much less how to stop one. I refused to let their blind faith in my abilities get them killed.

Fear consumed me as we drove off. Fear for my friends. For Jared and Cameron. For my future. But especially fear for my grandparents once everyone figured out what they'd done. Just the threat of sending me away had the Order up in arms. I couldn't imagine what the members would do when they found out I was gone. What my grandparents would face. Derision? Hatred? Hostility?

I turned to look out the back window. We were on an incline and Riley's Switch sat nestled in a lush valley below, its lights twinkling in the thick darkness. Jared was somewhere on the other side. The Clearing lay a couple miles out, and whatever he and the sheriff were supposed to be investigating would keep them busy for a while.

Hopefully it would be long enough.

Turn the page for a sneak peek at

death and the girl he loves

Coming October 2013

SAME DAY, DIFFERENT DEATH

The Bedford Fields Academy pitched itself as one of the most prestigious private schools in North America, promising a stellar education and a future brighter than an exploding supernova. Or something along those lines. In reality, it was a last-ditch effort for rich parents with kids who'd been kicked out of every other institution in the free world. The boarding school was insanely expensive, but those parents with unruly children and money to burn would pay anything for the illusion of a good education. They took their public guise seriously. Keeping up the pretense of good parentage took effort. And trust funds. And the school kept the children out of their hair. For that, they would pay extra.

I didn't know that when I started at Bedford Fields, of course, but a pretty blonde with too much eyeliner and too few scruples explained the rules and regulations of the school in the bathroom while cleaning her nails with a switchblade. She'd lifted the knife from a pickpocket while on vacation with her family in Cabo San Lucas the summer before, and she made sure to mention how she'd honed the blade to a razor's edge for ease of penetration. That was my first day and my introduction to life sans everything I'd ever known. It pretty much went downhill from there.

First of all, the reality of winter in the North was a complete shock to my system. I couldn't get warm, even bundled in seven layers as I was then. Second, I'd started school in the middle of the semester, thus I was behind in almost every class they'd assigned to me. And third, I apparently had an accent, a fact that some of the more irritating students reveled in making fun of.

But the worst part of all was the homesickness, which I took to a whole new level. I missed my grandparents, my friends, my old school to the point of feeling like I had the flu twenty-four/seven. I even missed Tabitha Sind, the bane of my existence. Luckily, I had Kenya here to take up where Tab had left off. At least Tabitha had never threatened me with a switchblade. Life was simpler in New Mexico. Life at a boarding school for rich kids in a state where the weather rivaled that of Siberia was far too complex. And hazardous to my health.

"Lorraine!"

I heard my nom de plume but kept walking. I hated nothing more than being late to class. These teachers at BFA could wither a winter rose with one look.

"Lorraine," she called again.

While my friends in New Mexico knew me as Lorelei McAlister, aka my real name, the students and faculty here in Maine knew me as Lorraine Pratt, a transfer student from Arizona. Fortunately, I'd been to Arizona a couple of times, and knew just enough to fend off questions from the more curious students.

I walked the halls with my head down and my gaze glued to the floor. Now that I was no longer a novelty, I could slip relatively unnoticed from class to class. At first, everyone had stared. Everyone. That's what I got for transferring in the middle of a semester. But once the other kids found out I was a scholarship student, and not a particularly interesting one at that, they stopped staring and ignored me altogether. Most of them, anyway.

I could handle being ignored, but the scholarship was a mystery I had yet to figure out. I'd been secreted away from everything I'd ever known in the middle of the night. Driven in four different vehicles with four different groups of caretakers for more than two days straight, and delivered onto the steps of Bedford Fields in the bitingly frigid pre-dawn hours with little more than a suitcase and a hair tie. How on earth did I suddenly have a scholarship? That was clearly a part of the plan my grandparents forgot to mention.

"Lorraine, wait up."

I finally slowed and let the eighth-grader catch up to me. She was the only student still enamored with my shiny newness. I'd been there for weeks. Hopefully my gleam would wear off soon, because she could be a little annoying.

She beamed at me when she caught up, her cerulean eyes sparkling behind 'round-rimmed glasses on a face framed by thick dark braids.

Well, annoying in a charming way. She was another scholarship student, a science whiz who was destined to be the next Stephen Hawking if I had anything to say about it. The girl's mind was like a supercomputer on steroids.

"Hey, Krystal."

"Hey," she said back, breathless from trying to catch up to me. "So what are you doing?"

I tried not to chuckle and indicated the door ahead of me with an index finger. "Just headed to class."

"Oh, right, okay, that's a good idea."

"Isn't your next class across campus?" I asked her.

She looked around in utter cluelessness and spun in a complete circle to get her bearings. I felt the crush of students acutely, especially when one knocked me forward as he rushed past. I felt a tug at my coat and started to say something, but I barely caught sight of the back of his head before he disappeared into the crowd.

"Yes, it is." Krystal's pale face had a light sprinkling of freckles over cheeks slightly chapped from the crisp winds of Maine, and she had a bow-shaped mouth like a doll's. She stopped then put one foot behind the other. "I guess I should jet, then."

I couldn't help but grin. "Okay, you jet. I'll see you later?"

After flashing me a smile that could have melted the heart of that Ice Queen in Narnia, she nodded and hurried away.

I watched her leave, a little enamored myself with such a guileless creature, then turned and ran right into the one girl in school I did *not* want to run into. The only one with a switchblade. Well, the only one I knew of.

She gaped then pushed me away. I stumbled back and barely kept myself from tumbling head over heels by grabbing on to another student's backpack. He scowled over his shoulder then jerked out of my grip before I could apologize. Or right myself. I almost fell anyway, but I managed to get my footing without any more humiliation than absolutely necessary.

"Nice save," she said, raising her brows as though impressed.

But I was still reeling from what I'd discovered from our little encounter. I wasn't fond of Kenya. She wasn't fond of me. But it disturbed me nonetheless to watch her die.

Unfortunately for me—and everyone around me—I have, for lack of a better word, *visions*. Sometimes when I touch people I can see into their futures or their pasts. It's heart wrenching on several levels. I never see the time they were laughing at a party or riding a roller coaster at the fair, screaming with exhilaration. No, I see the bad parts of their lives. I see the catastrophic. I see the pain and fear and anxiety. And now, thanks to this nifty skill I'd inherited, I knew exactly when, where, and how Kenya was going to die.

Her death had flashed before my eyes the moment we touched. The visions were thoughtful that way. And now I had a decision to make. I'd struggled with the question of divulgence before. Many times. And this scenario was no exception. I might be able to prevent her death if she listened to me, but that took a lot of faith. And since she threatened me with a switchblade every chance she got, I didn't figure faith was her strong suit. Especially faith in me. The new girl. The girl she most liked to harass and promise a slow and painful death to. I was pretty sure I'd developed a nervous twitch after meeting her.

But this was different. Maybe it was a timing thing. She was going to die too soon. Too young. She literally had only days to live. And the vision stole my breath with its vividness.

In it, a storm rolled in, darkening what had been a sunny afternoon. She was on a boat with her aunt, uncle, big sister, and little brother, but it wasn't a vacation or a pleasure trip. She was scared. Her aunt and uncle were scared too, terrified, in fact, running, trying to get away from something, to escape. The clouds roiling overhead like a cauldron of a dark witch's brew dipped lower and lower in the sky. If Kenya reached up, she could have touched them, but she was busy clinging to her brother for dear life. The water churned and crashed against her uncle's sailboat. Rain slashed horizontally through the sky, the stinging chill cutting to the bone. Her sister had wedged herself between two seats, huddled there, shivering, worried she'd fall overboard.

I could feel the unimaginable fear that blinded Kenya to everything but those clouds. Yet it wasn't the storm she was afraid of. It was something else. Something inside them.

Before I could ascertain the origin of her fear, another wave hit. It slammed against the boat causing one side to tip and rise with the swell until the small boat had no choice but to succumb to the fates. The water hit Kenya hard, slapping against her as she crashed into it. She tried desperately to keep ahold of her brother, reached blindly for her sister, but the pull of the waves was too strong. It sucked her deeper and deeper into its icy grip. She kicked. Fought with every ounce of strength she had. Then, left with no choice, she exchanged water for air and filled her burning lungs. Panic seized her with such a violent force, she gagged, tried to swallow the entire ocean, searching for oxygen in the thick liquid. Found none.

The last image that flashed in my mind was of her floating in the deep gray depths of the arctic water. Her eyes open. Her mouth a grim line as though she'd accepted her fate at last, but did so unhappily.

And she knew. She knew who was to blame.

Ricocheting back to the present, I sucked in a sharp gulp of air, fighting the feeling of suffocation, of drowning. I doubled over and coughed, then clamped a hand over my mouth when I felt bile slip up the back of my throat.

What were they running from? Why were they so scared? And why would anyone be to blame for a storm?

"Pratt?" she said, her voice edged with wariness instead of her usual menace.

I ignored her, turned, and began fighting my way to the bathroom when I bumped into a boy. Another vision gripped me and performed a hostile takeover of my brain function. And just like the vision of Kenya and her family, this boy's expiration date was rocketing toward him. And it was disturbingly similar to hers. The storm. The dark clouds. The roaring winds. The boy was running toward his dorm on the school campus, but unlike Kenya, he was scared of the storm and nothing else. He died when a tree was uprooted and took down some electrical wires near him. The currents hammering through his body brought me down, because I didn't just see what happened to people in my visions, I felt it. Every spike of fear. Every wince of anguish. Every spasm of pain. And being electrocuted to death hurt. An agonizing pain pulsated through me, attacking my nervous system until the boy breathed his last breath and his nervous system shut down.

I felt a hand on my arm. I pushed it away and stumbled to my feet, reeling from that experience when another boy reached out to help me.

Same day.

Same storm.

Same utter chaos.

Different death.

I jerked away from him and into a girl. I now had an audience. Students surrounded me, and every one I touched died.

Same day.

Same storm.

Same utter chaos.

Different death.

One after the other until I finally lunged into the bathroom and locked myself in a stall. The shock of each death shuddered through me as I heaved my lunch into the toilet. When the spasms eased, I spit out the sour taste and tried to clear my head. To understand what I was seeing.

Something changed. Something happened in the last few minutes that altered the fates of every kid at school. But they were in different places. On the water. In a storm shelter. In Town Hall. Fleeing the country in a chartered Leer jet. And it wasn't just them. It was their brothers and sisters, their parents and friends. In exactly seven days, everyone in the city of Bangor, Maine, was going to die. But somehow, I didn't think it would stop there.

Something was different. What could have—

Then it hit me. The boy. The tug at my coat. I reached into my pocket and pulled out a note. It was the third one I'd received in quite the same manner. Stuffed into the pocket of my jacket when I wasn't looking.

Dread consumed me as I opened it. This one had a stick figure drawing of two people, a boy and a girl. The girl—who I was going to assume was me since she had garishly red curly hair—was lying on the ground, presumably dead. Blood pooled on her chest and sat in puddles around her head and torso. The boy clutched a knife in his three-fingered hand, but he was leaning over her. Over me. And a darkness was leaving her mouth and entering his. Like he wanted what was inside me. Like he welcomed it.

And somehow he knew. When I was six years old, I had been possessed by a demon. A demon that was still inside me. But no one here knew that. How could they? And yet this boy did.

Five words made up the text of the note. I read them over and over in disbelief. Fear darkened the edges of my periphery. Five words. Five words that had the power to make the darkness inside me quake and buck inside my body. Five words that would change the fate of the world. Five words that read simply, *I know what you are.*

"Only Jones could make the Angel of Death crush-worthy!!"

—Lara Chapman

Book One

Book Two

And look for the third book in the series,

Death and the Girl He Loves,

available October 2013

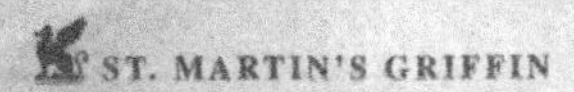

Made in the USA
Las Vegas, NV
11 September 2021

30092718R00187